CW01497862

BACK FOR GOOD

To Dee and Steve

With love

Jay Jacobs x

Back for Good

Jay Jacobs

The
Book
Guild

First published in Great Britain in 2025 by
The Book Guild Ltd
Unit E2 Airfield Business Park,
Harrison Road, Market Harborough,
Leicestershire. LE16 7UL
Tel: 0116 2792299
www.bookguild.co.uk
Email: info@bookguild.co.uk

Copyright © 2025 Jay Jacobs

The right of Jay Jacobs to be identified as the author of this
work has been asserted by them in accordance with the
Copyright, Design and Patents Act 1988.

All rights reserved. No part of this publication may be
reproduced, transmitted, or stored in a retrieval system, in any form or by any means,
without permission in writing from the publisher, nor be otherwise circulated in
any form of binding or cover other than that in which it is published and without
a similar condition being imposed on the subsequent purchaser.

The manufacturer's authorised representative in the EU
for product safety is Authorised Rep Compliance Ltd,
71 Lower Baggot Street, Dublin D02 P593 Ireland (www.arccompliance.com)

This work is entirely fictitious and bears no resemblance to any persons living or dead.

Typeset in Minion Pro and Adelle Sans

Printed and bound in Great Britain by 4edge Limited

ISBN 978 1835742 464

British Library Cataloguing in Publication Data.
A catalogue record for this book is available from the British Library.

For all spirit guides,
especially my own.

It All Started With a Big Bang

"How many times do I need to remind you, Zinnia?" said Hebron as he materialised next to me with a grumpy headmaster face on. "The rule book is there for good reason. Until you've mastered the contents, they are non-negotiable."

I hadn't even broken a rule (this time); I'd just been, let's say, considering it. And if you want to know how annoying The Spirit Guidance Rule Book is, this is the screensaver on my training tablet, tailored especially for me:

1. Remain emotionally detached from one's protégés.
2. Do not interfere.
3. Only assist when called upon by your human or advised by your mentor.

So restrictive and I didn't do restrictive well.

"You know this is only until you're qualified," said Hebron, his demeanour softening fractionally. "We don't want any more slip-ups before you've learnt how to make the right choices. If you practise the rules and follow my tuition, you'll soon get more involved."

Being involved was why I'd chosen to be a spirit guide: supporting an individual as they experienced their human life, sharing their ups and downs. I'd spent so much time with my soulmate Daziel, a revered spirit guide, I'd been sure I'd ace the role. And I loved being back on the Earth plane, albeit in spirit form. Okay, so it hadn't been as simple as I'd hoped and I'd failed Level II the first time round but I was getting there.

"So far, you've done an excellent job with Sasha," encouraged Hebron. "Remember you are free to present her with opportunities so long as they support the paths she chooses."

Unassuming Sasha, who I'd been matched with for my Level III field work, hadn't been difficult to guide. But now her marriage with Mark was heading for heartache and I could so easily help.

"All I want to do is give Sasha a tiny nudge," I said, totally ignoring Hebron's words of wisdom. "If a creature was struggling to cross a busy road and you pointed out the safest place, it would just be a prod in the right direction rather than changing the course of nature."

"Is that what you were thinking with Oswald?"

Ouch – that was a low blow. Oswald was the first human I'd been put in charge of. He'd been a hardworking serf, oppressed by a greedy landowner who always came up with new ways to keep the peasants down. One night, when I couldn't bear seeing him suffer any more,

I'd fed Oswald a few insights on what was happening, to encourage him to move to a better manor. I hadn't banked on him confronting his master with descriptions of his visions, which led to accusations of witchcraft and devilry. It hadn't ended well for Oswald. Or for me, to a less terminal degree; I was demoted to Level I.

Why did I bother arguing my case with Hebron?

"Don't lose faith, little one," he said. "I do listen to you."

Sure you do. The sarcasm slipped out before I could stop it. I peeked up at Hebron for his reaction, but he was concentrating on something else – which he blocked from me.

That's strange, I thought, *very strange.*

Hebron dissolved away, and I was back in the room with Sasha – her kitchen, to be precise.

***

Sasha jumped as her phone vibrated and started ringing. She dried her hands and answered the call.

"Hi, Mum. How are you?"

"I'm fine. Well, not really. Could I ask a big favour, please?"

"Of course. What's the problem?" Sasha asked, her heart thumping in her chest and thinking, This isn't like Mum at all.

"I'm at the hospital and not allowed to drive home, so I was hoping you could pick me up."

"I can, but why are you there?" Sasha fought to keep her voice steady.

"It's nothing to worry about – I'll explain when I see you. I'll be sitting in the main reception area."

"Okay then. I'll get the children ready. We'll be with you as soon as possible. Love you."

"Love you too. Bye-bye."

Sasha dropped her phone on the worktop, thinking, *What on earth is wrong with Mum? She's never normally ill, let alone needing to go to hospital. What if it's serious?*

My tablet suddenly lit up and started vibrating, prompting me to explain something you, dear reader, may not have considered but also maybe don't need spelt out. However, if I ignore it, there will be a really annoying audio warning which won't stop so I'll tell you quickly.

Spirit guides can listen to everyone's thoughts as well as spoken words. They mainly concentrate on the person they're guiding but they'll tune in to anyone remotely involved. And perhaps some randoms too, if the fancy takes them – or is that just me? Anyhoo, the point is I'll tell you people's thoughts, sometimes more than one in a conversation, as well as my own. Traditionalists say it's confusing but I reckon it would be dull if you didn't get the full picture. Of course I won't make a habit of tradition-breaking. (I had to say that in case Hebron was listening in; I don't really care about traditions. Oops, ignore that last bit.)

***

Resisting the urge to call her mother back, Sasha quickly finished preparing a bottle of formula milk before rushing into the living room, where Rosie and Noah were supposed to be playing nicely together. Four-year-old Rosie was doing as she was told, sitting cross-legged amongst the scattered patchwork of books and toys but two-year-old Noah wasn't. He wasn't in the room at all.

That's not normal, thought Sasha, racing up the stairs two at a time.

Sasha's "normal" was disappearing faster than a sandcastle at high tide and it didn't help that it was an unusually hot day, even for June in Milton Keynes. Her forehead was clammy with sweat when she reached the landing.

"What the…" She gasped, entering Noah's bedroom.

Sasha's stomach lurched as she came face-to-face with brown streaks on the wall and a matching deposit on the blue carpet, into which two small bare feet were squidging about. Yet there was no stench; quite the opposite. Sasha raised her gaze to the wide eyes of her little boy, who was nervously holding the remains of a family-sized chocolate bar in one hand and his now-brown cow, the indispensable cuddly toy known as Moo-cow, in the other. Quite how he'd managed such a mess, she had no idea but she heaved a massive sigh of relief – it could have been so much worse.

"It's all right, darling," she said, whilst picking him up (at arm's length) and rushing into the bathroom to place him gently in the empty bathtub.

"Wait there – I'll be back in a minute." *Oh God! What do I do first? Why did this have to happen today of all days?*

Sasha's anxiety was elevated by a soft whimper. Which wasn't soft – or a whimper – for long. Like a volume dial twisting to maximum, the noise became a flood-warning siren. Violet had woken from her nap and clearly she was hungry, thirsty and weighed down with a full nappy.

"Rosie, darling, please come to Mummy. Violet's woken up early. Come quickly, sweetheart," Sasha shouted down to her little second-in-command. "You can sing to Violet and give her milk whilst Mummy cleans up Noah. No! Don't worry about Noah. Sing her 'Old MacDonald'. You know she likes that. Please, *now*, Rosie."

Sasha left Noah where he was safely contained, skidded into the kitchen to warm up the formula milk, which she practically threw at Rosie as she raced back upstairs.

Rosie was a willing little helper. Holding a bottle to Violet's lips, who clung to the bars of her cot whilst teetering on wobbly legs, was almost as good as feeding baby goats at a petting zoo.

Sasha sprinted around, as if she were competing in a domestic version of the pentathlon, cleaning up Noah, changing Violet's nappy, dumping Noah's dirty clothes and Moo-cow in a bucket of soapy water and doing her best to clean up the mess in Noah's room. The living room, though, would have to wait.

As soon as the children were ready to go, she scribbled a quick note for her husband, Mark:

Gone to get Mum from hospital.
Sorry no time to make dinner – get fish and chips? S x

She left it on the kitchen worktop, with a neon-pink plastic spoon and fat yellow fork on either side to draw attention to the note – it was a standing joke that Mark never seemed to notice things.

With the children safely strapped in the car and the scent of Dairy Milk still wafting from Noah, Sasha fought to bring her breathing under control. Twenty minutes had passed, which was rather commendable considering the circumstances, but still longer than ideal. It would be another ten minutes to get to the hospital and she prayed she'd manage to find a convenient parking space – or any parking space, in fact. And she must make sure she remembered to pay for a ticket, whatever method that was going to be.

Off they set, along the tediously repetitive route of straight roads and roundabouts. The dashboard of the car displayed 32°C. Sweat trickled down her back and from her armpits as she turned on the air-con. It did little to cool her or slow her thoughts as she accelerated onto the penultimate roundabout.

What's Mark going to think when he finds no dinner ready and the house in a mess? I hope he doesn't—

A discordant symphony of screeching tyres, distorting metal and shattering glass accompanied the heavy transit van that slammed straight into her car door and silenced Sasha's thoughts.

Gaining a Fresh Perspective

I watched Sasha's soul rising from her limp body in a glowing, wispy curl before settling ten metres above the scene of the accident. "Welcome to my world," I wanted to say, but I wasn't allowed. I turned my appearance to a not particularly noticeable orb of energy.

Sasha knew she was separating from her body and becoming airborne but she didn't understand it. Her children were still in their car seats and she would never leave them unattended; what was she doing? What was going on?

I knew I was flouting the rules, but I communicated that the children were being protected – angels had placed metaphysical safety jackets around them to keep them safe – and there wouldn't be any lasting effects; they wouldn't even remember the event once they were older.

Sasha absorbed this information but it was like trying to work out an exam question that was far too complicated. She started by looking around and then realised that she didn't need to turn her head – she had three-hundred-and-sixty-degree vision. Ooh, this is so weird, she thought. She expected to feel nauseous but she wasn't. She looked down at her car. It had been harpooned by a big and, to be honest, rather dirty van in the middle of a large roundabout. There were thick, tarry skid-marks on the road, with a liberal scattering of broken glass and mangled plastic trim, which all looked like some prize-winning piece of abstract art. She could almost taste the stench of scorched rubber and was mesmerised by the brittle shards of glass glittering in the bright sunlight.

The two vehicles had made a good job of blocking half the roundabout and traffic was stacking back remarkably quickly. Sasha spotted furrowed brows on drivers' faces and watched others thumping their steering wheels in frustration at the inconvenient delay. Nobody was relaxed apart from Sasha as she observed everything in a curious state of detachment. It was just as well all the resentful people couldn't see her up there. Other vehicles were slowly entering and exiting the unaffected section of the roundabout, grateful they weren't stuck in the stationary traffic, though not particularly happy at having to amend their routes now.

Three cars had pulled over moments after the accident occurred, with various people jumping out and racing over to the scene. A professional-looking woman in a grey suit had pulled a mobile phone out of her jacket pocket. Sasha somehow knew this person was calling 999 to request the police and an ambulance.

Now she wasn't constricted by her body, she could enjoy the ability to study and understand any living being instantly, the same as I could, or any spirit for that matter.

She was enthralled by the woman's conversation with the emergency services operator and was impressed by her concise control.

I'd trust her to look after me any day, she was thinking.

Which was just as well, since that was exactly what the woman was doing.

Sasha looked at the other individuals, who were peering into the crashed vehicles, trying to assess the risk of fire and calculate whether it would be best to help the occupants out or leave it to the professionals who were yet to arrive.

She wondered who was in the van, and instantly, she found herself face-to-face with the driver.

Ooh, that's crazy. It didn't even feel like I moved.

The man's face was very pale, his eyes wide and staring.

Oh my God, is he dead?

I instinctively advised Sasha the driver was in shock, though not critically so; his seat belt and an airbag had prevented any serious injury. *Be careful,* I admonished myself. *Hebron's probably watching.*

Sasha didn't realise the knowledge came from me but it did help to spark her curiosity and she wanted to know more about this man. In the spirit world, when you ask a question, you receive an instant answer – unless it's not in your best interest.

Accordingly, she became aware his name was Colin and he was forty-three. He had two teenage girls who were adorable one moment and complete nightmares the next. He found his wife a bit of a nag, though he'd never dream of leaving her, and was looking forward to seeing his mates at the pub that evening, where he intended to sink a copious amount of beer.

Wow – this is fun! Eagerly, Sasha turned her gaze to her own car. Even though she knew it was herself inside, it was like looking at a stranger.

The car's bodywork was an ugly mess where the driver's door was pressing in against the woman's right side. She was slumped at a twisted angle with her head hanging over the gear stick, shoulder-length mink-brown hair obscuring her face. Her legs were also out of view under the wreckage of the bulkhead, whilst her right arm was awkwardly draped over the steering wheel, like that of an abandoned marionette. There were no signs of breathing or any movement: no signs of life at all.

Does that mean I'm dead? she suddenly thought, panic rising. *What happens to Rosie, Noah and Violet?*

I didn't have a chance to repeat my reassurances before Sasha was whisked away from the scene.

Sasha thought it felt like a giant vacuum cleaner had sucked her up, like dirt from a doormat, and then plopped her into the middle of the softest, comfiest blanket she could imagine. She was effectively distracted from the plight of her children as she was pulled away, higher and higher and higher. Glancing around, she had to double-take when she saw her grandmother, who had died four years previously, on her right. She looked a good few decades younger, but it was Gran for sure.

What Sasha hadn't seen was Gran coming to me first, giving me a proverbial high five and saying, with a youthful giggle, "Don't worry, I've got it from here."

You might well wonder how Gran taking over made me feel. Well, on our side, there is so much love and compassion that feelings of envy are redundant. We exist in a utopian wonderland where such emotions don't ever come into play. Who am I kidding? Whilst I couldn't help being charmed by adorable little Gran, a frisson of frustration rippled through me as Sasha's shock was followed by delight. I wasn't supposed to question the way things were but I couldn't believe my role was so limited.

"I'm a guide," I shouted to no one in particular, "so why can't I actively do some guiding?" I must have sounded like a petulant prepubescent.

"You will, Zinnia, once you've watched and learnt," said Hebron, who was with me in an instant. "Remember how humans are told they must walk before they run? You should take a leaf out of their book."

He loved quoting human idioms. I acknowledged Hebron more or less politely and rejoined Sasha.

"Gran! What's going on?" she was saying.

"Don't worry, my darling," Gran replied whilst taking her hand. "The children aren't hurt and I'm looking after you."

The reminder was timely, and Sasha put her concerns aside once more to focus on her surroundings.

"This doesn't make sense. I can't be travelling through a blanket."

The cosy-blanket-effect altered into what now appeared to be more like a traditional tunnel, albeit with a velvety-soft glistening lining.

"Did that just change because of what I said?" Sasha was finding everything exceedingly discombobulating. They seemed to be drifting quite sedately and yet she was sure they were covering a great distance at speed – faster than she'd ever moved before. "This is madness!"

"Just go with it, Sasha. Relax."

"That's easier said than done. Aren't you scared?"

"No, my dear. I quite enjoy it now."

The "walls" of the structure were made of myriad colours, with a range of depth and beauty that would have taken Sasha's breath away had she still been breathing. Up close, they were a mass of multi-coloured miniature stars, all pulsating and merging into a blurry haze, as Sasha and Gran whooshed through. A beautifully subtle harmony, far more delicate than the finest orchestra could make, was emanating from the haze.

Ahead of them, an intense point of light was visible. It was growing and growing into a dazzling disc that they were fast approaching.

The Grass is Greener on The Other Side

The disc transformed into a jaw-droppingly beautiful vista. As Sasha and Gran emerged into the landscape, the atmosphere became saturated with the most intense love Sasha had ever encountered; she was bathed in rapture.

They were surrounded by emerald meadows full of wondrous, unfamiliar flowers displaying brand-new colours Sasha couldn't even name. She looked closely at one that consisted of a single, seamless petal, shaped like a bell, containing featherlike fronds in a shimmering version of violet. Its perfume was glorious, mingling with the sweet scent of fresh grass.

Rabbits, foxes and animals she didn't recognise were ambling around fearlessly below exotic birds that swooped and soared in the pure blue sky, their cries hauntingly melodic. The pastures gracefully melded into rising hillsides and alpine mountains with glimmering lakes and tinkling streams. A magnificent waterfall cascaded from a verdant cliff, creating the most vibrant rainbow in its refreshing spray. Sasha could never have dreamt up such a marvellous place.

Her attention shifted to the path they were standing on – a track which appeared to be made of shimmery crystals yet was soothingly smooth underfoot. It drew them onwards.

Gran and Sasha walked lightly along the path, hands still linked, as Sasha tried to comprehend all that she could see. It was so incredibly new yet simultaneously familiar. Had she ever been here before?

Gran said, "Yes, before you were born. You could say this is home."

Home? thought Sasha. It was hard to think of anywhere other than Milton Keynes being home. And yet this all felt so right, so normal. It was very confusing.

Buildings rose ahead of them, varying in size and design but all constructed of radiant stone, akin to mother-of-pearl, in hues of pale orange, pink and gold. The closest were small and round, with domed roofs; they reminded Sasha of luxury yurts she'd seen in a travel brochure.

"Could we look inside one, please?" she asked. Back on Earth, she would never have been so bold.

"Yes, but we mustn't stay," replied her grandmother.

Sasha realised they weren't talking out loud as such, using mouth or voice.

Is this telepathy? she wondered.

"It's the standard form of communication used here, Sasha. Human bodies aren't developed enough to use it."

"Everything is so different, Gran. Like I've gone into some crazy sci-fi film."

Gran laughed. "I suppose it is, dear. Now let's go inside… oh, and just one thing." She stopped outside the entrance and took hold of Sasha's hands. "Everything happens for a reason here. And everyone you meet will be important to you when you go back to your family. Remember that."

"Okay," said Sasha, though a tremor of resistance pushed up from her core.

They opened the shell-like door into a circular chamber. The furnishings were sparse and Sasha couldn't see any windows or lights but the room was perfectly well illuminated. Pacing back and forth between chairs and a low table was a young man, around the age of twenty-five. His dark auburn hair was wild and swirly but his gingery beard and moustache were neatly trimmed. Caterpillar-thick eyebrows shrouded his eyes in a heavy scowl.

In response to Sasha's unspoken question as to why he was there, he launched into a tirade about leaving his wife Anita during an argument, racing away on his motorbike and having a fatal accident. Now he was stuck here without her.

"I'm so sorry," said Sasha, reaching out to comfort the distressed young man, her own heart aching with his pain.

They stayed in quiet sympathy until Gran said gently, "Time to move on."

Sasha followed her grandmother outside.

"Are there others like him?" she asked. "It's so sad."

"Oh yes. But they're getting support and they'll adjust in their own time," said Gran. "Now come look in here."

As they moved towards the next yurt, there was a flash of movement from the left.

"Excuse me, Miss," called out an older gentleman who seemed to appear from nowhere. He was short and stocky and looked a lot like Winston Churchill.

Sasha caught the man's pleading gaze and stopped to speak to him.

"Not now, Bernard; not this young lady," said another spirit from behind him, tugging him back out of sight.

Gran hadn't been expecting that interruption to the tour and propelled Sasha inside the next place. It was large and warmly lit, with crimson and tangerine velvet curtains draped from the centre of the ceiling, hanging in folds and pinned back against the curved walls. Four females occupied the room, ranging in age from teenage to thirty. One looked to be in her early twenties, with soft brown eyes and long wavy brunette hair that had a natural streak of grey just above her left ear.

As soon as she spotted Sasha and Gran entering the room, this young woman approached them and started chatting about her last days when she was a history student at Oxford University.

It was at this point that Hebron took me aside to explain that Sasha was having a near-death experience (or NDE for short), which meant her body had technically died at that point but she would be returning to life. During this event, she was receiving information on specific people who would be important for her when her NDE was over and she was back in her human body. It would be her mission to help individuals who were still living on the Earth plane and what she was being told now would come back to her in vivid detail at appropriate times. I vibrated with delight – Sasha's life was about to get a whole lot more interesting.

An older woman, whose long beige gown seemed to float around her with a life of its own, now walked steadily and reassuringly into the room. This lady radiated a cinnamon glow of warmth and understanding. All the women in the room smiled and greeted her as she travelled amongst them, chatting softly.

Gran explained to Sasha, "That's Indira. She's helping them adjust to their new circumstances. Some people need support, especially when they've come over unexpectedly. We'll move on, darling. This place isn't for you."

They returned to the crystal path and continued along it. Sasha inhaled the palpable peace as exquisite birds displayed their iridescent plumage and beautiful butterflies undulated on the gentle whispers of a breeze. A line of individual houses appeared, sprinkled along a curving lane.

"I'd love to live in one of these," said Sasha wistfully.

"Oh, you will, love," said Gran. "Would you like to look inside?"

Joy erupted from Sasha like a bubbling spring. There seemed to be one delight after another to sample and she was like a child given free rein in a sweet shop.

I was certainly seeing a new side to her now she wasn't bogged down by family-induced fatigue. My professional detachment was being tested like a saucer-eyed puppy begging me for a treat. Down, girl!

Sasha was drawn to the third cottage along and the door was opened by a sprightly woman with hair pulled back into a bun and piercing blue eyes that complemented her bright smile. A starchy white apron was tied neatly over her long grey pinafore dress.

"How delightful to see you, Margaret," she greeted Gran. "And this must be young Sasha."

Instantly, Sasha comprehended that the lady was her great-grandmother, Gran's mum, whose name was Dorothy.

"Do come through," she said as she opened the door on the right and ushered them into the cosy living room. There Sasha met her great-grandfather, Henry, who filled her in on part of the family tree she'd known nothing about, which included children Olivia and Billy, who were sitting at his feet, playing with a golden retriever.

"I look to you, Sasha, to go to their parents with reassurance that there was nothing they could have done to save the children," he said at the end.

"Of course," said Sasha, forgetting that under normal circumstances she'd run a mile from this sort of challenge.

By this point, I was reconciled with being the bystander. It wasn't as if I'd been allowed to be too "hands-on" when Sasha was on Earth, so it didn't need to be any different in my dimension. I scrolled through my tablet to see what rules or advice there was about NDEs.

Oh, in case you thought it odd that I have a tablet, it's because The Spirit Guidance Rule Book (which is the main course book) is always provided in whatever format matches the time span of the human being guided. When I was with Oswald, I had a dusty old tomb of a book with ye olde writing. Now it's 2018, I've got a small electronic tablet that is a lot easier to use.

Having moved on from the cottages, Sasha was approaching an imposing building with a façade like a grand old museum. It glowed and shimmered with the gold, pink, orange and yellow tones she was becoming familiar with, all intricately interlaced into a mesmerising sheen.

Walking between sculptured columns and through a studded door, she was struck by the vast emptiness of a cavernous room with nothing more than polished flagstone flooring and pale walls. She turned to ask where they were but Gran was no longer next to her. This was a shock; Sasha hadn't even considered how reassuring Gran's presence had been but now she felt very alone. And she thought about Rosie, Noah and Violet being alone too. They must still be in the back of her car, unable to move or even comprehend their situation. Her poor babies! How could she so selfishly enjoy this heavenly place when they must be terrified back on Earth? She had to get back to them straight away. Sasha spun round and sprinted towards the door.

A strikingly tall being with an undisguisable headmaster-like countenance but a contrastingly warm aura was blocking the doorway, and Sasha skidded to a halt.

Yes, it was Hebron. Just typical that he'd take centre stage, I thought.

A druggy mist of tranquillity descended over Sasha.

"Please, you've got to help me get back to the car," she cried, more quietly than intended.

"Shh," soothed Hebron. "The children are being looked after and you'll be back with them in no time. You've nothing to worry about, nothing at all."

"Nothing?" she asked, and deep within his eyes she spied a vision of her children enveloped in the love and attention of angels. Sasha's concerns evaporated into the ether as her very core was softly daubed with reassurance, her fears replaced by acceptance.

"You're an angel too, aren't you?" she said more to herself than directly to the being. Straight away she absorbed the knowledge that he was an archangel, therefore more evolved than an entry-level angel but it was fine for her to think of him as an angel. She had already been in awe of the love in this dimension but the compassion pouring from Hebron took her to another level. Waves of love washed over her so intensely, penetrating every tiny particle of her spirit. It was indescribably better than anything she'd ever encountered in her Earthly body. Now, nothing – absolutely, categorically nothing else – mattered and she could not imagine desiring anything more in the whole universe. Trembling, Sasha reciprocated her own appreciation and thanked him for caring for her children.

Just to be clear, her reaction would be the same with any angel or archangel who took on this role. Still, I softened. It was a good reminder for me of how special this dimension really was; it was easy to get blasé after a millennium or two.

Sasha turned to face the centre of the room. A holographic vision was rising up from the glassy floor, lifelike in size and colour. It reeled through her life, highlighting feelings and consequences for those affected by her actions. She had heard people say that when you die, your life would flash before your eyes and here it was, happening to her now. It started with her parents getting together and sped through her childhood, showing incidents both positive and negative, continuing right up until the van had struck her car.

There were two scenes which stood out to me.

First, when Sasha was twelve, she asked whether she could have a new grown-up bicycle for her next birthday. Her best friend, Louise, had just got one and Sasha wanted the same. That evening as she was getting ready for bed, she heard raised voices in the kitchen and tiptoed to the landing to listen in.

"But do you realise how much those bikes cost?" her dad was saying gruffly.

"I know they're really expensive," said Mum. "If we get her one, would we have enough spending money for the holiday?"

"I doubt it."

Young Sasha rushed into her bedroom. Her stomach twisted as she considered being responsible for ruining their summer holiday and she told herself she must never ask for anything again.

The second scene was less than a year later.

Her best friend Kya was sleeping over, and from the top bunk, she leant across and dribbled spit in Sasha's face. Sasha gasped and backed away to the wall. Why was Kya being so horrible to her? It wasn't even the first time she'd been mean. Sasha had had enough of it and she prayed for something horrible to happen to Kya.

On Monday at school, Kya apologised and said she'd

spat on Sasha because she was jealous of her happy family. Sasha felt sorry for her and they were back to being best friends forever.

But Kya didn't come into school the next two days. On Thursday, she arrived with a cast on her right arm, a black eye and bruises across much of her body. Young Sasha's hands flew to her face as she recalled her prayer. Was she responsible for Kya's accident? She'd never thought of herself as a bad person but this showed how wicked she must be. Not long ago, she'd decided to never ask her parents for anything; well, asking God was just as bad – actually, a million times worse. She made a vow to never ask parents, friends, teachers, God, anybody, for anything ever again. That would pay for what she'd done, wouldn't it?

Spirit Sasha was able to view what had really happened to her unfortunate friend, who lived with her mother and two younger half-brothers: Kya's mum had come home from a boozy argument with her latest boyfriend to find Kya making a mess of changing her brother's dirty nappy. Instead of being grateful for Kya's attempt at helping, she'd erupted, shoving Kya out of the bathroom hard enough to knock her down the stairs.

Getting this insight should have made Sasha realise Kya's difficult lifestyle wasn't anything to do with her and that continuing to punish herself by sticking to a childhood vow, which meant she wouldn't ask for anything that would benefit her personally, was pointless. Pointless and deleterious. But she didn't have any such thought process and she didn't even follow the other threads that related to this event. Such as her present-day issues with Mark, where her not asking him to help out when things were too much for her was having an impact on their relationship.

I'd have been shaking my head if I wasn't in orb-form.

Back to Reality

Sidetracked by the missed opportunity, my thoughts turned to the rest of Sasha's family. In my dimension, time order – past, present, future – didn't exist, so I could hop over, as it were, to anyone else and come back to Sasha without missing anything.

The children sounded like they were auditioning to be backing singers for a thrash metal or post-punk band. Their mother was in front of them, but for the first time in their little lives, she wasn't attending to their needs. Violet was emitting a near-continuous wail, only pausing for breath when absolutely necessary. Rosie was crying out, "Mummy! Mummy! Mummy!" and Noah repeatedly tried his hand at both techniques but nothing was having an effect. They saw strangers moving around outside the vehicle; one made eye contact and shouted something through the window at them.

I told the children that the bystanders were actually trying to help and everything would be okay very shortly but I was as inadequate as everyone else. Rosie was barely aware of me. Violet could see me but ignored me. Noah was clearly receptive, but he chose to copy his siblings' behaviour instead of taking any notice of me. I knew it wouldn't be long before emergency services arrived on the scene, so I turned my attention to Sasha's mum.

She was sitting in the reception area of the hospital, having been parked up in a wheelchair by a nurse. This was the place she'd called Sasha from around half an hour ago. Pauline was generally quite a placid person but it was evident she was getting irritable now. She was certain she could drive herself home safely but of course Sasha was on her way, so she couldn't leave now. She didn't want to phone as Sasha would be driving and, likewise, there was no point sending a text message either.

I prompted the idea of imagining what the other people in the reception area were there for and soon Pauline was distracting herself with stories in her head.

I once prompted Sasha when she was little and had to sit through the longest, most boring sermon ever, to imagine she had superpowers to make everyone fall asleep. She pulled the most extraordinary faces at adults and children in front of her, some of whom seemed to be responding, but after the sermon, the vicar took Pauline aside to ask whether Sasha had any issues that might need addressing.

Happy with Pauline, I took a quick look at Sasha's husband, Mark. He was sitting at his desk in the office, tapping away at his keyboard, blissfully unaware of his wife's predicament. Nothing to worry about there then.

I turned back to Sasha.

She was smiling serenely until Hebron stated, "It's time for you to return."

"No!" She gasped, falling to his feet. "Let me stay here with you."

Just before she'd started her life review, she'd been desperate to get back to her children; now she was begging to stay. Like, make up your mind, Sasha! I didn't mean it, though, this place has that effect on a soul; I'd witnessed it plenty of times.

"Your children need you to fulfil their own destinies," Hebron was saying. "Plus, you have a mission to fulfil, assisting the people connected to this experience of yours. But you won't be alone; we will always be here for you and will guide you appropriately. All you have to do is ask for help and it will be given."

Oh, that's all, is it? I thought. Easy enough for most people, but we're talking about the woman who's refused to ask for anything since she was twelve.

"I don't want to go back. Why did I ever want to go there in the first place?"

It wasn't that Sasha was selfish or cold-hearted; she was just so distanced from her primitive human ego and was certain Mark could find another woman to replace her.

Hebron spelt it out.

"Sasha, you have met those who have asked for your assistance and you have seen others you affected, who are also in need. Your plan involves asking for help, developing your new powers of awareness – which are granted to very few – and finding these people. Your life is moving into a new phase. Do you understand?"

"I think so, but..."

Sasha was proving to be one of the stubborn ones, so Hebron brought in some further reassurance; in other words, me.

"I'd like to introduce you to Zinnia, your spirit guide."

Following Rule 15 to appear relatable, I changed from the energy orb into my most recent human form: black hair piled up on top of my head, wearing my best embroidered white blouse over a full red skirt and a shawl around my shoulders. If Sasha focused – don't be silly, of course she didn't – she'd have seen that I'd tucked a few pretty flowers in my hair. She just glanced at me long enough to exchange polite greetings before turning away.

"Not many people get to meet their spirit guide face-to-face," Hebron said with impressive patience. "When you return to your body, your capacity to see Zinnia will be weak unless you practise your psychic abilities. However, you can be confident she will always be there for you. If you ask for help, she will point you in the right direction, and she can assist you with communicating with this side. Does that reassure you?"

"I guess, but..."

It clearly didn't reassure Sasha one little bit. She had no idea how privileged she was to meet her spirit guide in person and get all this advice spelt out. I don't think she listened to a word of it. And, no, of course I'm not sulking.

There was nothing left but emotional blackmail.

"Look to your right, Sasha," said Hebron.

Sasha turned. Noah was materialising in front of her, reaching out with his chubby little arms and big soulful eyes full of tears.

"Come back, Mummy," he wailed.

Her maternal instincts ignited and she stepped towards Noah in acquiescence. What felt like a hand gripped the scruff of her neck and propelled her back to the scene of the accident at supersonic speed. Coming to a halt just above her body, she hovered for a moment, unsure how to reconnect.

***

Sasha's spirit was squeezed back in through the top of her head.

"Oh, I don't fit anymore – it's too tight."

"You'll get used to it presently. Pull air into your lungs," ordered the voice of the angel.

Sasha concentrated hard and complied, drawing an excruciating, rasping breath into her desiccated throat. Her physical situation came into the sharpest of focus as pain that rivalled childbirth shot through her in all directions. The sense of constriction within her body was the least of her worries. Struggling to get sufficient air into her damaged lungs, she was vaguely aware of paramedics approaching the car. All she could manage were rapid, shallow breaths now.

Oh Jesus! exclaimed Sasha silently. *If heaven is where I've just been, then this is hell for sure.*

We could have had a lovely, deep conversation on

that topic, but now was clearly not the time. Though, for one delightful moment, I pictured her with the ability to communicate with me, doing just that.

It sunk in that the cacophony behind her belonged to her frightened children. She couldn't turn to face them but she managed to produce sufficient platitudes to calm them. A croaky mum was better than an unresponsive one and they seemed to understand they had not been abandoned after all. The screams and howls subsided.

Two paramedics strode over to the car and one of them grabbed the handle on the damaged driver's side. He wasn't surprised to find it stuck fast, so he tried to open the rear door, but it was no good either. He walked round the back of the car to gain access from the other side.

At the same time, the second paramedic who'd approached the nearside had instant success. She opened the front passenger door and squeezed inside to assess Sasha.

The paramedic was in her late twenties. She tugged her long fringe of platinum hair back behind the ear on the unshaved side of her head as she told Sasha her name was Jackie.

She could see her patient was breathing with difficulty, so she gently strapped an oxygen mask to her face and quickly started the injuries checklist as best she could under the cramped conditions. She couldn't see any external injuries to the head or neck but whiplash was common in a side impact collision, and fractured vertebrae were also a possibility. There was copious blood seeping through Sasha's T-shirt on the right side of her torso from the impact of the driver's door. Apologising for causing pain, Jackie taped a temporary dressing over the wound. She would have liked to put pressure on it to reduce the blood flow but Sasha's breathing difficulties pointed to internal thoracic and possibly abdominal injuries. Jackie craned her neck to view the patient's legs under the steering column but they appeared to be trapped by the distorted bodywork – so likely trauma to one or both legs.

She quickly realised it wouldn't be viable to get the patient out of the car from the passenger side, so she radioed for backup from the fire brigade to cut open the offside.

Meanwhile, the male paramedic checked the children over, one by one, and was astounded to find there were no obvious injuries. He told Sasha it would be best for Accident and Emergency staff to give them a more thorough examination considering the seriousness of the accident. She called back to the children that she loved them and she'd be with them soon. The paramedic gently removed them from the car and transferred them into an ambulance that set off straight to the hospital.

"What's your name, love?" asked Jackie.

"Sasha Denning."

"Well, don't worry, Sasha – we'll have you sorted in no time. Can you feel your toes?"

"I think so… aarrrggghhhh!"

The pain in Sasha's right leg ripped through her whole body when she tried to wiggle her toes.

"That's good," said Jackie.

Good? You've got to be kidding me! I hate to think what your idea of bad is, grumbled Sasha silently, not realising the pain was an indication that she could feel her toes and consequently Jackie knew Sasha was not paralysed.

Jackie gave Sasha a small dose of morphine to reduce the pain and kept a light conversation going with her the whole time to keep her conscious whilst she kept checking her pulse and oxygen levels. She also gave reassurance that the children would be fine.

Sasha was in less pain because of the morphine but her mind was crystal clear. She was sure it was a residual effect of what she'd just been through. She'd heard people talking about "near-death experiences", where someone should by all rights have died but instead had strange visions and then came back to life to tell the tale. She'd never taken much notice of these stories as they hadn't really resonated with her and she hadn't even been sure that it was a real thing. Some people said it was just your brain hallucinating and she'd been inclined to agree with them. Now, it resonated as clearly as if she were standing beside Big Ben at midnight and she was buzzing.

Why did this happen to me? Why couldn't I have stayed there? Sasha lamented.

I wrapped her in a blanket of affection, and as a brace was being carefully arranged around her head, I filled her mind with a picture of her mother.

"Oh, Jackie! My mum's waiting for me at the hospital."

"Don't worry – I can get a message to her. Do you have anyone else to tell?" Jackie had spotted Sasha's rings on her left hand.

"Mark. His work number is on my mobile. I'll tell you my pin."

Jackie opened the bulging bag in the passenger footwell and found a mobile in it. She called the hospital to get a message to Pauline and then called Mark.

Sasha imagined her mother panicking and her husband speeding towards the hospital, losing control of his own car or getting stopped by the police. It was too much and she shut her mind down to blank out all her horrid thoughts. But then, as if someone had switched a radio on, she heard Jackie. Not out loud, but what was going on in her head. Really clearly.

Why the hell can't Zara be more considerate? Sasha heard.

She got a vision of a pretty woman with come-to-bed eyes, spiky green hair and a quirky, outgoing character. She then saw, as if through Jackie's eyes, this Zara lounging next to a father figure, feet up on the coffee table, beers in hand, watching rugby. Jackie and Mum-in-law-to-be were at the side, bored out of their heads, waiting for the match to finish.

What's going on? wondered Sasha. *Things like reading minds don't happen to ordinary people like me.*

It was too much to comprehend and she succumbed to sleep.

Yet again, I wished I could communicate with Sasha to discuss her newfound ability. I could have reassured her that her so-called ordinariness, or quieter brain patterns, was ideal. It meant other mind "traffic" didn't fight for attention and her brain could switch vibrational level to that which she'd been using in the other dimension.

The firefighters finished cutting the side of the car away; Sasha was extracted from the vehicle, placed flat on a gurney and wheeled into the second ambulance that sped along to the hospital, lights flashing, siren screeching. When a pothole jerked Sasha awake, she found she was strapped down horizontally with big foam pads on either side of her head. A siren wailing above her and the bumpiness of the ride told her she was on the way to hospital. The intense pain, her vivid memories of the other dimension and her guilt at failing to reach her poor mum were altogether an unbearable load. Thankfully, Jackie noticed Sasha suffering and gave her a top-up of morphine.

Pauline's Problems

I went back to the hospital to see how Pauline was getting on.

The nurse had wheeled her to reception and positioned her next to the reception desk so she could easily ask for assistance if required. Now she was away from the oncology department, she felt back to normal and was itching to leave the hospital. She waited impatiently for the arrival of her daughter, her toes tapping out a tune on the footrest.

What on earth was taking Sasha so long? What a waste of an afternoon. Her thoughts sifted over what had led to this irritating inconvenience.

She'd recently attended a mammogram unit for breast cancer screening that was followed by a letter not giving her the all-clear but calling her back for further tests. After her initial palpitations, she'd reminded herself she was an experienced nurse, albeit retired now, so she should know better than to jump to conclusions. Maybe she'd twitched during the X-ray. A second X-ray was bound to be clear; she didn't feel or look like she had cancer and she was far more fit and healthy than most of her friends. Of course anxiety did creep in but she'd followed in her mother's footsteps, bearing the crown of a worthy martyr as she selflessly raised her children. Accordingly, Pauline decided she wouldn't bother anyone else about the letter. Off she'd gone for the retests on her own, without her husband Kevin any the wiser.

Unfortunately, she did have every right to be anxious. A further mammogram, ultrasound and biopsy later, she was back in the consulting room listening to the doctor.

"Now, let's have a look at your notes. Ah, yes, Mrs Carter, there's an issue with a small mass in your right breast. It appears to be no more than one centimetre wide and, so far as we can see at the moment, there are no signs of spreading. That makes it Stage One – a good position under the circumstances."

Pauline had gulped and gripped her hands tightly together. The words "good position" didn't seem very appropriate right now.

"There is a set procedure for treatment. You will undergo ten weeks of chemotherapy to contain and shrink the tumour. This will be followed by surgery. We have two choices: a lumpectomy or a full mastectomy. Clearly, the latter is a major surgical procedure but it does give more reassurance that the cancer has been completely removed and you can have a breast implant in most cases. The lumpectomy is less invasive. There is always a risk that some cancerous tissue could be missed; however, in your case the growth is small, so a lumpectomy is certainly a viable option. Following surgery, there will be fifteen weeks of radiotherapy."

Sour wafts of disinfectant clotted with Pauline's despair. Her sniffs rolled into sobs.

After an awkward pause, the doctor was telling her, "Take this information sheet to read and if you have any questions, you are welcome to call the number at the end of the leaflet. My secretary's number is listed. You will receive a letter in the post to give you a date for the start of your treatment."

As she rose to leave, buzzy bright sparkles whirled around Pauline's head, playing havoc with her balance, so she sat back down. After a couple of fruitless attempts to stand again – even getting up ever so, ever so slowly – the dizziness was replaced by stomach-churning nausea and Pauline called out for a sick bowl. The weary doctor now ordered her to lie down on the nearest examination couch where he checked her blood pressure, which was lower than ideal. As the nurse elevated Pauline's legs with a pillow, the doctor advised her she mustn't drive home and she'd need somebody to pick her up. Next, he asked the nurse to use a wheelchair to take Mrs Carter to the entrance area of Milton Keynes Hospital, where she could be collected and he could get on with his long list of patients.

But who can pick me up? Pauline had wondered as she was trundling along.

She didn't want to ask Kevin because she'd told him she was going to visit her old friend Sheila that afternoon. Plus, she had driven the car, so he'd have to order a taxi and wouldn't be too pleased with the expense. He was always very sensible with money.

What about Sheila? Kevin might not think twice about Sheila appearing back with her. The only problem was Sheila's driving was getting increasingly more erratic. The last time, she'd bounced off the kerb twice when driving along a straight road. Not the best for a dodgy tummy.

The next option was Sasha. She was always willing to help but she'd have to bring the children, which would be a bit of a palaver. Well, Pauline couldn't think of anyone better so Sasha would have to do, children and all.

Sitting self-consciously in the hospital wheelchair, concentrating on the issue in hand, she'd steadied her voice to near normality as she'd called Sasha with her mobile phone.

Checking her watch now, Pauline saw that thirty long minutes had turned to forty. What was Sasha doing? There was a woman around Sasha's age with a small girl at the reception desk and Pauline wondered what they were there for. She started creating stories for the miscellaneous individuals around her and the next twenty minutes passed more easily.

A member of the clerical staff by the name of Mrs Jones, according to her name badge, approached.

"Are you Pauline Carter?" asked Mrs Jones.

"Yes," Pauline replied, wondering what this could be about, as Mrs Jones sat down on the empty chair beside her.

"I'm afraid there's been an accident," said Mrs Jones. "The children are now in A & E but your daughter is still at the scene of the accident."

"Oh heavens," exclaimed Pauline, her hands flying to her mouth and tears filling her eyes. "There's nothing wrong with me anymore. Please let me see the children." She stood straight up, prepared to bolt towards the A & E department in the event of any resistance.

Mrs Jones had been fully briefed on Pauline's situation and couldn't help thinking that "nothing wrong with me" wasn't a good choice of words. The patient did appear to be in control and of normal pallor but people were always suing the NHS, so she wasn't going to take any chances.

"If you sit back down, Mrs Carter, I'll wheel you to A & E."

"Bugger that," muttered Pauline as she clutched her handbag close to her chest and sprinted off. She knew the route and nobody was going to stop her.

"Wait! Let me wheel you," shouted Mrs Jones at the receding figure. She scurried behind, propelling the vacated wheelchair.

Pauline's sandals clip-clopped on the solid linoleum as she speed-walked purposefully, trying not to fully break into a trot. All thoughts of her own predicament were left in reception. It was a ridiculously long way to A & E and she was acutely aware of Mrs Jones at her heels.

At last she entered the cubicle where the three young children were lying. As she shooed Mrs Jones away, Pauline patted her hair into place and endeavoured to reduce her audible breathing to normal levels. Thankfully, the doctor was more interested in the children than the anxious grandmother.

Violet was vigorously sucking her dummy, which had been clipped to her clothing when Sasha had got the children ready to go out, a virtual lifetime ago. It was clear that it wouldn't be long before she'd be spitting out the dummy and wailing with hunger again.

Noah was rather overwhelmed by all the recent and current events and he lay on the big bed with huge, watery, watchful eyes whilst being uncharacteristically still and quiet. I can confirm he was re-picturing his brief unearthly contact with his mother. It would soon fade into his subconscious though.

Dr Yeo was looking at Rosie, scratching her chin (that is the doctor's own chin, not Rosie's, which would have been weird). She was more than a little baffled. Having been advised that the car had been struck with considerable force, she'd expected to discover potentially serious injuries but it was hard to believe the children had been in the car at all. Apart from some minor grazes where the seat belts had scraped delicate skin, there was nothing to be seen and all tests came back normal. Dr Yeo was prepared to discharge all three children, provided there would be appropriate supervision to monitor them for the next forty-eight hours.

Should I Stay or Should I Go?

Now I turned my attention back to Mark. I liked his soul. He and Sasha had shared a few pairings in previous human lives; their bond so tight that Those Above made certain allowances for them. In his present incarnation, he'd been given a logical brain with a black-and-white filter and his intuition had been dialled down. To be fair, this didn't bring out the best in him.

When Mark had received the paramedic's call, he'd jumped straight up, the blood draining from his face and his chair knocking over his rubbish bin, scattering its contents. Oblivious, he ran into his boss's office where he shouted to John that Sasha and the children had been in an accident and he was leaving immediately for the hospital.

Once in his car, Mark risked almost every speed limit. He gritted his teeth and swallowed back tears as he gripped the steering wheel.

Let them be okay. Please let them, he pleaded all the way to the hospital as he squinted against the glaring sun. It hadn't occurred to him to put his sunglasses on.

He arrived and parked in the first available space he could find, cursing that he had to pay for parking before he could enter the hospital. He raced into A & E and waited in line for the front desk, where it was barely any cooler than outside. He kept clenching and unclenching his fists until it was his turn.

"The children are being assessed at the moment, so you'll be led through to them shortly, but your wife is still at the scene of the accident," a receptionist finally told him.

As he entered the cubicle where the children were, Mark forced a smile onto his face and tried to ignore his queasy tummy. He responded to all their requests for hugs before he and Pauline discussed what to do and came up with a basic plan.

Mark rang Kevin and asked him to get a taxi to the hospital so he and Pauline could drive the children back home. For convenience, Kevin and Pauline had bought car seats for the children from a car boot sale. It was certainly very convenient today.

Kevin was confused; he couldn't understand why Pauline wouldn't have picked him up on the way back from Sheila's, but the gravity of Mark's tone stopped him from raising the question.

Mark would wait at the hospital until Sasha was brought in so he could be by her side as soon as he was permitted. They decided not to tell Sasha's sister, Carina, or anyone else about the situation until more was known about Sasha's condition. As Carina was currently in France, working as an au pair, there was no point alarming her unnecessarily.

Mark, Pauline and Kevin each carried a child to the car and strapped them in. Mark gave them all big kisses and asked them to behave well for Nanna and Grandad. Noah cried and begged Daddy not to leave them, but it was Rosie's and Violet's turns to be uncharacteristically quiet – it had been a very peculiar day, to put it mildly.

Mark waved to the children until they were out of sight, then loped back into the hospital. He was desperate for news of Sasha.

The lady at the counter confirmed that she had indeed been brought in and was waiting to be taken for a full CT scan. She wasn't saying how long he'd have to wait, but he got the impression it might be a long time.

Mark paced up and down. What should he do? It made sense to go home, grab something to eat, have a quick shower and change into more comfortable, cooler clothes, but what if something went wrong when he wasn't there? He would never forgive himself if he wasn't with Sasha when she needed him. There again, it was only a ten-minute drive home. He could be there and back in half an hour.

A man who was moulded into one of the plastic chairs in the waiting area made eye contact with Mark. "I've been 'ere three hours, mate! Three bloody hours! I shoulda done what they said and waited for a call to come back. It's too late to go now, innit? Wish they'd bloody 'urry up."

"That's tough, mate," said Mark, his hand on his car key, ready to nip home. Then the main door was flung open by a man half-carrying a woman whose face was covered in blood. Mark blanched and sat back down. Change of plan. He wasn't going to risk not being there when Sasha needed him. Trying to ignore his sticky work clothes, he settled down for the long wait and sent a text to his boss to say he was unlikely to be in the next day.

So Tell Me About Yourself

I switched back to Sasha at the point where the ambulance was arriving at the hospital.

Hang on a minute – my tablet's flashing. Oh, it's another little explanation for you. Remember I said I can hop around to see what's going on? In human form, you're always stuck in the present moment, but time isn't linear in my dimension, so I can go backwards when I choose. If you're wondering about going forwards, too, it's a bit trickier going into the future due to variables and suchlike, but you'd be surprised what's possible.

Sasha's gurney was wheeled through the rear entrance straight through to an assessment bay.

Jackie briefed the registrar who immediately arranged for Sasha to have a barrage of tests. There could be a lot more injuries than the obvious broken thigh bone.

The mixed bag of results came back. No bleeding to the brain nor any spinal injury. However, two ribs had snapped and pierced the thoracic wall, causing a pneumothorax: a punctured lung, hence Sasha's difficulty and pain with breathing. No further internal injuries were detected. The hips were intact, but the right femur had a clean break through the middle. Blood tests revealed cardiac enzymes indicating she had suffered a heart seizure during the accident, so she was wired up to an ECG machine. The results showed no further issues with her heart, but time would tell whether there would be any lasting damage to her brain if it had been starved of oxygen during the seizure.

The respiratory physician, Dr Bowkowski, aspirated Sasha's right side using a needle to draw out air and fluid. This made it easier and less painful for Sasha to breathe. Once he was confident Sasha was stable, she was then passed over to Orthopaedics.

Because of the pneumothorax, the orthopaedic surgeon was reluctant to operate straight away. Instead, her leg was put into traction to place the broken bone back into alignment and to prevent the muscles and tendons from pulling the femur out of shape again. She was taken to a bed in a high-dependency ward and wired up to all sorts of monitoring equipment.

During this lengthy process, Sasha answered questions briefly and gave minimal responses to the small talk that anyone attempted with her. The hospital staff were used to all sorts of people and it was much better to have a diffident patient than a loud, aggressive one. Of course, they had no idea Sasha's responses were a million miles away from her well-mannered self.

There were two reasons for Sasha's attitude. The first was that everything around her appeared brighter, colours deeper and more vibrant. She would have liked to ponder this but another issue was much more intriguing. She could "listen" to the people around her. Just like with Jackie, Sasha was getting information on anyone around her whom she tuned into. She could blank her mind like flicking a switch and suddenly she was on their wavelength. It wasn't just what they were thinking and feeling, but background knowledge too, almost as if she had commanded, "So, tell me about yourself."

Dr Bowkowski, who was a short, rotund, middle-aged man, with chubby cheeks and a pleasant face, had been worried his decision to aspirate rather than insert a chest drain might backfire. If the aspiration went well it was the best plan, he thought, but it could fail, requiring a chest drain insertion which, of course, he could just do straight off but was less advantageous to the patient. No, he would stick to plan A and hope for the best. There could be unknown factors and it was rather like playing God at times. *Only nobody sues God if he doesn't get it right*, he grumbled to himself.

Sasha was staggered that Dr Bowkowski still felt uncomfortable, after all his years in practice, with the responsibility of choosing the right course of action.

Nurse Hannah, conversely, was oh-so-happy. She couldn't wait until her shift was over. She'd recently met a guy called James at her friend Laura's housewarming party. James was twenty-eight, worked in IT and went to the gym. He was well-fit with the sexiest Caribbean accent. She got butterflies in her tummy just thinking about meeting up with him later at Dino's. *Maybe he's the one!*

No, mustn't think that. Don't want to jinx things so early on. She would wear her favourite blue dress and silver high heels with the dainty ankle straps. *That ought to make a good impression on him. I hope he fancies me as much as I fancy him*, she thought. Hannah's excitement was like a mouthful of popping candy.

I made sure Sasha stayed well-sedated to keep her responses, such as telling Dr Bowkowski not to worry as she was sure he was doing the best he could for her or wishing Hannah good luck on her date, to herself. Whilst I would've had fun watching what happened if she did, I stuck to being sensible. I had exams to pass, after all. I enjoyed listening to Sasha mulling over her new abilities though.

This is so weird, she was thinking. *What if I "see" something really personal? Yuck! Or a serial killer planning their next murder? Ooh, I could help solve crimes. Ha-ha – as if!*

The next person, thankfully, wasn't a serial killer, but it didn't mean her story was cheerful.

The senior nurse on the ward, called Julie, was struggling. She did her job as if on autopilot without problem – after all, she'd been a nurse for the last thirty-three years – but she was constantly overwhelmed by the lowest of moods.

Why do I bother? she was asking herself. *All I've got is a knackering job I never get any thanks for and go home to a useless bugger who'll just moan or wind me up. It's all shit.*

Sasha's heart ached in sympathy. It occurred to her, without any input from me, that reading minds was certainly one way to keep her mind off the intense desire to be back in that other world. She'd thought about it much less since hearing other peoples' situations and contemplating their lives.

I couldn't resist flashing an image of myself to Sasha, which, pleasingly, she recognised.

That's a coincidence. Or is it? Maybe there's no such thing as coincidences, after all. Zinnia is my spirit guide, isn't she? That's cool! Maybe this is Zinnia's way of helping me cope with being back.

I was as chuffed as a lottery winner that Sasha actually saw me, but I sobered up the moment I was zapped with an image of the rule book. It was clear Hebron was warning me to back off, but I didn't feel it was fair. Me flashing the image to Sasha wasn't helping her do anything; I'd only wanted to see if it provoked a reaction. Being under supervision was *so* tedious.

Mark's Malarky

To get some distance from Hebron (not that he couldn't follow me if he wanted), I flew over to Mark.

A uniformed police officer entered A & E and was pointed in Mark's direction. He gave Mark the accident report number and a business card for the depot where Sasha's mangled wreck had been taken.

There were no further interruptions and the minutes dragged by. Reading the newspaper he found lying on an adjacent seat wasn't helpful; the words dissolved in his brain without meaning, so he gave up, letting his mind wander.

I listened in on his internal musings.

It's amazing how a shock like this can make you appreciate someone, he told himself as he shuddered, trying to block the thought of Sasha not being there for him and the children.

He pictured her now. Apart from a bit of a mumtum, she hardly seemed to have aged at all in the seven years they'd been together. Mark was proud of her looks;

he had the best-looking wife out of his circle of friends and acquaintances (and it never actually occurred to him other husbands were thinking exactly the same about their own wives). They had their three adorable children and he loved his family dearly. All his friends told Mark how lucky he was; how well-suited he and Sasha were. They were the perfect couple – the perfect family.

But then, what did his friends really know? Sasha no longer seemed to want him, or even care much about him. He could hardly remember the last time they'd made love – maybe it was when Violet was conceived. Whenever he made advances and suggested they have an early night, Sasha would brush him off and say she was too tired. Or the children might hear. Or she didn't feel very well. Or any damn excuse. He had needs and desires but what did she care? He used to be able to cheer her up and make her laugh but now she only seemed to smile and laugh when she played with the children. The children always came first now.

And then there was Natalie, an admin assistant at work. She appeared to be very interested in him. She was shorter than Sasha, with a considerably curvier figure. Her breasts were unmissably large and she often wore figure-hugging tops just low enough to show the top of her cleavage but not so much as to be criticised by the Human Resources department. He couldn't help imagining wrapping his muscular arms around her waist or holding her generous hips and an equally generous – but to him, attractively pert – backside. She had deep brown eyes you could trip and fall into and glossy black hair that tumbled halfway down her back. Mark's version of Natalie promoted her from pleasantly, plumply good-looking to Jessica Rabbit drop-dead-gorgeous.

What Mark wasn't aware of, but I'd noted very quickly, was that Natalie was nearly thirty and many of her friends had settled into coupledom, some starting families. And she was worried she'd be left behind. With her continued lack of success in finding her mate for life, she was getting rather less selective, to the point where she persuaded herself a married man wasn't completely "verboten", under the right circumstances.

Natalie was attracted to Mark Denning and had been watching him for some time now. After all, it seemed to her that Mark seemed less and less cheerful with every passing month, so perhaps his marriage wasn't right for him after all. Maybe she was destined to be his special soulmate and make him happier than his wife, Sasha, ever could. She knew Mark had three young children but she could grow to love them and hopefully she and Mark could have more of their own; she'd always dreamt of having a big happy family since she was an only child. Such were the egocentric, biological-clock-fuelled and rather unrealistic thoughts whirling around in Natalie's head.

Back to Mark sitting in the sterile hospital, all he was aware of were her boobs and bum and her "come-and-get-me" manner. When Natalie first started flirting with him, Mark's neck prickled, his face flushed and he'd busy himself at his desk. He did his best to ignore her as it was very much against his principles to consider another woman since he was married. He loved Sasha and would never want to cause her pain. He knew he should have told Natalie she was wasting her time but that moment had passed. Now, an appetising tingle in his tummy would erupt when she looked him deep in the eye and he had to exert mind over matter when she slipped a suggestive remark into conversation, in case his dick started to react too. He hadn't felt any surges of excitement like this in such a long time.

His loyalty to Sasha was stretched enough to let erotic fantasies about Natalie creep into his imagination, such as pulling her tight against his body and kissing her seductively, like the macho men in those black-and-white movies, all silent, powerful and manly.

Jesus, man, he admonished himself. *Your wife's seriously ill in hospital and you're fantasising about another woman. You're disgusting.*

Exactly what I was thinking. And we were both relieved when someone in a white coat approached. Mark looked up, hoping his guilty thoughts weren't displayed on his face. They were to me, but the doctor didn't notice.

"Mr Denning?"

Mark nodded.

"I'm Dr Stevens. Your wife has had quite a serious accident. She has two broken ribs, a punctured lung and a broken femur. In addition, tests show she suffered a cardiac seizure. She was breathing when the paramedics reached her but we don't know how long her heart might have stopped. There is no evidence of cognitive impairment but we cannot rule it out. Fluid has been removed from the lung and now we must wait until she is ready for the operation to mend her femur. In the meantime, she has a splint on the leg. Her condition is stable but she may not be very responsive due to medication and a need to rest. We are keeping her under observation but you can visit her now. Any questions?"

"Uh, no. I don't think so. She will be all right, won't she?"

"Well, she's not out of the woods yet but try not to worry. She's in Franklin Ward on the first floor. Take the lift or stairs just along the corridor and on your left. Good day, Mr Denning."

Mark's head was reeling with all the information the doctor had just given him. The worst thing was the mention of possible brain damage. That would be as bad as losing her.

His eyes prickling with the threat of tears, he mechanically thanked the doctor and made his way along the sterile white corridor, up the stairs and through to Franklin Ward. There were bays on either side as Mark walked into the ward. He approached the central desk to find out which bed Sasha was in and, as he waited for a nurse to put the phone down, he thought he could see Sasha in the bay opposite, over by the window.

This did turn out to be correct. Relief and anxiety flooded through Mark in equal measure as he approached his bedridden wife.

Hearing familiar footsteps, Sasha opened her eyes and looked up at her husband striding towards her. He was wearing his suit and she realised he'd come straight from work. His face seemed a little creased and stressed but he was smiling broadly at her. This was the man she'd fallen in love with and wanted to spend the rest of her life with.

Mark bent over and awkwardly hugged and kissed Sasha, one small tear dropping onto her hair. Sasha reached up gingerly to hug him back.

"Oh my goodness! Look at you." Mark took in the scene. Sasha was propped up in a semi-reclined position, with marshmallow pillows behind her back and head. She was wearing a white hospital gown speckled with some blue pattern; a sheet and lightweight cotton blanket were covering up to her waist. The traction splint on her right leg wasn't visible under the blanket and Mark also didn't notice the extending length of metal protruding beyond her foot, down to the end of the bed. There was a cannula taped securely into Sasha's left hand and a bag of saline solution had been hooked up. Her face was pale with dark shadows under her eyes and she seemed to have a bewildered, preoccupied expression as if she wasn't fully in the room. Could it be brain damage? An icy tremor zapped through Mark.

Sasha relaxed back down in the bed and used her left arm to pull her hair up from under the back of her head; it spread out across the pillow like a wonky halo.

"How are you?" they both asked at exactly the same time, creating spontaneous laughter.

"Ow!" cried Sasha, automatically clutching her right side then pulling her hand away. "Don't make me laugh – it hurts so much."

"Sorry; you first," said Mark as he settled himself into the blue armchair next to the bed. *Why are hospital chairs always blue?* flitted through his mind.

"I'm okay." Sasha made a split-second decision to mention only the physical effects for the moment, even though she was bursting to talk about everything else. "All down the right of me hurts really badly but they keep giving me pain relief, which helps a bit. The worst thing is breathing, which is kind of hard to avoid. Other than that, I'm fine – ha-ha."

"Make sure you ask for pain relief when you need it. You don't want to suffer more than necessary."

"I will," Sasha lied. The nurses had enough to deal with without a demanding patient. "Have you seen the children? How are they? It feels wrong to be apart from them."

"They're all good. It's incredible, really – they aren't hurt at all. Even the doctor couldn't believe it. Barely a scratch on any of them."

Of course, thought Sasha. *Gran kept telling me the children would be fine. I wonder whether angels could have stopped them from getting injured.*

She wondered correctly. It's not unusual for angels and spirit guides to get involved in situations such as car accidents, occasionally even preventing them.

"Your mum and dad have taken them back to our house and will stay until I get home. I expect your mum will stay longer to help look after them."

"Oh – how is she? Why was she in hospital in the first place?"

"What do you mean? I guess it was odd that she was here on her own before me but it didn't look like anything was wrong with her."

"She called for me to pick her up – she wasn't allowed to drive but she didn't say why. I really hope it's not serious."

Mark raked his hand through his hair. He didn't know if he could handle another problem on top of Sasha's accident.

Sasha saw him deflating. "You must be so tired if you've been waiting for me," she said. "I think everything's taken a very long time, hasn't it?"

"You could say that. It feels like I've been here a whole lifetime."

A smile flickered at the corners of Sasha's mouth. *Try having a life review*, she thought.

"I was really worried about you," Mark said. "What happened, and how bad is the car, by the way?"

Sasha squirmed. "I don't really know what happened. One minute I was driving onto a roundabout, the next…" She hesitated. She couldn't say that the next moment she was looking at the accident from above, could she? *Maybe not now*, she thought, and moved on. "The car is one hundred per cent going to be a write-off. You'll be shocked when you see it."

"Why?" asked Mark, frowning.

"Well, firemen cut the side of the car away to get me out. It must be a real mess. Oh, I don't know what's happened to it, as I got put straight into an ambulance as soon as they got me out. I wonder if it's still at the side of the road."

"Oh, I know about that. A policeman told me the car's been moved somewhere and he gave me a card for the place. I'll contact them tomorrow and get our things out of it. I'll call the insurance company and we'll sort it all out when you're up to it."

Sasha really wanted to tell Mark about her peculiar experience even though he'd probably think she was talking rubbish. She took a deep breath, pain shooting through her chest, before giving it a go.

Ignoring Hebron's warnings, I told Sasha not to bother, as I knew what Mark's reaction would be, but she didn't listen to me. I don't know why I butt in when there's clearly no point.

"Mark, have you ever heard of near-death experiences?" she asked tentatively.

"Well, yeah. Aren't they what some people say they've had when they've almost died? Don't they say they've gone through a tunnel and seen the light? Or been to heaven and back? As if! It's obviously just the brain playing tricks on them or they've just been hallucinating. Why do you ask – you're not going to tell me you think you've had one, are you?"

"No, no, of course not; I just wondered," backpedalled Sasha.

I stopped myself saying, "I told you so."

In cheerful ignorance, Mark chatted on for a while about how shocked he'd been when he'd got the phone call to summon him to the hospital, the frustrating journey there and then the order of events regarding seeing the children, her mum and her dad. He then spoke briefly about work, being careful not to mention Natalie's name at all.

When he paused, Sasha said, "You don't need to stay, you know. You look exhausted."

"Well, I'll stay for a little longer before I go home."

Sasha let her heavy eyelids slide shut. Mark stopped talking and sat quietly back in his chair, listening to the background noise and keeping an eye on Sasha's face in case she opened her eyes again, though he suspected she'd fallen asleep.

While she was pretending to be asleep, she was processing what she had "seen". When Mark had been talking about her parents and her children in the hospital cubicle, she could see his images as if they were her own – like she was standing next to him. Then he'd started talking about work and she could see the office in her mind.

First, his desk and computer, but then she also saw a young woman with big boobs, long glossy dark hair and an intimate smile, undulating along the corridor towards her. Abruptly, this image disappeared and she was back to seeing Mark's computer screen, paperwork and coffee cup. Instinctively, Sasha knew Mark was pushing this woman out of his thoughts but that hardly made it acceptable.

What the hell! Sure, things were strained between them at the moment but she'd thought her husband was decent, that he'd never be unfaithful. She'd had such an incredible experience today, followed by agony, both mental and physical, at returning to her body. The surge of renewed love for Mark when he'd entered the ward had been wonderful but now mistrust blasted it into a million brittle shards of misery.

I so wanted to reassure Sasha that things would be okay, but apart from the little issue of Sasha not being good at sensing me, I also couldn't be certain of the outcome on this one. There were too many variables ahead.

Her Life Flashed Before Her Eyes

Sasha was alone again – as much as she could be in a busy ward of course – and she was drawn back to her life review in the NDE.

Okay, I admit I put the idea in her head; I wanted to give her another chance to spot the significance of her childhood vows.

Straight away, Sasha was reliving everything exactly as it happened in the other dimension starting with the holographic vision rising up. The first scenes were of her parents before she was born. Even second time around, it was strange to see her mother in her twenties, training as a nurse at Northampton Hospital. Sasha watched Pauline falling in love with Kevin, a fellow nurse who was five years her senior, tall and kind. Confetti sprayed over the couple on their wedding day, and Kevin carried Pauline over the threshold to set up home in a modest semi in Milton Keynes. Sasha had a view of Milton Keynes as it was then – in its infancy as a purpose-built new town, full of promise for a clean, modern future.

She saw the moment she was conceived, in the resting hours following her parents' passion, when an incandescent spark of electric blue light erupted in her mother's abdomen.

The embracing security of being well-cared for as a baby followed, and family scenes continued with the addition of her sister, Carina.

She recalled her life review exactly as it had been in the other dimension and her reactions were replicated. With every detail, Sasha was not just hearing what was spoken but feeling all the emotions of those involved. She experienced the consequences of her actions, positive or negative and much of it was startling due to repercussions which she had been oblivious to at the time.

She watched her toddler-self at a picnic in the park, where she ambled away into the path of a woman on horseback. The horse reared up, then fell back onto the rider, damaging her spinal cord with life-changing impact. Adult Sasha felt sick for the suffering she'd caused.

In another scene at primary school, Sasha was protecting Carina from a bigger girl called Rebecca. It had been a fleeting moment in her childhood, but now Sasha was shocked to witness the knock-on effect on Rebecca's self-esteem and life choices.

Not everything in the review was doom and gloom though. There were many positive events and the angel often beamed with affection, making it clear that Sasha's good deeds, however small, were recognised.

I have to say, this had me glowing with pride too. Yes, I know certain religions tell you pride's a sin, but let's not get into religious dogma – that would be a whole different book.

As for the childhood vows to refuse to ask for help, she'd winced at her emotional response but there was no recognition of an over-reaction or anything remotely useful as she breezed right past the incident once again.

I shook my head in despair.

The next scene she paused at was when she was twelve, playing catch with a cricket ball in her friend Ryan's front garden. Sasha reacted to this replay, as it zoomed in on the neighbour, Mr Taylor, and followed the unfortunate line of consequences.

I could feel Sasha's relief that events were less dramatic from high school onwards; she'd learnt how to keep under the radar of teachers and bullies alike.

Leaving school at sixteen with unremarkable qualifications, she'd found her first job at a local printing company where she made endless cups of tea and performed repetitive general admin tasks.

God, that was boring, she reacted, and I wholeheartedly agreed. It was the dullest part of her life, for sure. At least she could see that the next job in a billing department was a step up with a bit of variety and workmates she could have a laugh with.

Sasha watched her eight-year-long relationship with Liam, a lad who worked in a sports shop in the main shopping centre, develop from a young crush to routine as they continued to live at their respective parents' homes. Everyone, including Liam and Sasha, had expected they'd get married one day, until Liam's head was turned by an

Australian woman who whisked him off to Sydney when her visa ran out. It had surprised everyone, including Liam. Sasha had cried a little, got drunk with her friends, then gone on a skiing trip and discovered there was more to life than Liam.

Sasha honed in on an evening at The Half Moon pub. As chief bridesmaid for her best friend Michelle, she'd arranged a hen-do with a DJ and disco, buffet food and stripper. All the friends and relatives were wearing the bright pink T-shirts that Sasha had organised, with BRIDE 2 B on Michelle's and NOT 2 B on the others.

That was the best time ever, Sasha thought with a wistful smile.

Mark was at the same pub with his mates Phil and Paul, having their regular Saturday night of pool and pints of lager. Phil, who didn't possess an ounce of social boundaries awareness, charmed his way into the party, dragging Mark and Paul along with him. They drank and danced and chatted up the girls over the course of the evening, with Mark having eyes only for one girl. He'd seen her before but never had the courage to approach her. Mark thought her hazel eyes, slightly upturned nose and cupid-bow lips were worthy of a beauty contest winner. He stood self-consciously on the periphery of the dance floor, transfixed by her hair bouncing around her shoulders as she danced but not quite brave enough to approach her.

That's me, of course! observed living Sasha with delight. It was just as fun to watch second time round.

The DJ put on "Girls Just Wanna Have Fun", so Sasha downed her drink, jumped up unsteadily and headed back to the dance floor. Her attempt at a sexy sashay was thwarted by the slippery flooring and she skidded precariously, arms wind-milling madly.

Mark rushed forward to save her from falling. Instead, his feet slid straight into hers and they toppled like two bowling pins. Disentangling, Mark spluttered profuse apologies, which Sasha, in her state of intoxication, found utterly amusing and charming.

Encouraged by Sasha's demeanour, Mark said, "Well, that wasn't exactly the way I'd planned to sweep you off your feet."

"But it worked, didn't it?" replied Sasha.

"Did it? Does that mean you'll go out with me?"

"I suppose it does."

Bedbound Sasha grimaced with embarrassment and sped through the rest of the review.

It showed her moving into Mark's house and his marriage proposal that Christmas, with positive reactions from all her friends and relatives. They took in Georgie, a rescue cat, and the review showed Sasha the dreadful events he'd suffered before he was rescued.

Then came Mark and Sasha's wedding. She looked amazing in a stylish wedding dress with pink flowers in her hair to match her bouquet. Mark and Phil, his best man, wore cobalt blue three-piece suits and gold cravats that had a small motif of pink to complement the flowers. The day was full of sunshine and warmth with only one small glitch. At the time for the parents' photo, Bob was moving into position when he tripped over the train of Sasha's dress and glided face-first into Pauline's bosom.

Her Bucks Fizz erupted from its glass, baptising Bob's bald spot. With Pauline shrieking in horror, Gail and Kevin rushed in to extricate Bob, headbutting each other as they did so. There were many scarlet-cheeked apologies but they joked about it afterwards; quite a long time afterwards.

Next, Sasha was pregnant with Rosie. *Oh God, please skip over the morning sickness,* she pleaded. God had better things to deal with elsewhere, so the nausea and fatigue engulfed Sasha all over again.

Well, that's one way to make sure I never have any more babies, she thought.

Sasha relived the joy, fatigue, anxiety and enchantment of their first baby. Planning to have more children, Mark and Sasha moved into a four-bedroomed semi in time for baby number two.

The following year, they had to turn the spare bedroom into a nursery as unplanned baby Violet was on her way. Sasha steeled herself for the final onslaught of nausea.

Now she was witnessing the familiar sense of exhaustion. No longer in paid employment, their income dropped and all-inclusive holidays became a thing of the past whilst bargains of all sorts gained attraction. Fun boozy nights were replaced by dozing in front of the television.

Sasha didn't really want to watch how she shouldered all the housework but a brief segue into Mark's past was enlightening. She saw his mother at home, doing everything for her sons. They didn't have to help with laying the table or washing up, dusting and vacuuming or even keeping their own bedrooms tidy. Gail did it all.

Since that's the way he was brought up, I don't suppose he'll ever change, Sasha sighed as she emerged from the flashback into the hospital ward.

Had I done the right thing making Sasha revisit her life review? I really wasn't convinced. I frowned at my tablet as the three horrid rules glared back at me.

Which is Worse?

Sasha's parents let the children watch CBeebies whilst they prepared a simple dinner and put down food for Georgie, who was winding himself round their legs, meowing.

The aroma of fried eggs, baked beans and chips relaxed them all as they ate at the kitchen table, the adults assisting the grandchildren as necessary. Violet didn't complain about her meal from a jar and she guzzled a bottle of milk, sitting on Pauline's lap once the meal was complete. Following plenty of cuddles and a nappy change, Violet was put to bed by Pauline whilst Kevin poured the wooden train track pieces out of a toy box onto the living room floor and helped Rosie and Noah build a track and have a bit of fun before bedtime. He was in his element, making different voices for the engines and inventing little stories to keep the children entertained.

When Rosie and Noah were finally in bed and settled, Pauline sank down on the sofa with her husband, heaving an involuntary sigh as she hugged her mug of tea to her chest.

I leant in to listen closely to their thoughts as well as conversation.

"Something doesn't seem right, love," said Kevin as he turned to face Pauline.

"Oh, Kevin. I'm really sorry but I hadn't wanted to worry you if there wasn't a problem. I didn't actually go to Sheila's. I had an appointment at the hospital today."

Pauline didn't want to accept what she had to face. It was a good distraction when Georgie jumped up onto her lap, purring loudly.

"What for?" asked Kevin, thinking, *Will this day never end?*

Pauline stopped stroking the cat. "I've got a lump in my breast," she said, avoiding looking directly at Kevin. "The good news is it's only small and they don't think it's spread yet, so it's Stage One. The bad news is that treatment goes on forever. I've got to have ten weeks of chemotherapy first of all. That's followed by surgery: either a lumpectomy or mastectomy. And after that is fifteen weeks of radiotherapy. That's the programme. What a nightmare."

Kevin put his arms around Pauline and she collapsed onto him. He gently drew back the hair that had fallen across her face and planted soft kisses on her forehead. He wasn't sure what to say but he was determined not to let her down.

"Okay," he said at last. "You'll get through this. It's Stage One, so you've got every chance of a full recovery."

"I know, but it's still such a worry. What keeps going through my head, when I'm not thinking about Sasha, is which type of surgery to choose and losing my hair. My hair wouldn't win any awards but I'd rather keep it, all the same."

"I thought they give you a cooling hat to wear after chemo to stop the hair falling out."

"I think so too, but don't most people end up going bald? I suppose I've just got to prepare myself for it, but easier said than done. Anyway, what about the surgery? What should I choose?"

"I don't know, love. What are the pros and cons of each option?"

"Well, if I remember correctly, having the lumpectomy means a shorter recovery time but I'll probably end up with a bit of an odd-shaped breast. If they remove the whole breast, there's less chance of the cancer coming back and I could have an implant but I'd lose my nipple. Since they've caught the cancer early, I'm thinking the lumpectomy should be good enough. Which is worse: an odd-shaped breast or no nipple on one side?"

This was worse than a "does my bum look big in this dress?" question. Kevin batted it back to Pauline. "Which would you be more comfortable with, do you think, love?"

"Oh, I don't know. I can't imagine not having a nipple on one side, so I think that's worse. And I'd worry in case the implant leaked, so I don't like that choice much. They said a mastectomy was best if I was worried about the cancer coming back – like who isn't going to worry – but I'm not at the worst risk of it coming back. I think maybe I'll go for the lumpectomy. They did suggest that first, after all."

It was a great relief for Pauline to talk to Kevin about it, and now they had other worries with Sasha being in hospital, she felt far more pragmatic about her own situation. In her job, she'd seen so much and thought it was all a bit of a lottery. Sometimes people who seemed in a really bad way made a full recovery but there was also the time when the person you thought least likely to have complications ended up on the mortuary slab.

Just stop worrying and over-thinking everything, she scolded herself. "At least I don't have to make the decision straight away. And you never know, maybe I'll be lucky and the chemotherapy will get rid of all the cancer, so I won't need surgery in any case. It was strange the way I over-reacted in hospital, you know. I might be a bit of a worrier but I've never got that upset before. I almost fainted and got really nauseous. That's why they wouldn't let me drive home. And that's why Sasha was driving to the hospital. Oh God – it's all my fault."

"Don't be ridiculous. You didn't make her crash. I love you, Pauline, no matter what happens. Just let me know what's going on from now on, please."

Kevin wasn't going to let Pauline see how worried he was about the cancer and the possibility of losing his wife but it was clear to me.

"Of course I will, love. I'm sorry I didn't tell you before I went to the appointment. I'd convinced myself the X-ray had been faulty and there was nothing there. Now I've had some time to get my head around it, it doesn't seem quite so bad. Probably because Sasha's accident has put it into perspective. I'm more worried about her at the moment."

"Well, just let me do the worrying for both of you now."

Kevin was never one for lots of chit-chat, which was just as well as Pauline was happy to do the talking for both of them. She continued, still churning over events.

"This has been the most awful, bizarre day, hasn't it? What with me not coping at my appointment… I know they say doctors and nurses are the worst patients, but… and I don't care what you say – if I hadn't called Sasha, she wouldn't have crashed."

"No, Pauline," interjected Kevin. "You didn't make the van run into Sasha's car. It's just one of those things, so stop blaming yourself."

"Well, I don't know. And that's the other thing…" Pauline paused as she reread a text from Mark. "Sasha has some serious injuries, yet there was barely a scratch on the children. It's all very odd."

"It's been a long day, Pauline. Let's just try to relax now. It shouldn't be long before Mark's home."

My heart went out to Pauline and Kevin. They were such good-natured humans, always putting their children first. They had also been ideal nurses, naturally caring and giving, and it was a shame to see them suffer now. Pauline knew this was no ordinary chain of events but she didn't have the courage of her convictions. Shame I couldn't confirm that her uncharacteristic reaction to the breast cancer news must have been the chosen catalyst for Sasha's key life-event – not that I had been in the know at the time. (I did keep wondering why that was; I'd have expected to be forewarned of all major events for Sasha.)

Mark arrived home a short while later, threw his

keys down on the kitchen worktop and collapsed into an armchair.

"How is Sasha?" asked Pauline, shuffling to the edge of the sofa.

"She's doing well considering," said Mark, wondering how much to say. He'd already texted them the main details, but he held back the heart seizure for now as he could imagine what Pauline's reaction would be like.

"It must hurt like hell but she's not complaining, and I think she's been dosed up to the eyeballs. She started nodding off when I was talking to her, so I've left her to get some sleep. If you're okay to look after the children in the morning, I'll go back then and take some clothes and things for her – maybe you can help choose what – and then you could go see her in the afternoon. Oh, unless you'd prefer to see her in the morning."

"No, that's fine," said Pauline. She wondered how difficult it would be to wait until the afternoon to see her precious daughter, but she wasn't going to ask Mark to change his plan. "We'll help you out with the children and meals and everything, won't we, Kevin? You can't do it all on your own. At least we're both retired now, so it won't be a problem at all."

Pauline also tried to ignore her cancer problems and whether her treatment would have any impact on them helping. She didn't know how soon the chemo would start but she was sure it wouldn't be immediately.

"Thank you so much," said Mark, genuinely grateful he could rely on his in-laws and also thankful they were easy to get along with. His own parents lived too far away to help but he made a mental note to give them a call soon to let them know what had happened.

"We'll head off now," said Kevin, "so you can get a good night's sleep. See you around nine if that suits."

"That's great," replied Mark and he let them out, looking forward more than he ever had to getting into bed and sinking into oblivion.

Angels

I was dancing metaphorical jigs when I found out Those Above had chosen to provide Sasha with psychic healing. It had to be given sparingly on Earth because the medical field only accepted its own principles of science despite it being relatively rudimentary from a cosmic point of view. Anything that couldn't be explained in a "rational" way made them very uncomfortable and too many "unnatural" healings would disrupt the good work they did.

Despite all the clanking, chinking and chatting in the ward, Sasha was sleeping soundly; at least I was allowed to assist with that. Deep into the early hours, I roused her gently from her slumber so she would be privy to her special treatment. As she became aware of a bright yet reassuringly warm glow expanding around her prone body, I could tell she was uncertain whether she had woken up or was still dreaming.

As the glow came into focus, she could make out the shapes of three tall, enrobed figures bending over her. Her instinctive fearful reaction was immediately replaced by curiosity. These figures looked like humans except for their unusual height, towering up to seven feet or so. It seemed odd to Sasha that they seemed to be female, considering their height. Their gowns were pale and plain but when she focused in on them, the material appeared to contain a kaleidoscope of sparkling colours, twinkling delicately. It reminded her of things she'd seen in her near-death experience. Sasha could hardly see their faces under the shadows of large, droopy headdresses but she felt certain they would be kind and caring.

They must be angels, Sasha said to herself, rather awestruck. *Wow!*

I was quite charmed by Sasha's delight. There was such naïve innocence to souls in human form when they encountered other dimensions, which had the same effect on me as babies and young animals have on you humans.

The figure who appeared to have her hands on Sasha's thigh where the bone was broken had a dry, serious demeanour, like an elderly spinster aunt. Sasha was aware of intense concentration coming from her into her leg, which tingled with a peculiar heat. It didn't feel quite the same as having, say, a hot water bottle against her skin; perhaps it was more like the heat was within her leg rather than on the outside. Whilst she pondered this, she was also aware that the other right-hand-side figure, who was less spinster aunt but still quite matronly, had her hands over the chest wound, causing more tingling. The lone angel on the left, though, was like a tendril of summer breeze as she wafted up and down Sasha's body in a more general fashion. Sasha would've loved to get to know her but something (me) stopped her calling out to the angel. Her body twitched and tingled involuntarily as it responded to their collective action but there was no pain. Actually, was her breathing getting easier and were her injuries hurting less?

The angels bathed Sasha in wave after wave of loving reassurance and she lay there transfixed and overwhelmingly content. To have these other-worldly beings caring about her so single-mindedly and tenderly was very humbling. All her Earthly worries paled into insignificance in the presence of these awe-inspiring beings. They worked on Sasha for several hours but she was not aware of this as I helped her drift back to sleep before they had finished.

When she awoke in the morning to the sounds of the shift change-over, Sasha was infused with serenity. She recalled the night's events and smiled, feeling strangely confident the angels had done much more to make her better than any hospital treatment could achieve. It had also sent thoughts of Mark and the wicked woman at work to the back of her mind – for the time being.

One of the nurses noticed Sasha's smile and approached her bed.

"Good morning. How are you feeling today?" This nurse, called Juliette, had listened to the patient reports at the start of her shift and was expecting this one to be feeling somewhat sorry for herself rather than smiling away at nobody in particular.

"Oh, much better, thank you," Sasha replied.

"Well, I'm pleased to hear it," said Juliette, wondering whether she'd misheard Sasha's situation. "I'll bring you a nice cup of tea and see what medication you're due."

"I'd love a cup of tea, please, but I'm not sure I need the morphine any more. Just a couple of paracetamol will be fine." Sasha had heard horror stories about morphine addiction and her pain was significantly lower today.

The nurse noted her pulse and blood oxygen level, checked her blood pressure and took her temperature. All were now normal. She glanced through Sasha's notes and struggled to hide her confusion. The woman in front of her and the notes just didn't gel. Still, there were more patients to deal with; at least this one was concerning in a good way.

Sasha had her cup of tea and breakfast when it was brought round and lay back, examining her surroundings.

Something is different to normal. What is it? It's not much different but there's definitely something. Like when I came into hospital yesterday. Maybe everything's a little clearer or sharper. Are colours brighter? It's like the angels have charged me up with love. I'm radiating love to everyone and everything – wow, that's so weird – and lovely.

That was good to hear.

Sasha tried to stop thinking and just bask in her tranquil aura of love but her thoughts kept on tumbling out.

Now I feel like I'm a soul inside a human body, I can sort of imagine the souls inside everyone else. Each body contains a perfect loving soul, no matter what their human self is like. I wish I could reach out and speak to their souls. Does anyone else feel like this? Or have I gone mad?

As Sasha's brain struggled with the enormity of her thought processes, she fell asleep. She slept peacefully through most of Saturday and Sunday, just waking for breakfast each day. The nurses put her back on a saline drip to ensure her hydration remained satisfactory.

Mark had told Pauline and Kevin about the heart seizure when they'd arrived at the house on the Saturday morning. They worried about her, misconstruing her unresponsiveness as a symptom of brain damage, fearing how long her recovery would take and wondering how much the accident would affect Sasha. Would she be the same woman as before or would her personality be affected? Would she be able to look after herself and the children fully? Would the broken leg heal well or leave long-term effects on her physical abilities? They knew she would hate to be restricted.

And I could relate to that, for sure.

Saturday afternoon, with Pauline sitting beside the hospital bed, Sasha was brought out of her slumber by her mother's voice. Straight away, she realised she was hearing her mum's internal monologue and she kept her eyes shut so she could continue to eavesdrop unnoticed. She was getting good practice at feigning sleep.

Pauline was mentally replaying what the doctor had told her: "Ah, yes, Mrs Carter, there's an issue with a small mass in your right breast…"

Sasha felt like she was watching from a seat right next to her mum as she stared at the dispassionate doctor telling Pauline about the discovered breast cancer as if he were reading the football results. When her mum burst into tears, Sasha almost cried too.

As Pauline reached the point where she tried to stand up and say goodbye, Sasha immediately felt the room tilt with tiny, bright stars whizzing around her head.

Ooh, I don't like that feeling, she thought.

Watching Pauline stumble and sit back down on the edge of the chair, followed by her repeated attempts to rise, Sasha's stomach lurched.

Thanks for that, Mum. What is it with all the nausea?

Pauline was then being propelled over to the examination couch to lie down and the doctor was telling her she mustn't drive home.

So that's what it was about. Oh, poor Mum. It's so unfair; why should she get cancer? But then, I suppose, why should anybody? She's got to get better! I couldn't bear to lose her.

Kevin walked into the ward, handed a coffee he'd bought from the vending machine over to Pauline and pulled up a chair next to her. Pauline's thoughts turned to the sub-standard coffee and whether to bring in a flask of her own the next time.

Not being in the least bit interested in her mum's coffee conundrum, Sasha drifted back to sleep.

British Bulldogs

Sunday morning, the clink of cups and saucers and the scent of toast and bacon got Sasha's tummy rumbling. Normally, she'd be in her kitchen, making a fried breakfast as a Sunday treat. She raised onto her elbows and watched the lilac-uniformed lady serving breakfast from a trolley.

"Hey, Andrea, do you remember Bernard?" the lady called out to one of the nurses.

"Oh, yes. He was a sweetie, wasn't he? Always so appreciative."

"I know. And yet, you'd never have thought it from the way he looked. Heh-heh. Like a little old British bulldog."

"Actually, I thought he was just like Winston Churchill. All he needed was a big fat cigar."

What? Sasha jack-knifed upright like a released spring. She had been listening in on the conversation as soon as she'd heard the name Bernard. Their descriptions of the man matched perfectly with the spirit she'd seen.

"Excuse me – was this Bernard a patient here?" she cut in.

"Yes, love. He – err – left a few months ago. Did you know him then?"

"No, not really. I just met him once. He seemed nice." *Hope they don't ask how I met him*, she thought.

Personally, I hoped they would. I'd have liked to see Sasha deal with that, but she was let off lightly.

"Oh, yes. He was one in a million." The trolley lady moved on to another patient, leaving Sasha to breathe a sigh of relief.

If he was such a nice man, I don't see why I couldn't have heard his story, she mused.

That made me curious too. I requested the answer but the response wasn't available. I scrolled through my tablet, which contained The Spirit Guidance Rule Book, lessons, records of all people who interacted with Sasha and all my writing and notes. Nothing linked to Bernard. Why wasn't I supposed to know what was going on?

Buy Your Near-Death Experience Here

There was barely a cloud in the sky as Sasha stared out the window. Not much to look at other than the tops of trees and the side of the hospital wing. Someone had opened the windows, as far as the safety locks allowed, but it was never going to make much difference to the stuffy air in the ward. Lying in a hospital bed gave Sasha more time than she'd ever had since having the children to just rest and think. It was strange how she was bursting with gratitude and compassion for anyone and everyone since the angels had visited her. Suddenly her little world of worry for her family seemed insignificant. Even better, her positivity meant she was no longer dying to return to the other realm. She smiled at her own pun. But recalling how much she'd resisted returning to life led Sasha to recall the astral conversation before she'd left. The part about having a mission acted like a sharp pin against her ballooning self-assurance and she quickly changed her thoughts to images of her beautiful young children. She and Mark had agreed that the three of them would be a bit much for anyone else in the ward, and, anyway, visitors were limited to two per visit. It wouldn't have been easy to bring in one at a time, but with her heart almost physically aching for them, Sasha wondered whether they should try it out. Would it be fair on the children though?

She sighed and fished around in the bag of belongings Mark had brought in for her – she was a connoisseur at distracting herself from unwanted thoughts. Her fingers found the reassuring shape of her mobile. As she waited for the phone to finish its booting-up sequence, it occurred to Sasha to look up near-death experiences. It would be good to know for sure whether that was really what she'd had.

I was beginning to realise just how many times I interfere. I wasn't convinced she'd look into the situation without a little prompt since she seemed to have forgotten the part about having to develop her psychic abilities. Prompts aren't as bad as interference, are they?

Sasha typed into the search engine "near-death experience", and the first result was "Death in service quote"; followed by "Somerset House Online – Re-Issue of Official Certificates & Wills".

Well, that's not what I'm looking for, she thought with disappointment.

Next was "Near-Death Experiences – at Amazon" followed immediately by "Near-Death Experiences" on eBay saying "Seriously, We Have *Everything*".

Seriously, really? Sasha laughed out loud at the suggestion of being able to buy an NDE online. That was so funny.

Spotting Wikipedia, Sasha opened the page and read the lengthy definition.

Well, that sounds like what happened to me.

Reading on, there was a list of likely occurrences in the "Common Elements" section:

"A sense/awareness of being dead." *Yes, once I was in the other dimension.*

"A sense of peace, well-being and painlessness. Positive emotions. A sense of removal from the world." *Oh definitely.*

"An out-of-body experience. A perception of one's body from an outside position…" *That's what happened when I was looking down on the accident.*

"A 'tunnel experience' or entering a darkness. A sense of moving up…" *Yes, I had the tunnel experience and moving up.*

"A rapid movement towards and/or sudden immersion in a powerful light (or 'Being of Light') which communicates with the person." *I moved rapidly towards a powerful light but it didn't speak to me.*

"An intense feeling of unconditional love and acceptance." *Oh, one hundred per cent.*

"Encountering 'Beings of Light', 'Beings dressed in white', or similar. Also, the possibility of being reunited with deceased loved ones." *Tick.*

"Receiving a life review, commonly referred to as 'seeing one's life flash before one's eyes'." *Yes, that's exactly what happened.*

"Approaching a border or a decision by oneself or others to return to one's body, often accompanied by a reluctance to return." *Certainly had that.*

"Suddenly finding oneself back inside one's body." *More like being shoved back into my body.*

And finally, "Connection to the cultural beliefs held by the individual, which seem to dictate some of the phenomena experienced in the NDE and particularly the later interpretation thereof." *You what?*

Well, apart from not understanding the last bit, I ticked every single box. So it definitely was an NDE. Oooh – I just knew it. I'm not mad, and it wasn't a dream. I don't care what Mark thinks; I don't have to doubt myself anymore.

And then Sasha found another website all to do with near-death experiences that was a lot simpler and very informative. It also had examples of other people's accounts, which now gave Sasha the sense of reassurance and connection she had been seeking. She read a few accounts before she started yawning.

At least I can keep coming back to this when I've got time. Oh, that's such a relief.

I was glad Sasha had done this but it fell short of what I'd hoped for. Was she really going to learn anything from her experience?

Losing His Marbles

"So how are we feeling today, Sasha?" Dr Bowkowski asked as he scanned through the notes on the clipboard at the end of her bed.

Sasha had stayed awake for longer today and even eaten lunch.

"Much better, thanks," she replied, smiling brightly. It felt like when she was back at school, eagerly awaiting her teacher's approval after handing in a piece of work she was particularly proud of. She remembered standing next to Mrs Johnson, her geography teacher. They'd had homework on the evolution of oxbow lakes, which Sasha had found interesting enough to be able to write about. She'd been so pleased when she got a B+ for her homework, with a tick and "v. good" next to the pictures she'd drawn to illustrate the lakes. Regarding Dr Bowkowski, she had a sneaking suspicion she was doing far better, after her angelic intervention, than the average patient.

Dr Bowkowski applied his stethoscope to Sasha's chest and asked her to breathe in and exhale. He checked both lungs and was astounded to find little difference between them. There should still have been a marked impairment on the right lung due to the pneumothorax but there was no evidence for this.

"How big a breath can you take?" he asked Sasha to check his findings.

Surprisingly, Sasha breathed in deeply, expanding her chest visibly.

"Does that not cause you pain, Sasha?" the doctor asked, unable to cover his surprise.

"Hardly any really. It's nothing like it was at first."

It just didn't make sense to poor Dr Bowkowski. He was sure that even if the lung had somehow been healing at a rate of knots, Sasha still had broken ribs that would surely be very painful with pressure against them.

Scratching his ear, Dr Bowkowski then looked at Sasha's leg. The swelling around the fracture had receded and the bruising was already progressing well through the colours of the rainbow. Broken legs were not his line of expertise but there was noticeable improvement from three days ago.

"On a scale of one to ten, how would you rate the pain in your leg?" he asked.

"About two or three now. I honestly feel so much better today. It's like my whole body is healing really quickly."

Sasha so wanted to mention the angels she had seen on the Friday night and had felt around her as she slept during the weekend. *Best not*, she decided; Dr Bowkowski didn't seem the sort to believe in supernatural healers.

Sasha tried to hide her amusement as she listened in on Dr Bowkowski's confusion (as did I, of course). It did not seem possible to him that her injuries should be healing as quickly as they appeared to be. It should be at least a week before they would consider surgery on Sasha's leg but having checked Sasha as well as he could at her bedside, she seemed unbelievably better than expected. He decided to give it another couple of days before reassessing the situation. She couldn't possibly be ready yet! Clearly, if she were, it would free up a bed for the next patient, which was always ideal but, no, it wasn't worth taking the surgical risk. Dr Bowkowski also wasn't prepared to risk his credibility by suggesting Sasha might be ready for surgery after just three days. What would his colleagues think of him? That he'd lost his proverbial marbles, he expected.

Sasha instinctively wanted to reassure him he wasn't mistaken. However, an unfamiliar voice in her head was telling her quite firmly she definitely wouldn't need an operation on her leg.

I bet you were thinking that voice was me but not this time; it was one of the angels who'd attended Sasha (the dry, serious one) managing to get through to her. I knew Sasha wouldn't have said anything to the doctor but the angel wasn't taking any chances.

***

Although the breast cancer was constantly on her mind, Pauline carried on as normal – well, as normal as possible, considering she and Kevin were spending most of their time at Mark and Sasha's house, doing school runs or visiting Sasha. They didn't mind; in fact, it was good to have a lot to deal with, to keep their minds off the impending treatment and worries for the future.

They were also impressed with Sasha's rapid recovery. Whilst both of them had occasionally seen patients appear to make miraculous recoveries, it was as rare as a snowflake in June and they were very thankful Sasha was one such snowflake. From Monday onwards, Sasha was awake for longer periods of the day and seemed to have a very positive frame of mind in terms of her recovery. Each time they visited her, their fears of diminished capacity or long-term physical restrictions lessened. They were very proud of their girl.

***

Mark was given a week's compassionate leave from work so he could visit Sasha every day and he put all other straying thoughts to the back of his mind. He too could see Sasha was improving day by day, but he didn't share the positive outlook Kevin and Pauline talked of. For him, Sasha was harder to work out and more emotionally withdrawn than she had been before the accident – not that she'd been exactly open back then. She had seemed so pleased to see him when he'd first appeared by her bedside but she was nothing like that now. It wasn't that she was critical; sometimes she was almost as warm and loving as she used to be, ages ago. But then she withdrew to a polite distance, like a stranger. At other times, she would snap at him crossly, like he'd done something wrong. He'd never mentioned Natalie, that he was sure about, and nobody else knew about her. How could it seem like Sasha did? How could he be paranoid about something that hadn't even happened?

How Long?

Due to a punishingly busy schedule, it was mid-afternoon on the day Dr Bowkowski came back to see Sasha. He listened to her chest, asking her to breathe deeply, which she did without difficulty, and decided to send her off for a chest X-ray before making any decisions. As her leg was still in traction, a hospital porter came along to trundle her down to the X-ray department in her bed.

An hour later, Dr Bowkowski was looking at the X-ray images on his computer screen. His face was a picture: eyebrows raised, brow furrowed and mouth open in a little "o" shape as he peered at the X-rays. Not only was the right lung looking healthy and fully inflated, but the fractures on the two broken ribs had knitted together with new bone structure, which looked perfectly well-formed. It was comparable to three weeks or more of normal repair. If an uninformed doctor looked at these X-rays, they would never have suspected Sasha had been involved in a serious road traffic accident a mere six days ago.

Dr Bowkowski rubbed his right earlobe. Clearly, if the ribs were healing at such an accelerated rate, wouldn't the femur too? He didn't want to authorise surgery that wasn't necessary, so he organised a leg X-ray for the next morning. Dr Maron in Orthopaedics could review the results at the end of his morning clinic.

Sasha was greatly relieved to have another day of healing before a decision was to be made on whether to operate or not. The angels, who never seemed to be far away, were still insistent that surgery would not only be unnecessary but detrimental.

On Friday morning, Sasha was heading to the X-ray department once more. The technician was very gentle with Sasha but all she could think was, *it doesn't hurt. I'm not a baby.*

She was impatient to get back to Rosie, Noah and Violet. Picturing herself back at home, Sasha remembered the mission.

I don't see how I can help anybody – I've got no idea where they are, other than maybe Mr Taylor, just supposing he still lives in the same house. And what would I say to him? "Sorry I ruined your life; just thought you'd like to know it was me." That's hardly going to help, is it?

Sasha was clearly in a negative funk. I wanted her to be looking forward to her mission. Whilst she was in hospital, she had so much time to practise her psychic listening skills and reach out to me – she'd met me, for goodness' sake; how much easier could we make it? Clearly, her avoidance of confrontation was going to be another hurdle.

The rest of the morning and early afternoon dragged by for Sasha. When her mum and dad visited at 2pm, her mind was distracted by what the Orthopaedics doctor might say to her. With her belly shooting spiky warning signals, she was steeling herself for the unwelcome conversation. How could she convince the doctor that she, who'd only scraped a C in Science, knew what was best for her? Could they force her to have an operation against her own will?

At last Dr Maron arrived at Sasha's bedside. He was a tall man, possibly in his fifties, with a balding head and broad shoulders. He stood with feet squarely planted as he crossed his arms over his gently protruding belly, looking down on Sasha.

"Good afternoon, Sasha," he said. "I have read through your notes and examined the X-rays thoroughly because they rather defy science as we know it."

He coughed a little, and he raised his left hand to soothe the skin on his neck under his now-chafing collar.

"Under normal circumstances, Dr Bowkowski would have been informing me whether you were fit enough for theatre. I would then perform an intramedullary nailing to fix your fractured femur. However, it appears your body has been healing at an unprecedented rate. With the splint holding the femur shaft in the correct position, new bone tissue has already been bonding very well at the site of the fracture, to such a degree that there is no advantage in giving you surgery. This is highly unusual. I have decided to keep the splint in place for a further two weeks to keep pressure off the bone whilst it continues to heal, then take another X-ray. The bone is not fully repaired, and we cannot be certain it will continue at its current rate; obviously, we do not want any setbacks. We will move you to a low-dependency ward."

"Another two weeks?" Sasha's chin wobbled.

I put the thought in her head that at least she didn't need to argue against surgery.

She gave Dr Maron a weak smile and thanked him as he turned to go.

I could see how frustrated Sasha was being bedbound.

Because the splint had a metal rod extension about eight inches beyond the bottom of her foot, it meant walking just wasn't possible. She could shuffle out of bed on her good leg, leaving the splinted leg resting on the bed, in order to use a commode, and she could even stand on her left leg, still with her other leg resting on the bed, if she held onto the bed frame. This got her circulation running through her buttocks and left leg but she couldn't hold the pose for long.

At first, she had enjoyed the opportunity to read books undisturbed. Since having children, books were pretty much reserved for holidays, and even then, her reading time was limited. The *Divergence* trilogy was sitting on her cupboard, like a box of chocolates waiting to be savoured, whilst she was in the middle of *The Invention of Wings*.

She also had puzzle books her mum had brought in, plus magazines and newspapers. But she was getting bored with looking at print. Using her phone for games apps, social media and funny videos was also losing its appeal.

She discovered there actually was a saturation point for watching funny cats and dogs after all.

On the plus side, she still had the distraction of mind-reading – when she remembered, which she had to admit, wasn't often. She could sense whether people were happy or sad, just plain weary or irritated – though that wasn't easy to witness when she was the cause.

A Bit of Bother

Sasha tried to blink her eyes into focus and gauge what time it was. Her curtained bed-space was dark; well, as dark as it got in the ward. There was usually an inspection lamp turned on somewhere or other, whatever the hour. Ah yes, she remembered hearing "lights out", and that seemed like a while ago. The scratchy voice of a nurse conversing quietly with a patient confirmed it must be the middle of the night then.

Next problem, what's woken me? And what is pressing against my leg?

Sasha raised her head to look at her legs; there was a distinct feeling of pressure against her left shin and ankle.

What the hell?

Sasha drew herself up to a semi-sitting position, pulling her legs away from the body sitting on the side of her bed. Winston Churchill was staring at her.

"Bernard!" she exclaimed in a forced whisper.

"Hello, dear. I do hope I haven't given you a shock."

"Um, not so sure about that. What are you doing

here?" *And how can I see you?* she added in her head.

"Well, I do need your help, so I thought I'd try to make contact. People who have NDEs have a better chance of seeing us so-called spirits when we return."

Sasha was unnerved by him answering her silent question as well as the whispered one. In fact, she felt very jittery. It just wasn't normal to have a dead person sitting right there on the end of her bed, looking as three-dimensional and normal as if he were still alive.

"You see, I've been watching my wife ever since I passed over and it's clear she's in a bit of bother."

"What do you mean – a bit of bother?"

"Well, we have an independent bakery. She's doing a grand job of keeping it going but I can see that our office manager is fiddling the books. I've watched him for about a month now and he's very sneaky. He's set up payments to go into his own accounts. Someone's got to stop him. I want you to let Ursula know she needs to get rid of Clive quickly. And he ought to be prosecuted."

"Gosh, how am I supposed to do that?"

"Well, for a start, you can go and talk to Ursula. She's usually out-front serving customers."

"Serving where exactly?"

"Oh, silly me. At Bernard's Bakery, on Pagnell High Street. Do you know it?"

"I'm not sure. I haven't been to Pagnell for a while."

"Well, it's opposite the Co-op, and you can park round the back. It's very straightforward."

"I really don't know, Bernard. Why would she trust me? She'd think I was mad if I told her how I met you."

"Ah, I've thought of that. Tell her to look on top of the display unit. There's an envelope with fifty pounds in it. I put it there as emergency money after the newsagent's got broken into about five years ago."

"Okay, but is there anything personal I could tell her that only you would know?"

It was clear to Sasha she was getting sucked into the situation but she couldn't help herself.

She might have been reluctant but I was enjoying this.

"Tell her my first dog's name was Blackie."

"Lots of people call their dog Blackie. Something to do with her."

"Hmmm. Ah, I've got it. She's got a photo of us from our wedding day on the bedside table. She kisses the photo and says, 'Goodnight, darling' when she goes to bed."

"Okay, that should do it. But, Bernard, do you know any details about the money being stolen? I don't know how I'll be able to prove it."

"Ursula can give you the accounts. You'll need statements for the last five years."

"Aren't they on a computer?"

"I always insisted on the statements being printed out as you can't rely on computers. You could lose everything if they go wrong."

"What would I look for?"

The curtain around Sasha's bed suddenly parted as a nurse popped her head through.

"I thought I heard your voice. Sounded like you were having a conversation with yourself. Are you feeling all right?"

"Oh yes, I'm fine thanks. I, err, was just talking through a dream I'd been having. I do that sometimes." Sasha hoped it sounded plausible.

"Okay, love. Well, as long as you're fine. Goodnight then."

"Goodnight. Thank you."

When Sasha looked back at Bernard – or where he had been – she saw nothing.

Did I imagine it? No, I couldn't have. Oh gosh, this is weird.

Sasha lay back and ran through the whole conversation in her mind, wondering how she'd agreed to find this Ursula, who she'd never met before – well, not unless she'd popped into the bakers for a sausage roll on a Friday. As a cloud of fatigue descended, Sasha closed her eyes and fell into a restless sleep.

I was doing some wondering as well. At the stage in Sasha's NDE when Bernard had popped into the scene and been swiftly removed, I was curious but thought it was perhaps just a minor glitch, which can happen. However, if this was a glitch rather than intentional, I wanted to know why, but the answer wasn't available. Everything to do with Bernard was being withheld from me, and I didn't like it.

The Opening Act

Rain was dribbling down the windowpanes when the clanking of crockery and wafts of toast and bacon woke Sasha. Tears that mirrored the weather slid from her eyes, and she snatched a tissue from the box beside the bed, wiping away the evidence before anyone noticed.

Without me doing a thing (for a change), memories of her NDE entered her mind as frequently as a toddler asking, "Why?"

Every time Sasha thought about her experience, it was like she was transported back to the other world and she was reliving the heady, loving atmosphere once again. Often this filled her with euphoria but there were still moments, like this morning, that it left her bereft, lonely and resentful of being stuck in the living world. Now, on top of that, she needed to get her head around the spirit of Bernard persuading her to help his wife. He wasn't even part of her "mission", and yet it appeared he'd just jumped the queue. Not that she was planning on starting the mission…

She really wanted to talk to her friend Michelle but she'd avoided the subject when Michelle had visited since most of the ward could have listened in on the conversation.

Sasha sighed as she let her thoughts slide to Mark. As always, her first reaction was a surge of love for her husband; she'd never felt so strongly about anyone else and sometimes thought that she and Mark had been lovers in a previous life, if that were even possible.

This was another instance where I could have confirmed the case and told her more about it, if only Sasha would communicate with me.

But then her mood would darken as she turned to the woman she'd seen in Mark's mind. She'd had a few further glimpses of the office bint. Usually Mark was concentrating on the children but now and then his thoughts would stray briefly before stopping himself. *Was he trying to stop me seeing his thoughts? No, that's silly – he doesn't know I can read him. He must be trying to control himself. Well, I suppose that's something. Maybe it won't come to anything after all.*

Mark's viewpoint showed Sasha giving more affection to the children, hugging and kissing them, than to him. Not surprisingly, he wasn't happy about it. And she could see that when she made excuses to avoid sex, his reaction was like popcorn on the heat, spluttering and bursting with pent-up frustration. She felt bad until she remembered his lust for the cow at work and she drew the cloak of righteous indignation back around herself. She knew she could make things better if she reacted to him more lovingly, but it was a Catch-22 situation. Even if she could successfully pretend she wanted him, she couldn't overcome her resentment, which was stubbornly saying, "No way, José."

In the first few days after the accident, Mark had tried to take on the household chores, and Sasha's heart had swelled with hope. But, by the end of a week, Pauline and Kevin had insisted on taking over. When Sasha found out, she was seething, especially now her mum had breast cancer to contend with. He might not have been brought up to do chores, but it was no excuse really. How could he take advantage of her mother, whether he knew of the cancer or not?

***

After his week off work, Mark swapped to visiting Sasha in the evenings, with Kevin and Pauline taking turns with each other to cover afternoon visits and childcare.

I could see Sasha was in need of some light relief, which gave me something to do. It would be harmless enough to be within the rules. I persuaded a nurse to tell Mark where he could find a wheelchair with a suitable elevating leg rest so he could wheel Sasha to the cafeteria, which was open until 8pm.

Sasha's grin couldn't have been wider. She would have leapt up to kiss the nurse – but leaping up wasn't an option with the splint on her leg.

There was one little problem, though. Mark had zero experience of steering a wheelchair, let alone one with a leg splint extending out the front. They'd only moved a metre before the splint snagged on the privacy curtain between Sasha's and Wendy's beds. The grey curtain slid smoothly along its rail as if to present the opening act at a West End show. This show happened to be Wendy, on her commode, having a wee.

"Aaarrrggghhh," cried Wendy, horrified and helpless.

"Sorry – so sorry," spluttered Mark, fumbling to close the curtain with his beetroot face averted. Sasha also avoided looking at Wendy, whilst trying ever so hard to stop her shoulders shaking as she silently creased up with laughter.

It was probably a good thing she couldn't see or hear me laughing too.

Mark steered very carefully from then on and only collided with a couple of chairs – mercifully empty – whilst parking Sasha at a table, and their laughter erupted in unison. Sasha inhaled the aroma of sizzling burgers and chips and relaxed. It was heaven compared to the steamed salmon and soggy broccoli she'd eaten for dinner. Even though she wasn't hungry, she asked Mark to get her a doughnut and a diet cola. The opportunity was just too good to pass by.

Sasha flashed Mark a rare smile as he returned with the tray of treats. He sat down and basked in the warmth of his wife's glow.

Oh For Acting Lessons

Pauline's chemotherapy appointment came through for the twenty-third of July, which gave her a few weeks to keep helping out.

I could see she felt fine physically but mentally was more of a challenge. She'd say she wasn't worried but I observed all her exhausting thoughts: she went through so many possible scenarios of things going wrong that she often ended up in tears and then she'd get cross at herself for over-reacting. At least she had the grandchildren to look after and a second household to keep her mind occupied.

Unexpectedly, her cancer provided some more light relief (for me, anyway) when Kevin decided to tell Sasha about her mother's illness.

"You must be wondering why your mother was at hospital the day of your accident," Kevin said to Sasha at his next visit.

"No, I... oh, err, yes, of course," said Sasha, remembering just in time that nobody had actually spoken to her about her mother's situation. This probably wasn't the best time to tell her dad about her ability to read minds.

"Well, she's been diagnosed with breast cancer, love. But don't worry – they picked it up at an early stage and she's going to start chemotherapy on the twenty-third of this month."

"Oh no!" said Sasha rather woodenly. *Acting lessons sure would come in handy*, she (and I) thought. "But I'm sure she'll be fine, Dad. I just know she will."

The bit about knowing things would be fine took Sasha by as much surprise as it did her dad. It was as if someone had spoken through her.

I was amused to see that Gran had popped in on this conversation and put her penny's-worth in.

"Well, yes, of course," Kevin said, thinking, *she's taking this a lot better than I'd expected.* "I'm glad you're being so positive, Sasha. It will really help your mum deal with it."

"I'll be there for her, Dad. Just like you both are for me. We're not too shabby a family, are we?" Sasha smiled, trying to lighten his mood. "Have you told Carina?"

"Yes, we spoke to her last night on Skype. She'd really like to come home to be with you both but I told her not to worry. It's not like she can just take a few days' holiday in that job."

"No, that's true," agreed Sasha.

Sasha's internal vision was filled with Carina in a large old-fashioned kitchen, kneading bread on a broad wooden table in the centre of the room, with a young girl standing up on a footstool next to her, kneading a smaller piece of dough. This cute little girl, with curly hair spilling out of two high pig tails and wearing a bright pink apron, was giggling happily as she copied Carina's exaggerated movements: pushing and pulling the dough, slapping it down on the tabletop. The sprinkled flour puffed up into gentle clouds. Near to them was a much younger girl in a baby walker, watching the others whilst chewing methodically on a teething ring and rocking herself back and forth by her tiptoes.

Sasha saw that Carina was tired but pleased she was coping well with the children and chores, and she was looking forward to the evening when she'd be meeting up with another au pair she'd become friends with in the village.

"Well, don't worry," Kevin was saying. "With Stage One, you know there's every chance of a complete recovery." He couldn't work out why there seemed to be such a disconnect with this conversation; after all, he'd prepared himself for an emotional outburst, like Carina's. Still, this was easier than tears.

"And I'll help in any way I can," came Sasha's reply. Something was telling her she could help with her mum's recovery. But she hadn't a clue how.

Oh, Sasha. All you've got to do is ask.

Hearts and Flowers

Mark cursed under his breath as he stared at the frozen screen – the accounting system had crashed when he was in the middle of approving payments. Which, of course, were urgent. Grumbling to himself, he strode off to the small kitchen area to make a coffee and think about what he could do now. As he was filling the kettle, Natalie came sidling up behind him.

"Hiya, Mark! You alright?"

"Not really. The bloody system's down again and I can't get anything done. John'll be pissed off."

"Well, he can't blame you. Do you want to go for an early lunch while it's down, then you'll have more time this afternoon?"

Last night Natalie had gone to the pub with her friend Lucy. They'd had a few drinks, talking about men, and of course Natalie talked about Mark in particular. Lucy had called her a wimp and said nothing would happen between her and Mark unless she made the first move.

The kettle was building up to its crescendo and Natalie

fiddled with her hair anxiously as she waited for Mark's reply, wondering if she'd just made the biggest fool of herself ever.

Mark was rationalising that if he said yes, it was only having lunch with a work colleague. "Alright," he said. "How about the White Hart? It's a bit further away but they do a good ploughman's." *And hopefully others from work won't go there,* he thought.

"Okay," beamed Natalie. Her feet were going to hurt walking any distance in high heels but it would be worth it.

***

As they settled themselves into a high-backed booth, Mark's gut was quivering; was it foreboding or anticipation? He looked all around to check there wasn't anybody he recognised in sight.

He fiddled with a beer mat while they waited for the food to come. They talked about work and colleagues in an effort to avoid mentioning Mark's wife and family, but it wasn't easy.

"Any holiday plans, Natalie?"

"I'm going to Ibiza with my friend Lucy in September. I can't wait to do some proper sunbathing. And the clubs should be good – you get the best clubs in Ibiza."

"Sounds great," replied Mark. He'd zoned out at the sunbathing part, picturing Natalie's breasts saluting the sky and his hands rubbing sun cream all over her body.

Their food arrived, and Mark snapped back. He

ploughed into his ploughman's as Natalie nibbled at her cheese toastie, her appetite failing to compete with the butterflies in her tummy.

Mark's resolution to resist Natalie's charms was as solid as a lifeboat made of jelly. Every smile and giggle pulled him further away from self-control. As soon as they'd finished eating, they drank up and walked back to the office, side-by-side. Every time their arms or hands brushed each other's, tingles zapped between their bodies. Natalie returned to her desk on Cloud Nine but Mark sat at his frozen screen with maggoty guilt gnawing holes in his gut.

The computer sprang back to life at twenty past two, and Mark managed to get through the priorities of the day, though it took him until 6pm to do so.

Stopping for petrol on the way home, he spied the buckets of cut flowers beside the door to the shop. This seemed like the perfect time to buy a bouquet for Sasha; he hadn't actually given her any flowers yet because she'd received plenty from other well-wishers. He chose the nicest bunch of pink and white chrysanthemums.

This should be a lovely surprise for her, he said to himself.

Later, Mark walked into the hospital ward, holding the bouquet behind his back. He bent over, kissed Sasha on the cheek and produced the flowers with a theatrical flourish.

"For my beautiful wife!" he proclaimed.

Sasha's reaction began with surprise, melding swiftly into grim realisation before settling down into irritation.

Even if Sasha wasn't currently endowed with seemingly supernatural powers of mind-reading, she would have immediately wondered what her husband had been up to. Mark only ever gave her flowers on their anniversary or Valentine's Day; he hadn't even given her any after the accident happened. These had to be classic guilt-flowers.

All Mark had been expecting was loving gratitude. He couldn't quite read the fleeting emotions on Sasha's face but he was sure loving gratitude wasn't one of them. His own face transitioned from confusion into disappointment.

Whether he was conscious of his need to assuage his guilt or not, he was determined to make the situation better. Recalling his boss telling him earlier about his wife going off to a spa for a special treat, Mark was sure that could work for Sasha too.

"You've had a tough time with the accident and everything, Sasha. How about you and your mum go to a spa to relax and get away from it all? I'm sure she could do with the break too and I can look after the kids for a weekend."

First flowers – now this. What the hell has he done? wondered Sasha.

She probed into Mark's mind, dreading what she might find.

At that moment, he was kicking himself for getting stuck with the children on his own for a weekend. Searching past the panic, she found the scene of him and the girl from work sitting in a pub enjoying lunch together. Then they were walking back to the office, followed by a stuck computer screen and Mark feeling guilty as hell whilst reassuring himself nothing had happened. And now she could see Mark starting to regret his generous offer as he started wondering how on earth he'd manage to cope.

Sasha was cross and jealous he'd had lunch with the witch but at least he felt bad about it. *Maybe it will teach him a lesson if I do go to the spa, especially now he's regretting it,* she thought.

"Well… I suppose that would be good for Mum," she said. "With any luck, there'll be a week between me being discharged and Mum's chemo starting. It's rather short notice, though, isn't it? Places might be fully booked. And, anyway, wouldn't it be too expensive?"

"It shouldn't cost too much for a weekend or midweek break. We could see what there is online," said Mark.

They got out their phones and scrolled in silence.

"How about this one? It's in Henlow in Bedfordshire – that's not that far away," said Mark, pleased to see it was cheaper than the other offerings.

Sasha had a look at the pictures and the description.

"It looks lovely," she said, impressed by the grand old building, attractive decor and the lush green gardens that backed onto a river. The main pull, though, was the spa's indoor swimming pool, which looked so bright and inviting. Sasha pictured herself gliding smoothly through the sparkling water, relaxed and invigorated.

"Since it's not far away, we could just go for a day visit on a Saturday or Sunday. That would be cheaper than a weekend break."

"Sounds good to me," said Mark.

***

The very next morning, Dr Maron confirmed his plan to take X-rays with a view to removing the splint on Friday the thirteenth.

"That's perfect," said Sasha. "Would there be any problem with me going swimming a week later?"

"If we've removed the splint, it means the bone is strong enough and as long as the thoracic wound has healed, you should be fine. In fact, gentle exercise will be a good thing. Bear in mind you will have lost muscle mass and won't have much strength in your leg, so you will need to take things easy to start with. And you mustn't drive until your leg is strong enough."

Sasha was convinced the splint removal would go ahead, so she suggested to Mark they book the spa for Saturday the twenty-first.

"As long as Mum is okay with it, of course." Not that she really doubted it – whose mother would turn down an offer to go to a spa with their daughter?

Sasha asked Pauline that afternoon and, surprise, surprise, she was thrilled with the idea. Determined not to behave like an invalid, she also volunteered to do the driving. Everything seemed to fall into place perfectly when Henlow Grange was able to book them in on the twenty-first, in spite of the short notice.

It's as if we're supposed to go, thought Sasha.

No, really? was my reaction. Why don't you hone your intuition skills instead of letting them slide? It was getting more and more frustrating that Sasha had the opportunity to enhance her life experiences yet appeared to have no interest in doing so. She hadn't once tried to contact me. Maybe it was asking too much of her...

Sala the Slow One

"Your attitude does seem a little harsh towards your charge, Zinnia," said Hebron as he appeared by my side.

"I'm not supposed to get frustrated, am I?" I said, hoping I wasn't going to be told off for anything else.

"Frustration and impatience don't help you or your human," said Hebron. "What has shaped us in our previous incarnations can leave a residual influence on our current behaviour. Have a think about yours."

My earliest memories came from when I was the soul of a star, drifting in space for millions of years. Whilst you might think that being in one place for so long would be boring, it really wasn't. Such existence is peaceful, joyous, a constant state of bliss. Other stars, asteroids, meteors and planets would be around so I was never lonely. We communicated with each other lovingly.

When one particular asteroid rumbled by, it triggered a desire in me to move on – to change my existence. I shot through the universe and entered Soul Central. This was the realm Sasha entered in her NDE, where many souls continue to retain their appearance from when they were on Earth. I spent a long time here and met Daziel. We observed and learnt about all the different interventions and experiences involved in this environment. Some souls who had passed unpredictably required the help of higher-level spirits, like Indira. Other souls were happy to enjoy this realm whilst they waited for other souls who were on Earth to join them. There was a lot going on. I was in my small, glowing orb state at the time, a miniaturised likeness of my previous incarnation.

It was obvious my star-life and my visit to Soul Central had nothing to do with my present tendency for impatience. It had to be one of my human incarnations. My most recent one was growing up in rural Mexico in the 1800s. It was hard for inquisitive girls like me when education was male-orientated and the men in my large family weren't interested in bending the rules for me; all they cared about was themselves. At least my job of looking after the sheep kept me sane and gave me a chance to visit wise old Rosa. She gave me my nickname, Zinnia, because I adored the vibrant flowers of that name and I was always being told off for picking them when I shouldn't. They could make me smile when my heart was heavy.

Hebron cleared his throat. "Maybe start looking at your human lives from the direction of your first one," he said. He was normally very patient with me but he clearly didn't want to listen to me going over every single human life I'd experienced.

For my first one, I was born into a Central African tribe, years before foreigners had usurped indigenous territories. Unsurprisingly, living off the land was tough without electricity, power tools or modern weapons. Still, it was natural, surrounded by beautiful lands and animals, which fascinated me from an early age. As soon as I could walk, I was put to use in any way possible: fetching, sweeping, watching the goats. Everyone had to play their part in tribal life but I was a bit day-dreamy and was often shouted at to bring me back to the task in hand.

When I was still young, a day when the rain was like an all-round waterfall from heaven, I slid into a rocky ditch and broke my ankle. It didn't heal properly and I was left with a painful limp for the rest of that life. From then on, I was berated for holding the others back. I was even less reliable than I'd been before – which was going some – and they got impatient with me; I became known as Sala the Slow One. It was soon the norm for one person or another to be shouting at me.

As I grew older and lost one brother due to a leopard attack and another to a spear wound, I came to appreciate the need to be alert, seize opportunities and work hard. Once I was married with children, I found myself harrying and snapping at my own offspring. On the plus side, I was happy in our moments of relaxation or celebration. On the minus side, I'd become a dab-hand at chivvying others along and would get frustrated when they didn't respond as I wanted. What had been done to me by my parents and siblings I was now doing to the next generation.

Hebron was leaning back, nodding with a "so now do you see?" expression on his face. So it was my African life he meant, when I was a tall, willowy woman with the richest shade of skin and beaded hair, usually wearing a dusty cotton tunic held around the waist by a decorative belt.

Hebron's ah-hem noise stopped me reminiscing any more. Clearly, I was treating Sasha much like one of my offspring from that time, even though circumstances couldn't be more different. There was no threat to Sasha's life or fear of the family failing to put food in their bellies. I really should be more understanding.

"You don't need to be hard on yourself about this," he told me. "You're still learning as you go."

His words made me feel a little better – now that was a first.

Good Riddance

From the moment she woke up, all Sasha could think about was going to the X-ray department. An eternity later (in reality half past ten), a porter with Nick on his name badge ambled along and wheeled Sasha off to X-ray.

Sasha recognised one or two of the porters but Nick was new to her, so she decided to look into his mind on the way back to the ward.

Yay! She was making an effort to flex her psychic muscles.

Nick was cheerfully picturing wandering round to his mate Wally's place after work, with his cigarette papers and a stash of weed tucked neatly inside the secret pocket in his natty knitted hat he would put on his blond mullet the moment he was off hospital grounds. He'd saunter along, doing his best impression of the Rasta dreads he so admired. Then they'd be getting wasted, man – out of their sweet little heads.

Sasha watched Nick's recollection of the previous Sunday night, when they'd killed themselves laughing as they stumbled around the flat, making elephant impressions. Or was it tigers? Maybe that was a different time? He moved on to marginally clearer thoughts. Getting the munchies; going for a late-night kebab...

Sasha's stomach was sensitive to kebab odours (after regurgitating one when she'd been inebriated in her early twenties), so she quickly shut the image down and concentrated on the ceiling tiles instead. She didn't consider herself a prude; after all, she had once shared a joint at a party – though that had also made her throw up. She just wasn't a fan of the whole stone-head culture. Worrying whether Nick was stoned right now, she was grateful to see her bed was moving in a straight line.

What a shame she'd picked Nick to mind-read. I hoped it wouldn't put her off doing any more since it happened so sporadically nowadays.

Once back on the ward, there was another endless wait for Dr Maron. Sasha was reading and rereading the same paragraphs without a single word going in so she threw her book to one side. She wasn't in the mood for code-word puzzles and the view through the window was as dull as dust. She settled back in her bed, attempting to daydream about swimming and massages. Lunchtime was a welcome break and finally, at two o'clock, Dr Maron marched in.

Crossing his arms in his usual stance, he looked down at Sasha.

"You have made incredible progress. The repair is clean and straight; in fact, it is hardly possible to see where you've had the fracture." *Which just isn't normal*, he added silently, though Sasha heard as she made a point of tuning in to medical staff.

"I will remove the splint now. The muscles in your right leg, in particular, will need to build up gradually, so no sudden bursts of activity. As I believe I mentioned before, no driving to start with; give it three weeks at least. If there is pain or swelling, take ibuprofen. Any concerns, please contact the Trauma and Orthopaedics Department. Here is a card with my secretary's number."

Dr Maron then proceeded to remove the splint. Sasha sighed with pleasure as the nylon straps and metal frame came away. She rubbed her leg and slowly bent her knee upwards – for the first time in three weeks. She was surprised how floppy her calf muscle looked and couldn't resist poking it with her fingers, making it wobble from side to side.

She slowly swivelled round in bed to swing her legs over and with Dr Maron supporting her on her right, she stood up and took a few unsteady steps.

"I'll get the physio to bring you a pair of crutches, Sasha," Dr Maron declared. "I'm sure you won't need them for long, but it's best not to take any risks. Then, when Physio are happy with you, you're free to go."

"Thank you, Doctor. I do appreciate all your hard work."

"Not at all," he said as he scribbled away in her file. He updated the ward sister and moved on to his next patient.

At quarter to four, Tony the physiotherapist sauntered into Sasha's ward with a pair of aluminium crutches. He asked Sasha how tall she was, eyed her up and down, and adjusted the length of the crutches accordingly.

"Now stand up carefully, putting all your weight on your left leg. Slowly place your right foot on the floor and balance the weight between both legs. How does that feel?"

"It's fine," replied Sasha curtly. Putting her feet to the floor wasn't a problem but Tony was. Sasha cringed and bristled as she "heard" Tony's coarse assessment. She bit her lip to stop herself exclaiming that people shouldn't say – or even think – "I'd give her one" any more. How rude!

"Now take a step carefully. Don't worry, I'll catch you if you fall," said Tony as he moved alongside her, a few inches closer than required.

I bet you will and you'll get a crutch in the crotch if you lay a finger on me, said Sasha – but not out loud.

Thankfully, she stayed upright. Tony kept his hands to himself and Sasha managed to walk increasingly confidently.

"Well, looks like you'll be good to go," said Tony. "We just need to show you how to deal with stairs, if you think you're up to that now."

"I'm ready," Sasha snapped. His slick smile and even slicker hair that he casually brushed back from his forehead made shudders go up and down her spine, so the sooner she was done with him, the better.

They walked carefully out of the ward to a nearby stairwell. Tony showed Sasha how to hold the banister with one hand whilst using a crutch on the other side. She confidently navigated the stairs, down and back up again, and they returned to her hospital bed.

"Okay, Sasha. I'll let them know you're ready to go. Take care, darling."

Don't darling me, you creep! was Sasha's internal response whilst she said out loud, "Thank you. Goodbye." *And good riddance, you horrible little man.*

As soon as she could get the ward sister's attention, Sasha asked whether she could actually go. The nurse checked her notes and confirmed Sasha was finally ready to be discharged from hospital. Eyes sparkling, she picked up her phone and called Mark.

Home Comforts

Two hours later, Mark was helping Sasha out of the car and into their house. She gazed around, noticing the pink and blue hydrangeas which were now in full bloom in the corners of their small front garden. The heather border under the lounge window had been weeded and the grass smelt sweet, like it had recently been mown.

Thank you, Dad, thought Sasha gratefully. *I bet Mark didn't do any of it.*

She walked into the entrance hall and paused on her crutches to look into the kitchen. Everything was gleaming. Clearly, her parents had been very busy looking after the home as well as the children. As soon as Sasha was comfortably positioned on the sofa, Pauline and Kevin brought three hyper children to her. On seeing their mother, Noah and Rosie raced towards her shouting, "Mummy! Mummy!"

"Oh, my sweethearts!" exclaimed Sasha as Violet was placed in her arms and the other two clambered up either side of her, snuggling in tightly. "I've missed you so, so much."

She tried to hug all of them at once and they giggled gleefully. Sasha's eyes welled up with the sudden rush of emotion. There had been times when the decision to keep the children at home had been unbearable.

Georgie, the cat, had initially slunk upstairs upon Sasha's arrival. Now, he padded cautiously back down the staircase and entered the lounge. He stood in the doorway, with his big eyes locked on Sasha, sniffing the air, before strolling over with his tail pointing up in a quirky question mark and leaping onto the sofa. He threaded his way over little limbs into the remaining space on Sasha's lap, turned full circle on her thighs and settled down, purring as loudly as a fat man snoring.

"Are you sure he's okay on your leg, love?"

"Yes, Mum. It doesn't hurt at all. Honestly."

Mark sat down at the other end of the sofa, and Kevin and Pauline sank into the armchairs.

"It's good to have you back, Sasha," Mark said. "We've all missed you."

"Has it been strange? It feels it to me. I've never been away so long before."

"Yeah, but your parents have been amazing. How on earth do you manage to look after the children, the house and do all the cooking and washing and everything else? I never realised just how much there is to do."

"Well, now you know," said Sasha, hoping maybe this was the epiphany Mark needed to start doing more around the house. It was an achievement in itself that Mark acknowledged how much she did for the family.

Turning to her parents, she said, "I've been told not to

drive for three weeks, but apart from that, I should soon be back to normal, so you won't need to help out so much. Oh gosh, I guess we'll have to get a new car now."

"Don't start worrying," said Kevin. "You know your mum and I will keep on helping for as long as you need us. I can have a word with Steve at the garage to keep an eye out for another car. They're always getting trade-ins to sell on as well as newer cars. When you both know what you're looking for, let me know."

"Thanks, Kev," said Mark. "That will be a real help and the sooner the better. The insurance company has already written the car off and they've offered us £5,000. I had a quick look at the prices of cars online and that seems about right to me."

"I'd be happy with another Focus," said Sasha.

"What, even after the state of it?" asked Mark.

"Yes, I don't suppose it would have mattered what I'd been driving, unless it was an army tank. Though I don't really mind what we get. Anything similar as long as it's not red, please."

"Do you remember our old Datsun Cherry that was red, Sasha?" said Pauline. "The perfect colour for a Cherry."

"I remember you saying that more than I remember the car, Mum. That was years ago. It always stunk of wet dogs and cigar smoke from the people before us. Maybe that's why I don't like red cars."

"Maybe so. Anyway, Sasha, I'd better start getting dinner sorted. These lovely darlings of yours are starting to get hungry, and so am I. No, you stay there," Pauline said as Sasha reached for her crutches. "Just keep the children occupied. You've got lots of catching up with them to do. Here are a couple of books we got them last week which they really enjoy."

Sasha took the books and stared at the one on top. It had a picture of a monster looking down at a little boy, and the title was *Not Now, Bernard*.

An uneasy feeling rippled from the crown of her head to the soles of her feet as Sasha remembered those were the exact words of the female spirit calling Bernard away in her NDE. She shivered involuntarily and thought about Bernard sitting on her hospital bed. He seemed harmless enough, so why was she so worried? Looking at the book cover again, Sasha decided it was just that the monster was rather scary. She rubbed her arms to warm herself up and selected the other book instead. Thankfully, it was an amusing story about a calamitous duck and his friends, which was written in delightful rhyming couplets. Sasha enjoyed reading it as much as the children enjoyed listening.

I had been finding all the domestic bliss rather soporific until Sasha picked up the books. I wasn't being informed of any issues regarding Bernard or otherwise but I told myself to keep a metaphorical eye open for any more surprises.

Mark turned the television on to watch the news with Kevin.

A reporter was saying, "An end-of-terrace house in Glenisbrooke, County Durham, collapsed today into what is believed to be an old mine shaft. The owners, Mr and Mrs Parker, were at work when the disaster happened around midday, so the house was vacant at the time. The adjoining house received major structural damage. All the occupants of the terraced row have been evacuated pending a full structural survey and repair..."

"They didn't mention the poor old Jack Russell that was crushed in the kitchen. At least Smudge, their cat, managed to escape unhurt," stated Sasha, without stopping to think.

"What?" queried Kevin, surprised by Sasha's unexpected comment. "Oh, you've always had a good imagination for stories; I expect you could be right, love."

I know I'm right, thought Sasha, *but where did that come from? I keep thinking nothing else will happen and then it does. Have I actually become a psychic or something? That's scary.*

"Don't be scared," I wanted to shout at Sasha. "Think how useful this could be, if you'd only develop your skills."

After the children had gone to bed and Kevin and Pauline had left, Sasha and Mark sat watching telly on the sofa. Mark shuffled up to Sasha and put his arm around her shoulder. Rather than turn her face towards him for a kiss, she leant her head onto his chest and told him how exhausted she was. That wasn't quite what he had been hoping for.

***

Violet's crying was doing its customary build in volume.

Sasha opened her eyes and tried to make her brain focus too.

"Why does she always wake so early?" grumbled a voice next to her.

It took a moment to recognise where she was and to process what her husband had just said.

"Don't suppose you want to help, do you?" He turned to Sasha with a soppy, pleading voice.

Seriously? she thought as she threw back the duvet and fumbled for her crutches before following Mark to Violet's room. He'd been dealing with his daughter all the time she'd been in hospital; was he going to stop the moment she was back, even though her legs were still not at full strength? She only used the crutches for walking from one place to another and no doubt Mark had noticed that she wasn't using them so much indoors.

Sasha picked up Violet, breathing in her baby scent. Even though it included a dirty nappy whiff, it was more persuasive than her husband.

"You don't really need me, do you?" he said as he watched Sasha taking over. "Do you mind if I go back to bed for a bit?"

Sasha shrugged, and Mark slunk away.

"By the way, if you're going to get Rosie's and Noah's breakfast ready," he called over his shoulder, "they now like eating Weetabix with brown sugar on since that's what your mum's been giving them. She put a bag of sugar in the cereal cupboard."

Oh my God, thought Sasha. *What a lazy bastard!*

She didn't consider that Mark hadn't had a lie-in since her accident and would have been looking forward to the first opportunity. But shame Mark hadn't mentioned this before they'd gone to bed to see how Sasha felt about it. Maybe he could have left it one more day? Just communicate, I wanted to shout at them. Honestly!

Sasha grabbed bowls and spoons, which clattered as they landed on the table. She was peeved at her mum giving the children unnecessary sugar, whatever colour it was. Coming home was turning out to be a big let-down. She'd almost rather be in hospital, with breakfast being brought to her. However, when Rosie and Noah bounced into the kitchen with excitement, Sasha's bad mood burst like a piñata receiving its final blow, her sweet delight spilling out.

"I'm the luckiest mum alive," she said, hugging her children close, inhaling them deeply.

Why Me?

Sasha had been trying to ignore the mission she'd stupidly agreed to but flashbacks kept occurring. The clip that recurred most often was from visiting her great-grandfather, Henry.

Spirit Sasha was in Henry's cosy living room where two-year-old Olivia and five-year-old Billy sat on an indigo rug. Henry, wearing a formal pin-striped suit and tie, was sitting in the largest of two armchairs, his dark crinkly hair, bushy moustache and beard reminding Sasha of old sepia portraits of Victorian gentlemen. He was telling Sasha who everyone was.

"Your grandmother's sister, Winifred, was fourteen when the schoolmaster took advantage of her. She was taken to relatives in Leeds to give birth to the baby. He was called Arthur and was sent off for adoption."

Sasha watched another woman walk into the room to stand behind her great-grandfather. This woman looked quite similar to Dorothy, with the same distinct eyes but a reticent appearance. Sasha knew this was Winifred.

"Arthur grew up in Leeds with an affluent couple as their only child. From an early age, he yearned to act but his parents would only tolerate a prestigious career. He studied medicine and moved to Northampton, where he would become a specialist consultant in urology at Northampton Hospital. He married a young lady called Nancy and they had a son, Michael, who followed his father into medicine and still works at the same hospital now. Six years ago, Michael married Tanya and they had these two delightful children who you see in front of you."

Sasha watched the children stroking a placid golden retriever on the rug.

"Last summer, the family went on holiday to Crete," Henry continued. "Their first evening, Michael and Tanya put Olivia and Billy to bed before sitting down to enjoy a bottle of wine and a game of Scrabble. They marvelled at how well the children slept that night, seeing as they didn't normally settle well in new places. When they checked on the children before they retired, both appeared to be sleeping soundly. In truth, they were succumbing to carbon monoxide gas due to a faulty boiler in their bedroom cupboard. When the children failed to rise the next morning, Michael and Tanya's world imploded. They continue to struggle with their loss. I look to you, Sasha, to go to them with reassurance that there was nothing they could have done to save the children. Billy and Olivia will continue to grow up here, wanting for nothing. They will all be reunited in due course but Michael and Tanya must continue their lives with love, not grief, in their hearts."

Coming out of the flashback, Sasha was struggling to breathe properly. How had she agreed to it so readily?

***

In the evening when she was curled up on the sofa next to Mark, she couldn't concentrate on the television programme that was flickering in front of her.

I don't see why I should do it, she thought.

Because it could make some people feel better, she argued back to herself.

But somebody else could do it; someone who knows what to do. Can't the angels do it themselves?

Most people can't see or hear angels, so that wouldn't work.

Well, anyone else?

It was you the spirits chose to speak to.

I know. But what would I do? Most of the people are strangers – how on earth am I supposed to find them? I can't do it; I just can't. They'll still be okay without me sticking my nose into their business.

Sasha tried to convince herself but her mind turned to the horse rider, Rebecca at school and Mr Taylor.

It was my fault things haven't gone well for them. D'oh, understatement of the year for the horse rider.

Sasha sighed heavily.

I suppose I've got to try but God knows how.

Her mind zoomed in on a specific moment in the cottage scene with Henry.

Okay, I admit it. I put that picture in her mind because

she was getting nowhere on her own. I knew Hebron wouldn't be pleased, but I didn't think Sasha was ever going to get round to asking. I amplified the part where Henry was telling her about Arthur and his son Michael working at Northampton Hospital. Finally, Sasha latched onto that nugget of information.

Hmmm, I don't know their surname or anything but Michael still works there. Well, Mum used to work there too so maybe she'll remember them – it's quite unusual to have a father and son work at the same place, isn't it? Oh, God – what do I tell her though? I don't want her to freak out. Well, what about if I just say it was a dream? Yes, that's it. Some people have prophecy dreams. It's worth a try.

"You alright, Sasha?" said Mark. "You looked like you were miles away."

"Sorry, just zoned out for a moment." Sasha was back with *Celebrity Pointless* once more.

***

The next day meant Sunday lunch round at her mum and dad's house. After they'd eaten, Pauline and Sasha were dealing with the dirty dishes in the kitchen.

Sasha put away the plate she'd just dried and turned to face her mum, twisting the tea-towel between her hands. "Mum, do you remember a consultant in urology called Arthur at Northampton Hospital?" she said.

"Hmmm, let me think... ah, yes! There was a consultant called Arthur Young. I remember because we always thought how funny it was that someone with an old-fashioned name like Arthur had the surname 'Young'."

"Didn't he have a son called Michael, who was also a doctor at the hospital?"

"I'm not sure I remember, love. It's a long time since I worked there. Why are you asking?"

"Well, when I was in hospital, I had a dream. In it, I was with Gran and we went to visit her mum and dad. Your grandfather, Henry, told me your Aunty Winifred got pregnant when she was fourteen and the baby was taken away and adopted. The baby was Arthur. He married a lady called Nancy and they had Michael, who grew up to be a doctor too. Father and son both worked at Northampton Hospital. Michael married Tanya and they had children called Olivia and Billy."

Sasha's mum gripped the sides of the washing-up bowl as she interrupted. "But if this was just a dream, why are you telling me this? It's not real, is it? It must be a coincidence you dreamt of a doctor called Arthur."

"No, Mum! I swear it's real! I'd never remember all those details from a normal dream. In fact, I hardly remember dreams at all. Gran was just like I remember her, only younger, and her mum – your grandmother – was called Dorothy. She was your height with bright blue eyes, just like yours and Carina's."

Sasha had always been disappointed that she'd missed out in the eye colour stakes.

"She was wearing a grey pinafore dress with an apron. Your grandfather wore a navy pin-striped suit, had wavy dark hair, a beard and moustache and had grey eyes. I'm sure I never knew their names before. Doesn't this sound like them?"

"Well, yes, actually. Apart from remembering them with grey hair. But how?" *Just supposing for one moment that it's true, which it can't possibly be, it would mean we've got relatives I never knew about,* she thought.

Pauline threw off her washing-up gloves and thudded down on a kitchen chair. She couldn't believe she'd just been drawn into this ridiculous conversation and yet, the descriptions of her grandparents was spot-on. Had Sasha actually suffered some kind of brain damage after all?

Sasha pulled up another chair next to her. "Well, I guess it was a psychic dream. Anyway, I haven't even got to the important bit. Michael and Tanya took their children on a holiday to Crete last year and the villa they stayed in had a dodgy boiler. The children died in their sleep of carbon monoxide poisoning."

"Oh, how dreadful! I can't imagine!" It crossed Pauline's mind for a moment that perhaps the accident could have given her daughter some psychic abilities but that was an equally absurd explanation.

"I know. Your grandfather wants me to find Michael and Tanya to tell them they are looking after the children. I need your help to find them."

Sasha watched closely. It was impossible to gauge her mum's reaction.

"I don't know, love. We'd be a laughing stock if you tried to do this."

"Then don't tell them everything I've told you. How about saying I've been looking into our family tree and found out we are related, so you'd like to get in contact with them?"

"Well, I'm not sure, but if you really want to go ahead with this, I can call my friend Barbara. Her daughter Laura works on reception in A & E, so we should be able to find out what department Michael works in and maybe which days he works. She won't be able to give us any personal details though."

"That's okay. She could give him our phone numbers and my email address and ask him to contact us."

"Hmmm. Alright then."

"One more favour – would you mind driving us to wherever we'd meet, please?"

"You really are determined to do this, aren't you? Well, I don't mind driving. Northampton isn't far away."

Despite her misgivings, Pauline called Barbara that evening, giving her the family tree version of the story. Barbara promised she would try to get Laura to give contact details to Michael Young.

As soon as she ended the call from Pauline, Barbara rang Laura, who was happy to play her part in bringing Pauline and Sasha together with their distant relatives. She, in turn, said she would pass the contact details on to Michael Young the very next day.

I triple-flipped my tablet in the air and twirled around like a giddy teenager. Something to celebrate at last.

Frustrations Make a Heart Go Wander

I watched Mark set off to work at his normal time, deep in thought. The flowers and spa day hadn't shrunk the gulf that was growing between them and he didn't understand why Sasha was still giving him the cold shoulder. I was doubtful he'd ever work out how much better things would be if he did more to help with the household chores. It was true that in the past he'd been criticised for his inept attempts, which had put him off trying; plus, Pauline and Kevin had taken over with relish when Sasha was in hospital but seriously, getting Sasha back to work on her first morning home? I couldn't help thinking that when it's Mark's time to leave his Earthly body, he'll be mortified by his behaviour. Of course, he'll be literally mortified.

The accident had been a huge blow to Mark's sense of equilibrium, throwing his emotions all over the place. He knew how much he loved Sasha and he desperately craved some amorous reassurance but she had shown no carnal interest since the accident whatsoever, although the broken leg and ribs certainly gave her a good exemption clause.

He contemplated discussing the sexual drought with Sasha but the last time he'd tried, she'd shouted that he didn't understand and until he saw things from her point of view, it was useless to discuss it. Then she'd stormed off to do the washing up or something. If only they could have a sensible discussion, he was certain they could sort things out but he didn't know how to see inside her head and she clearly wasn't looking inside his.

I burst out laughing – if only he knew.

The situation was doing no good for Mark's rising frustration. In fact, at work he had to stay tucked behind his desk whenever Natalie walked into view, as "rising" was the key word. A hard-on was the last thing he needed on show. He definitely didn't want the others in the office to think there was anything going on between Natalie and himself. In his mind, he was still innocent. He just hoped he could keep it that way for as long as possible, so he did his best to keep his head down – in both ways – and concentrate on his daily tasks.

***

Back at home, Sasha was having some difficulties of her own.

Rosie and Noah were both in nursery now that Noah had started that term. Normally, these two would walk to school alongside Sasha pushing Violet in the buggy, or if Noah's legs got tired, he'd coast along on the buggy board at the back of the pushchair. Sasha – with Violet – would return at lunchtime to collect them.

Day One of the school routine, Sasha had put her crutches by the front door as she got the pushchair outside. She confidently picked up the crutches to set off but the pushchair handle was too high to hold together with the crutches. Before they'd moved two steps, Sasha's right crutch went flying and clipped Rosie.

"Owwww!" she cried.

"I'm so sorry, darling! Come here and let me rub it better."

Noah began to giggle.

"Book!" he said, which really meant "look".

"Aarrrgggghhhh!" cried Sasha as she leapt, surprisingly gracefully, to grab the pushchair that was gliding down the driveway whilst her other crutch pirouetted to the ground.

Rosie and Noah were both laughing now.

"Well, I give up," huffed Sasha. "We're going back inside and asking Grandad to take you to school."

Teenage Kicks in the Teeth

The next day, Sasha decided to accompany Kevin on the school run so she could catch up with the other mums. Her friends had heard about Sasha's accident and been kept up to date with her recovery; however, they had no idea just how much impact the accident or, more to the point, her NDE had had on her.

Sasha hadn't yet lost the ability to "see" inside their heads. Thankfully, her curiosity had kept this going.

She still found it a novelty and rather a privilege too. Conversely, it was also tricky to deal with when she was supposed to hold a conversation. The impressions she viewed sped through her mind at break-neck speed but if someone said "hello" and then the visions started, there could be an awkward pause before Sasha responded, which was often embarrassing. On top of that, what Sasha saw could be upsetting or downright odd. She had to carry on chatting with these people as if she hadn't suddenly discovered intimate details of their private lives and that wasn't easy at all.

This was certainly the case when she spoke to Meena, whose boy Jake was in the same year as Rosie.

Meena was in her mid-twenties, thin as a flag pole, with glossy black hair so long she could almost sit on it. Her deep fringe was like a curtain to hide behind. Jake was sweet-natured and rather quiet; he was small for his age as he'd been born nine weeks premature and had been in and out of hospital ever since with various ailments. Sasha didn't know the exact problems as Meena always seemed to avoid the subject and Sasha was far too polite to pry.

"Hi!" said Meena. "It's good to see you back! How are you doing?"

Stuck on pause, Sasha was connecting with Meena's past.

Meena was a little girl being yelled at, shaken and slapped by an angry father. Then, she was wearing a shabby uniform at school, with a gang of bullies taunting and pushing her around. Aged thirteen, she was with two other girls, smoking cigarettes and drinking stolen booze behind the playing field sheds.

Scenes of teenage Meena in various short-term jobs flickered by, and in parallel, Sasha saw Lance, a trendy street-wise guy who looked at least ten years older. He showered Meena with gifts and affection, drugs and alcohol until she was having sex with his "friends" at parties. If she protested, he punched her, branding her "an ungrateful cow who deserved what she got". She covered the bruises with make-up.

Then she was pregnant. When Lance detected her

swollen belly, he said, "You stupid slut. I'm not paying for no baby – you 'ave to get rid of it."

That night, when he was asleep, she took cash from his wallet and left. Walking three miles to the station, she waited nervously for the first train to Milton Keynes.

Always looking over her shoulder in case Lance should appear, Meena was a bag of nerves. She struggled to get a job and couldn't afford anywhere to live. She ended up buying a cheap thick coat in a charity shop and joining the anonymous homeless, begging, getting more abuse and more suicidal. When everything became too much to bear, Meena closed her eyes and stepped off the pavement onto a busy boulevard full of rush-hour traffic. A lad on a moped tried to avoid her but struck her arm with his handlebar, sending her flying. Meena was taken to hospital with a broken wrist, cuts and bruises and went into premature labour. Her tiny baby boy was born and put straight into an incubator in the neonatal unit.

A lady called Angela, who worked for a charity for the homeless, visited Meena in hospital and managed to find Meena a small room in a hostel with part-time work in the kitchens. When Jake was ready to leave hospital, he was looked after in a funded crèche. Over the next few years, life improved. It wasn't easy on her low income, but she had support, made a few genuine friends, slowly learning to trust again and come out of her shell. She loved her little boy with all her heart and was determined he would have a better life than hers had ever been.

She fell in love with a plumber called Tom, who'd also been rescued by Angela and was given the job to update the rickety old kitchen when the charity managed to raise sufficient funds. In time, they rented a small house not far from the nursery where Meena and Sasha met.

Sasha saw all this in an incredibly condensed timeframe, but it didn't go unnoticed.

"Are you sure you're okay, Sasha?" asked Meena. She knew about petit mal seizures, a type of epilepsy that Jake suffered from where he would lapse into a vacant stare for anything up to twenty seconds. Maybe Sasha got these now after the accident.

"Oh, sorry, Meena. Yes, I'm fine thanks. How are you?" said Sasha, with rather more concern than was appropriate under the circumstances.

"I'm all right – I'm not the one who's had a big accident," retorted Meena, certain now of brain damage.

"No, of course not. Sorry. I guess I don't feel quite back to normal yet."

Sasha really wanted to tell Meena how much love the angels were sending out to her, how proud they were of the way she had pulled herself back from the brink and how wonderful a mum she was to little Jake, but Meena's tent-shaped eyebrows were shouting doubt and pity.

"Um, when I'm driving again – which shouldn't be long – do you want to take the children to the park? It'll be the summer holidays by then, so we could have a picnic too."

"Sure. That would be nice," said Meena as she scooped Jake up, giving him a big hug and noisy sloppy kisses to make him giggle. "See you later!"

"Yeah, see you later," replied a rather shaken Sasha.

Oh my God! she thought. *What Meena's gone through is so awful. How much is going on with everyone we just never see?*

The Burden of Proof

Later that evening, Sasha received an email:

Hello Pauline and Sasha,

I hear you are long-lost relatives! My father is especially keen to make contact as he has always wondered about his birth mother and would like to find out more.

Do you know Salcey Forest? It's about halfway between Northampton and Milton Keynes so we could meet in the café there. I apologise for the incredibly short notice, but we could meet you this Friday, say at 2pm. Otherwise, it will need to be after August due to various commitments.

It would be my mother and father, myself and my wife Tanya coming along.

I look forward to hearing from you,

Michael Young

Sasha called her mum.

"We've had an email from Michael. Could we meet them on Friday at Salcey Forest at 2pm. What do you think?"

"Yes, I don't see why not. Friday's the day before we go to the spa, but it's not as if we have to pack or prepare much."

"Apart from shearing a bikini line hedgerow, legs and pits. But we should be able to fit it all in if we start early enough."

"Speak for yourself, madam. Well, do get back to Michael and tell him we'd love to meet them. I'd better look up how to get there; I don't think I've been to Salcey Park since you and Carina were little girls."

"Do you think Dad will be happy to have the children whilst we go, or will I need to take them with us?"

Pauline quickly checked with Kevin.

"He says it's fine, love."

"Thanks, Mum. I'll email Michael back."

***

According to plan on the Friday, Sasha managed to prepare for the spa day before lunch. She was already an expert with the crutches – when she bothered to use them – and she was rarely in pain now. It was another sunny day, so she set up the little paddling pool in the garden, which the children were very excited about. Sasha thought that would be a good way for her dad to keep them occupied whilst she was away.

Sasha and Pauline covered the children in sun cream, kissed them goodbye, then set off at 1.30pm. The journey along the country roads went smoothly and they arrived in good time, found a space in the car park and walked into the café.

How are we going to recognise the others? wondered Sasha with concern as she looked around the busy room. She didn't like the idea of drawing attention to herself by shouting out their names in the middle of the café and she didn't see four people waving as she had kind of hoped for. She and her mother queued up for drinks, allowing them to scan the room less obviously. Whilst in the queue, a lady turned loudly to her partner, who was just in front of Sasha.

"Bernard, what do you want?"

"Help."

"You what?"

"I mean, a cheese and pickle sandwich, of course." He cleared his throat and fiddled with his wedding ring.

That was weird, thought Sasha. She had the distinct impression this Bernard was prompted to say "help" for her benefit rather than his own (and she wasn't wrong, though I couldn't tell where it came from).

She paid for the drinks and pushed Bernard back out of her mind as she started making her way amongst the tables. Pauline followed behind with the tray. A man, who appeared to be in his forties with short brown hair and noticeably blue eyes stood up, looking in their direction.

At his table was a pretty lady of a similar age and an older couple. There were even two empty chairs pushed in at their table, covered by jackets and handbags. This had to be them.

Sasha and Pauline walked over.

"Hi! I'm Sasha, and this is my mum, Pauline. Are you Michael?" said Sasha, surprising herself (plus Pauline and me) with what looked suspiciously like confidence.

"Yes, and this is Tanya, my father, Arthur, and my mother, Nancy," said Michael before sitting down. "Please come and join us. We're all intrigued by what you have to say."

"Well, it's a bit long-winded, so I hope you'll bear with me." Sasha glanced at her audience but couldn't gauge how sympathetic they'd be. "Mum had an aunt called Winifred. At the age of fourteen, the schoolmaster got her pregnant. Her baby boy, who was Arthur, was then adopted by a childless couple in Leeds."

"This is all very colourful," interrupted Arthur, who wasn't too happy to be considered the result of a sexual assault on an underage girl, "but how exactly did you discover this?"

Michael hadn't been altogether truthful to Sasha when he'd written that his father was looking forward to meeting her. In fact Arthur had been imagining all sorts of unsavoury scenarios arising, with unknown relatives flying out of the woodwork. He'd almost refused point-blank to go along but Nancy and Michael had worked hard to persuade him.

"Well, it's a bit of a long story," started Sasha, now unsure about how to carry on.

"What proof have you got?"

"Well, not proof in the normal sense…"

Arthur scraped back his chair and stood up abruptly. "In which case, young lady, we have no reason to believe whatever you say. I'm not prepared to waste my time. Come on, Nancy – let's go." He marched away.

"Oh dear," said Pauline, thinking it was a shame Sasha had never got to say her piece.

"He's such an obstinate fool at times," Nancy said quietly.

"Do you think we should go?" asked Sasha, very disappointed with the way things had turned out.

"No. I'll speak to him. Just wait here, please," said Michael as he stood up and hurried after his father. He caught up with Arthur outside the café.

"Dad! For goodness' sake, let's hear what Sasha's got to say before we go. What's the worst that can happen? Nothing we can't handle. Please come back and listen," pleaded Michael.

"Why should I?" asked Arthur, thrusting his hands into his pockets. "We don't know them from Adam. They're probably after money. What with the girl on crutches, to get our sympathy."

"You're conjecturing, Dad. Remember? You told me that was the worst thing a doctor could do. We are both strong enough not to fall for any clap-trap and if she is doing this for some ulterior motive, I'm sure one or the other of us will spot it. I asked Mum and Tanya to wait at the table, so let's go back, politely listen and drink our tea. Why spoil what might be an entertaining afternoon?"

"Humph," was Arthur's response as he reluctantly turned around. "It's bound to end in tears."

He wasn't wrong there; that was for sure.

The men returned to their seats, and Michael made light of the interruption.

"Do carry on. We're all ears."

Sasha took a deep breath, then said, "I know this is very peculiar but I'm honestly not trying to con you in any way. There is nothing for me to gain with this." Having lost her newfound confidence, she was struggling to stop her voice shaking. "I expect with your medical backgrounds you will be sceptical of what did happen, but please hear me out before you decide.

"I was involved in a serious car accident about a month ago. When I got hit, I somehow left my body and was led away to another dimension by my dead gran. I believe what happened to me is called a near-death experience. One of the places I was taken to was a lovely home, which seemed as real as here on Earth, where I saw my great-grandparents, Dorothy and Henry, with Winifred and a little boy and girl. Oh, and a lovely golden retriever. I had wanted to know who the children were and my great-grandfather started off by explaining to me about Winifred having Arthur."

Arthur's back was iron-rod upright and his feet were braced to rise again at a moment's notice. His chin jutted out as he crossed his arms across his chest.

It was clear to them all Sasha was describing dead people, and Michael and Tanya both blanched at the mention of two children. Arthur and Nancy were reminded of their beloved golden retriever that had died ten years ago. Sasha's mum, meanwhile, sat open-mouthed as this account varied considerably with Sasha's initial story of a dream. She was trying not to be sidetracked by thoughts and emotions related to being lied to – which version was the truth even?

Sasha continued: "Henry told me Arthur had wanted to become an actor but went into medicine to please his parents. He became a specialist consultant in urology."

"I thought you hadn't told anyone but me about wanting to be an actor," she heard Nancy whisper to Arthur.

"I hadn't," he hissed through gritted teeth. Everyone turned to look at Arthur but he remained stony-faced, refusing to validate the statement.

"Arthur met Nancy and they had Michael, who chose to follow his dad into medicine. He married Tanya and they had Billy first and then a girl they called Olivia."

Michael grabbed Tanya's hand protectively as he anticipated what was coming next. He swallowed hard as Sasha looked directly at Michael and Tanya.

"Oh gosh! This is so hard – I'm really sorry! He then told me the lovely children in the room were yours and how they died of carbon monoxide poisoning from a faulty boiler in their bedroom when you were on holiday. They weren't in any pain when it happened – they were sleeping when their souls left them. Henry said I needed to find you, to tell you there was nothing you could have done to save them and they are growing up and being looked after on the other side, wanting for nothing. His final words were that you will be reunited with them in due course but must continue your lives with love, not grief, in your hearts."

Sasha stopped at last, nervously aware of the enormity of what she just told them. She looked around at everyone. Tears were sliding down Tanya's and Nancy's faces. The men's faces were frozen.

"Could this really be true?" asked Tanya. "I so want to believe, but…"

"Please describe the children you say you saw," Arthur asked Sasha, his voice mechanically cool and controlled.

Sasha could recollect her NDE as clearly as if she were still standing in the front room of the cottage, so she described the children's features and what they were wearing in as much detail as she could possibly manage and she also described the dog. Sasha knew this was the only way she could convince her audience. When she stopped, nobody said a word, and even Pauline was in tears now, empathising with Tanya and Michael and imagining how she would feel if she lost either or, God forbid, both of her girls.

Sasha looked around. People on the surrounding tables shifted to avoid eye contact, suddenly needing to sip their tea or pick up a piece of cake. *Next time you share this sort of news, make sure you don't sit in the middle of a busy public place,* she thought. She'd been bursting to tell somebody about her NDE but not this way.

Sasha might have been feeling uncomfortable but this was probably my best day since she'd had her accident. All the interaction and melange of emotions was fascinating. I would have so many notes to put in my tablet which would be useful for my next assignment.

Arthur wasn't finding it easy to admit to being wrong, let alone have to accept what Sasha was telling them. He'd been dragged round Next to get some holiday clothes for Billy and Olivia and had obligingly offered his opinion on the outfits so he actually remembered their clothing for a change. Which of course matched perfectly with Sasha's descriptions. The dog matched too. He – and Michael – knew many people happily believed in psychic phenomena but it was excruciatingly difficult to join the gang. Arthur was still going to confirm the family history on an ancestor-tracing website before he was anywhere near satisfied.

"Well, Sasha," he said at last after clearing his throat. "This certainly wasn't what we were expecting. For pragmatic scientists like Michael and me, it is rather a lot to think about."

"If you're related," said Nancy, rather more softly, "it would be good to know about your family too. Do you have any siblings, Pauline?"

With the atmosphere gradually warming to room temperature, Pauline told them about her brother Carl and his family in Norwich. The new acquaintances continued to chat for a while, agreeing they should get together again sometime. Then they stood up and the women gave each other hugs goodbye.

"Thank you, Sasha," said Tanya. "Life's been so hard since last summer but what you've said is very special. If I can believe we will see them again, it will be a little easier. I'll try to look forward now…" She paused, words catching in her throat. "Just maybe, I might even have the strength to campaign for more awareness of the dangers of carbon monoxide, especially for families going on holiday."

"Well, I'm glad to be of any help," said Sasha. "I can't possibly imagine what you're going through but I know somehow your beautiful children did what they were supposed to do on Earth and haven't suffered. Even if you can't feel it directly, just believe they are sending you and Michael so much love and they want you to be happy in your lives. If you can achieve that, then everything will be according to plan."

Sasha hadn't intended this little speech – it just came out of her mouth as if someone else were in control of her tongue – but she was quite chuffed with it.

It was Hebron who helped her out there, in case you were wondering. He told me to make notes as it would be relevant to a module on purposeful prompts.

"Yes, thank you very much," joined in Michael. "I'm sorry if I was a bit off with you, but this goes completely against the grain of everything I've ever understood. Tanya and I will have lots of discussions about this, I reckon."

Tanya nodded.

"It was lovely to meet you," Sasha said, though not so much at first, she added silently. "And you're welcome to call or email any time. If there's anything else I can do, I'd be honoured. Actually, you're the first people I've tried to help since my accident."

"Well, then I think we're honoured," said Nancy. "Safe journey home and see you soon!"

***

Back in the car, Pauline shifted to face Sasha before setting off. "Well, that was a whole heap more than I had been led to expect. Don't get me wrong; it went very well in the end but you told me you'd had a dream, madam, not a near-death experience."

"I know. I'm sorry, Mum. I didn't want to tell you all about it until after you'd had your operation, in case it made you anxious. But I could see they wouldn't accept it if I told them it was a dream; Arthur and Michael aren't as open-minded as you. I should have anticipated that – after all, I knew they were doctors. Then I could have told you on the way up but it didn't occur to me. It's weird; half of what I say now just seems to come out as if someone else is talking, not me. I don't really understand it."

"Hmmm. Well, I won't take it personally." Pauline started the car and set off. "I was a bit hurt at first but I understand. Goodness, life seems to be getting a bit surreal at the moment."

"You can say that again!" replied Sasha. Even though she was relieved the meeting was over, she was glowing inside. Dealing with Arthur had been horrible but Nancy and Tanya were lovely. Then she wondered how the rest of the mission would go and her glow flickered and dissolved away.

Just Like Buses

Next morning, Kevin and Pauline arrived early to collect Sasha for the spa day. Kevin went inside to spend the day with Mark and the children.

The sun was smiling in the bright sky and the temperature was expected to rise into the mid-twenties. Sasha kissed the children and Mark goodbye, chucked her crutches in the back of her mum's car and got in. She waved until they were out of sight.

At the health spa, a receptionist directed them to the dining area for fruit and yogurt, which was a welcome surprise. They relaxed before getting changed into the fluffy white robes and towelling slippers provided, ready for their facials at 10am.

Sasha and her mother were taken to separate rooms so, for lack of anything better to do, Sasha tuned in to the member of staff who was giving the treatment. This lady was in her early thirties. Her ash-blonde hair was tied up, away from her face, which was carefully masked by full make-up. Judging by the other staff Sasha had seen, this seemed to be management policy. Her white overall-dress was also uniform issue and there was a badge on her left breast pocket showing her name to be Lydia.

Sasha was engulfed by Lydia's despondency before her series of events began.

Firstly, a contrastingly radiant Lydia was walking up the aisle of a rustic church. The backdrop of traditional wooden chalets and mountains dressed in pine trees was charming. The tall, blond groom was in awe of his new bride and the wedding babbled with joy and excitement.

Next scene, Lydia and husband, Johan, were gazing at their newborn baby boy – but he died of cot death. A second baby boy was born and he contracted encephalitis within a year, dying in Lydia's arms in hospital.

Lydia and Johan grieved and grieved and grieved. He wanted to try for another baby – third time lucky – but Lydia was far too traumatised; how could she possibly survive the probable torment of losing another child?

She convinced herself he'd be better off with a wife who was capable of providing children and packed her bags to move to England, where she stayed with an elderly friend of her parents in Luton. Lydia polished her English by attending local evening classes. As a qualified physiotherapist, it was easy to obtain a job at a nursing home, where she stayed for ten years. She avoided any personal relationships with men but made a few close friendships with other women who worked at the nursing home. Sasha then saw her training as a masseuse and going for her interview at Henlow Grange.

Full of curiosity *(and a nudge in the right direction*

from me), Sasha followed the thread of scenes relating to Johan. He married again after several years but there wasn't the spark he'd experienced with Lydia. His wife gave birth to a little girl, called Anya, who looked so much like her daddy. The couple stayed together for Anya's sake for eight years but the wife left for a woman she'd secretly desired. Johan was more shocked than hurt and his thoughts often strayed back to Lydia. His parents helped where necessary with childcare and his life plodded on.

In the final scene, Johan and his daughter were packing to go on holiday. Clearly displayed on Johan's bed, next to his suitcase, was an open travel brochure with their destination circled in bright red ink: "Holiday Inn, Hampstead Heath, London". August 4–18 was underlined.

Sasha heard a voice so clearly in her ear it made her jump.

"Tell Lydia to go to the Holiday Inn. She and Johan are meant to be together," said Hebron.

Hebron didn't make me jump but I was hacked off. I wasn't allowed to give Sasha directions but he seemed to enjoy doing it. Still, it was better than him reprimanding me for nudging Sasha.

But what if she doesn't want to be with him anymore? Sasha silently asked.

"Don't worry. They will be very happy," came the reply.

How do I tell her? She'll think I'm mad.

"Tell her an angel told you. Trust."

Oh, my! exclaimed Sasha to herself. She swallowed hard and addressed Lydia.

"Um, Lydia…"

Lydia had just put the finishing touches to a pale green face mask which made Sasha look like she was ready for a Halloween party. Lydia, meanwhile, was standing at the sink washing her hands.

"I'm really sorry, but you're going to think I'm mad. Sometimes I see things and I get messages from the other side," said Sasha.

"The other side?" queried Lydia. Towel in hand, she turned to face Sasha. She hadn't personally had any problems with clients, but she'd heard stories from her colleagues. Lydia's eyes darted to the phone on the desk as she contemplated how easily she'd be able to call for help if she needed it.

"Well, you know – angels."

"Oh!" said Lydia, her body tensing as she dried her hands.

"Well, I've seen what you've been through with losing two beautiful baby boys – I'm really sorry. I could see how hard it was for you, and how you left your husband rather than risk losing a third baby. Your husband remarried and had a little girl but he didn't love his second wife as much as he'd loved you and she left him. But he misses you more than her. Johan and his daughter, Anya, are going on holiday to London this summer; they will stay at the Holiday Inn, Hampstead Heath, from August the fourth to the eighteenth. An angel just told me you must go there to see them; you and Johan are meant to be together and will be very happy with his lovely daughter."

Lydia went to sit down on her stool but she misjudged

its exact position, skimming the edge of it and bumping down on the floor with legs akimbo.

Sasha shot upright and peered over the side of the treatment bed. "Oh my God! Are you okay?"

Lydia stared up at Sasha's disconcertingly ghoul-like face. For a fleeting moment, she considered whether she'd been transported into a budget film with a very warped director.

Which I found amusing since she reminded me of a discarded doll in Toy Story (I watched it with Sasha and her children many a time).

"How can you possibly know this?" she demanded.

"I had a car accident last month. I almost died and I had an out-of-body experience. Ever since then, I've been able to see inside people's minds. I know I'm not imagining it. I saw you getting married in a traditional village with mountains behind. I saw your babies die of cot death and encephalitis – sorry, it must be painful to be reminded – and I saw you leave your husband because he was putting pressure on you to try again. Err, can I help you up?" Sasha added, feeling rather awkward that Lydia was still sat on the floor.

"No, no, I'm fine," replied Lydia as she got to her feet and straightened her uniform. Her eyes welled up but she held back the tears.

"Okay, I will think about this. The Holiday Inn, Hampstead Heath, you say? August fourth to eighteenth?"

"Yes," replied Sasha, relieved Lydia wasn't hurt and hadn't called for security. She could feel the beaming love of an angel around Lydia and could see two pre-teen boys standing either side of her too, looking lovingly at their mother. Sasha really wanted to tell Lydia about the boys but was afraid it might be one step too far. After all, she was here to get a facial, not to be some batty "Mystic Meg", and she definitely didn't want Lydia collapsing again.

Lydia finished off the facial in distracted silence as she contemplated what Sasha had told her. She'd have rung for assistance if Sasha hadn't mentioned angels. Lydia had started believing that angels did exist after a beautiful white feather had floated down to her feet at Jacob's burial. Since then, she'd asked for angels to help her whenever she was falling apart and somehow, she'd always pulled through. Could angels possibly be helping now?

When it was time for Sasha to go, they said "thank you" to each other awkwardly and Sasha found her mother walking out of her treatment room at the same time.

"How was your facial, Mum?" asked Sasha, switching her thoughts to her mother.

"It was lovely, thank you, darling!" replied Pauline. "Just what the doctor ordered. How was yours?"

"Not what I was expecting," said Sasha. "but very good."

***

With over an hour before lunch, they went to the changing room to put on their swimwear and try out the pool.

It was glorious to slip into the water, which was just as refreshing as Sasha had hoped. She needed to build her leg muscles back up and this was perfect. The water supported her as she swam alongside her mum, up and down the length of the pool. It wasn't long before she tired, though, so she got out to lay on a lounger whilst her mum carried on swimming.

Sasha had planned to close her eyes and relax, but Opportunity Number Two was beckoning. She felt drawn – pushed, even – to walk to the changing room.

Pleasingly, Hebron encouraged me to do the pushing.

Sasha tied her sumptuous robe securely around her waist, picked up her crutches and complied.

Sitting on a long wooden bench at the far end of the room was a lady who looked to be in her forties. She was hunched over, hugging her arms around herself as she rocked back and forth, quietly weeping.

I directed Sasha to go over to comfort the woman.

Sasha put her crutches to one side and sat down next to her. Without stopping to consider her actions, she put her arm around this lady to give her a gentle side-on hug.

"Can I do anything to help?" asked Sasha kindly.

"No, no, sorry! I should be able to keep my emotions in check," replied the lady, glancing obliquely at Sasha. Her face flushed as much as Sasha's did.

"Don't be silly," replied Sasha. "You're perfectly entitled to be upset, I'm sure."

"Well, if you're wondering what it's about, I… I recently lost my daughter. She was studying at Oxford, in her first year, and she… she died."

"Oh, I'm sorry," said Sasha.

The mention of a daughter studying at Oxford triggered a flashback of Sasha's NDE.

The girl in the yurt was saying, "I studied very hard for my exams at school and got into Oxford Uni to study history. My parents were so proud of me. I'd always been shy and kept to myself and I was still the same when I was at Oxford. I hardly ever socialised but that was okay. I wouldn't have felt safe in the pubs and clubs; my parents had warned me about the men who'd take advantage of naïve girls like me. Not that I was interested in men but I'd never have told them that. Anyway, then we got to the end-of-year exams. There's this tradition at Oxford where students get 'trashed' after their last one. I got caught up in it – loads of people were standing at the side, squirting silly string and throwing flour and champagne at us. It was actually good fun and people I knew got me to join in with everything. Stupidly, though, I tried to keep up with them and we drank so much. When I started feeling sick, I went back to my room but as soon as I walked in, I tripped over and threw up. I banged my head on the hall table and passed out, choking on my own vomit. I remember waking and sitting up, feeling remarkably well, so I stood up. It didn't make sense when I looked down and saw my actual body in a mess on the floor. I kept staring at it until I was sucked into a tunnel and ended up here. Now I realise I died and I'm coming to terms with it. Please tell my mum and dad I love them and I'll always be close to them. Mum thinks I committed suicide but I didn't. I was happy – really happy that day – but it just went wrong. I'm fine now and I'm not shy anymore. I can talk to anyone – see, like I'm talking to you!"

Despite the chances of a match seeming ridiculously

small, Sasha was sure the crying lady must be the girl's mother.

"Was she reading history by any chance?" Sasha asked tentatively.

"Yes, she was," exclaimed the lady, now turning to examine Sasha through her tears.

"And she was tall and slim with brown eyes and wavy, auburn hair with a grey streak, just here?" said Sasha, pointing above her left ear.

"How could you possibly know this?" the lady gasped.

Talk about being like buses; I don't tell anyone for ages, then it's one after another, Sasha thought, and she observed the lady's face turning pale. She braced herself ready to catch should this one start to keel over.

"You don't have to worry," she said. "I had a serious car accident last month in which I had a near-death experience and entered another dimension. I hope you won't think I'm crazy but in one of the first places I visited, I saw a group of girls who were being helped to adjust. The one who sounds like your daughter came over to talk to me. She told me she was reading history at Oxford and her parents were very proud of her. She said she'd been shy and kept to herself, as she didn't feel comfortable in the pubs and clubs."

"Oh my goodness – that sounds just like Belinda! I'm Val, by the way," said the lady, dabbing at her nose with a large soggy tissue.

Sasha introduced herself and relayed what Belinda had told her, finishing with, "She said you thought she'd committed suicide but she hadn't; she was really happy but it just went wrong. She also said she's fine and not shy anymore."

"You know, I did think she'd killed herself," Val replied as tears coursed down her cheeks again. "I thought it was my fault for pushing her towards an Oxbridge degree and it was too much for her. Oh, thank you so much for this. You're an angel. This is such a relief to hear and I can't wait to tell my husband, though I'm not sure he'll believe me. You truly must have been sent to help me."

"Perhaps I have," Sasha said.

"Yes, you really have," I said. She didn't hear me, or perhaps, just didn't acknowledge me.

Sasha was almost as stunned as the lady at what had just transpired. It wasn't like her to go up to strangers and hug them. This was the moment she realised her mission had well and truly begun – and it wasn't nearly as bad as she'd been imagining.

I was so pleased to hear this.

"I'd better go find my mother; she'll be wondering where I've got to and might start to worry. Are you sure you're alright?" Sasha placed a reassuring hand on Val's arm.

"Oh, I'm a lot better, thank you. I'll just sit here for a while longer to think it all over. I can never thank you enough."

"There's no need. You'd do the same if it were the other way round, I'm sure."

Sasha picked up her crutches and walked out of the changing room, relieved that Val had been so open to psychic revelations. A million miles from the likes of Arthur.

***

When Sasha returned to the sunlit poolside and sat back down on the lounger, her mother was just climbing out of the water.

"Hello, love. I was wondering where you'd got to."

"Oh, I got chatting to a very nice lady in the changing rooms. Did you enjoy your swim?"

"It was super, thanks. I'm starting to get hungry now – are you as well? Shall we go get lunch in a bit?"

"Sounds like a plan, Mum."

Sasha lay back and shut her eyes. She was more than happy to have a short break to centre herself and regain some energy. She felt quite drained from the latest encounter and all it signified.

Ten minutes later, they changed out of their swimwear, wrapped their robes back around themselves and padded off to enjoy lunch in the café area.

Afterwards, they received back and shoulder massages and spent some more time in the pool. When Sasha mused over her earlier conversations and whether the day had been of use for her mother to de-stress, she was pleasantly surprised to hear what seemed very much like a voice from the other side saying yes.

Which I was doing. Whoo-hoo! This really was a breakthrough day. I could see the incremental improvement in Sasha's confidence, in regard to her interaction with other humans and in starting to accept she now had gifts to make use of. And best of all, she actually noticed me.

One Down, Nine to Go

Bright and early, Kevin was ready to drive Pauline to hospital for her first chemotherapy session. They had been warned to keep the whole day free and to bring plenty of things to pass the time. When Pauline went to pick up the bulging bag Kevin had packed, she had to brace herself to lift it.

"What on earth have you put in here, Kevin? It feels like a ton of bricks!"

"Well, there's a bottle of water for each of us, a flask of coffee, some snacks, books, puzzle books, a magazine, pack of cards…"

"Honestly, love, I really don't think we need all that."

"Well, I'd rather have too much for your first day than too little. We'll know better after this session, won't we? Anyway, I'll carry the bag, so you don't need to worry."

Pauline pursed her lips to stop herself saying, "I'm not worrying – I'm embarrassed." She wasn't looking forward to people staring at them.

They were familiar with most of the hospital but the

Oncology Day Unit was not one either of them had ever needed to enter. Inside the entrance area were a number of chairs and low tables where people could wait before they were called in. There was a water dispenser against one wall and several doors with toilet signs on them; this fitted in with the information Pauline had read that encouraged a regular intake of water to keep hydration levels up. It smelt cleaner than most wards and was very quiet.

"Name, address and date of birth, please," said the receptionist.

"Pauline Carter, 21 Fairhaven View, Milton Keynes, the twenty-fifth of March, fifty-three."

After a rummage through the files in front of her, the receptionist directed Pauline to sit and wait. Soon a nurse called her name and led Pauline into a cubicle to take bloods.

"We have to check you have enough platelets and red and white cells before the chemotherapy can take place," she explained. "It's the way we'll start each time you come."

Pauline's height, weight, pulse and blood pressure were also measured and then she was sent back out to wait for the blood test results.

Kevin and Pauline chatted quietly while they sat in the waiting area. Next, they were sent into a consulting room where a doctor asked various questions, confirmed her blood readings were fine and calculated the dosage for the drugs that would be administered.

They were then sent back to the waiting area whilst the drugs were being prepared.

"Goodness, Kevin. I can see why they said to bring things to do. I think it's going to be a long day."

Both of them were conscious this was only the first of many sessions to follow and I'm sure I saw their shoulders sag in unison.

Around an hour later, a nurse called out Pauline's name again and led the two of them into the main room, which was more like a care home than a hospital ward. There were comfortable high-backed chairs instead of beds, together with visitors' seats alongside. Pauline was directed to one of the chairs, and Kevin sat down next to her. A cabinet was on the other side of the patient's chair alongside a trolley with medical equipment. Two members of staff checked and double-checked that Pauline was about to receive the correct set of drugs. The nurse hung the chemo bag onto a drip stand and connected it to a cannula in the back of Pauline's hand.

The cool fluid seeped up the vein in her arm and Pauline became aware of an unexpected strange metallic tang. It seemed to lodge at the back of her throat, and later, she wondered whether that was the cause of her feeling a little nauseous. As the day began taking its toll on Pauline, she didn't have the energy for books or challenging puzzles. Instead, she asked Kevin to read out easy crossword clues which she could half-heartedly attempt as he wrote the words in. She tried her best to keep her mind off the cancer in her breast and the toxic chemicals that were swimming around her body, but it wasn't easy.

About an hour after the infusion had been completed, a cooling cap was placed on Pauline's head. She endured it in the slim hope of keeping her hair. Once the cooling cap had been removed and staff were satisfied she was good to go, Pauline and Kevin finally escaped the hospital. They were mentally drained by the ordeal. Pauline didn't feel very strong physically either.

One week down, only another nine to go, Pauline thought grimly as they trudged out of the hospital.

***

Sasha phoned her parents later that evening.

"Hi, Mum. What was the chemo like?"

"Well, they weren't wrong when they said about it being a long day. We seemed to do one thing and wait, another thing and wait – all day long. It's really quite wearing."

"Oh, you poor thing. I did keep thinking of you. Would you like us to visit?"

"Well, give me a few days to recover. How about Thursday? Oh, but you can't drive, can you?"

"That's all right – Mark said he'd be able to leave work early any day this week so we can come over."

"That would be lovely then. Thanks, darling."

***

Thursday, after lunch, Sasha got the children ready for Mark's arrival and they all went round to her parents' house with flowers, chocolates and soft hugs. Pauline was sitting on the sofa with a magazine on her lap.

"Well, this makes a change, doesn't it?" said Sasha, trying to appear as cheerful as possible as she entered the living room. She was grateful she was no longer the invalid but wished it wasn't Mum replacing her.

"Thank you for the gorgeous flowers, love," said Pauline.

Sasha snuggled up close to her mum on the sofa. She was transported back to the occasions when, as a little girl, she was allowed to get ready for bed and then come back into the sitting room for a cuddly bedtime read.

As they were chatting, Sasha became aware of a curious sensation of warmth emanating from her body towards her mother's. There was a sense of energy too, almost like static electric prickles. She'd never felt anything like it before; it was most peculiar and definitely more than just normal body heat. She even glanced down, half expecting to be able to see some sparks. The words "you're giving her healing" popped into her head.

Gosh, thought Sasha. *I thought I was just supposed to talk to people. I'm not a healer. I don't see how this can be healing – I'm not doing anything.*

"Trust, Sasha," Hebron said. "You must have trust."

"Trust, Sasha," I mimicked peevishly. "You could try trusting me..."

Trust! That's easy for you to say, Sasha was thinking in response to Hebron.

I smirked as I realised she was reacting to Hebron much like I did. She clearly didn't realise he was the one she'd felt so much love for during her life review.

Impossible Thoughts

By now, Sasha was desperate for Michelle to arrange a night out. It had been good to tell people about the NDE over the last couple of days but it was nothing like a satisfying discussion with a best friend. She'd thought she'd have to wait at least another week since Michelle had messaged that she and Rob would be visiting his brother and family on Saturday. Sasha felt very lucky when the plan was dropped the night before. Clearly it wasn't so lucky for the daughter who had projectile vomited over her favourite teddy bear and was now in isolated confinement.

What? Are you suggesting I might have had anything to do with it? That's a bit presumptuous. But astute, I admit.

Up until now, it was rare for Mark or Sasha to go out without the other, so Sasha told Mark that Michelle had asked for a girls' night out Saturday; she hoped he wouldn't mind her going out.

"No, that's fine," he said without hesitation.

This response had me honing in on what was going on in Mark's head. I saw he had worked out that Sasha going out with Michelle gave him the perfect excuse to go out on his own as well.

Mark didn't want to leave Sasha or have an affair but all he could think about was his sexual drought. He tried to imagine a lunchtime quickie with Natalie. He could pre-book a hotel room but checking in, having lunch and sex and then getting back to work all within an hour seemed to be pushing it. Besides which, there was the cost and it would show up on a bank statement or credit card bill.

He thought about having a tryst after work but he was pretty certain Natalie lived at home with her parents. He couldn't imagine she would be any keener than he would to have sex while her mum was making dinner and her dad could be anywhere else in the house. It was bad enough if you were a teenager but he was heading towards forty. Definitely not an option. What about staying late at the office? But the cleaners would be there and probably security cameras. Going out in an evening – same problem, unless they had sex in the back of his car down a dark country lane, but that hardly seemed practical. The only thing he thought might be a possibility was getting Sasha to go away for a weekend. The spa day seemed to have been a success so maybe he could suggest she and Pauline went to one further away and stayed overnight. But then there were the children. He could hardly expect her to go away and take them too. Palming them off to Kevin was also out of the question.

It was all ridiculous. Why couldn't he just have sex with his wife like normal people? Suddenly, a possibility entered his head: he could go to a prostitute. But… for starters, he had no idea where or how he'd go about it; plus what about picking up diseases or getting caught? Even worse, he wasn't sure he could get aroused by a stranger in some sordid set-up. It would be the ultimate humiliation if he couldn't rise to the occasion.

God, this is impossible, he thought.

If only I didn't have to stick to the no interference rule I could get him to consider why Sasha wasn't interested or, better still, encourage him to do more to help her and open up the lines of communication. I knew he did do some of the jobs round the house, like occasional DIY, mowing the lawn, putting the bins out and entertaining the children at times. It wasn't enough but he wasn't quite as useless as Sasha thought. They just needed to talk things through.

A Cup of Tea and Croissant in Bed?

Sasha had stopped using the crutches around the house and they had really got in the way that morning when she and Mark had gone to look for a new car, so she decided to do without from now on. Her leg felt strong enough on its own now.

After dinner, she read the children a story before she and Mark put them to bed.

Michelle arrived soon after, wearing a patterned tangerine top, with chunky jewellery, over skinny black jeans and high heels, and she wafted expensive perfume. In contrast, Sasha hadn't put much thought into going out; she still had on the same pink T-shirt she'd grabbed that morning but she'd changed from shorts into jeans in anticipation of the evening temperature cooling down. And her only scent was eau-de-housewife.

"Hi, Michelle! You look lovely as usual. Sorry for letting the side down."

"What are you on about, Sasha? You always look lovely."

Once inside the pub, Sasha bought a gin and tonic, and a diet Coke for Michelle, then they found a small table in a corner of the bar.

After they'd settled down and caught up on their current news, Sasha said, "You'll never believe it – guess what happened on my first morning back home."

"A cup of tea and croissant in bed? Has Mark turned all domestic since he's had to do everything himself?"

"As if! I had to get up early and do everything as if I'd never had the accident while he went back to bed."

"No way! I always thought Mark was one of the kindest, loveliest men around. What a shit. Sorry – I shouldn't have said that."

"Well, it's what I thought. Even the crutches didn't make him feel guilty. And he hadn't been doing much extra while I wasn't there; Mum and Dad did just about everything. The house and garden were better than they've ever been."

"I can't believe it. Haven't you said anything to him? It's about time you did."

"It's complicated. And I might as well just get on with it. At least things get done properly. You don't have that problem, do you?"

"No, Rob's really good. He does all the ironing, the washing up after I've cooked and he'll share the general housework. Maybe I should get him to have a word with Mark."

"Like that would do any good."

Sasha played with her beer mat. Would Michelle be as sceptical as Mark about NDEs? That would be awful. She looked over at the bar and took a sip of her drink.

"What else is going on, Sasha?" Michelle asked intuitively.

Sasha looked at Michelle and still she hesitated.

"Go on. I know there's something you're worried about."

Sasha sighed. She'd just have to try.

"Okay, well… have you heard about near-death experiences?"

"I think so. Isn't it when somebody sort of dies but then they come back?"

"That's right. It happened to me when I had the accident."

"Oh my God! What happened?" Michelle leant towards Sasha, her elegant braided hair extensions tipping forward.

"Well, I don't really remember the accident itself but everything straight after is crystal clear. First, I was in the air above it but as soon as I thought about something – like the drivers – I was suddenly back down, right in front of them."

"My God – that must have been so scary."

"Well, it was and it wasn't. And then I was whisked away before I could say anything to the children. I did panic for a moment but Gran – my gran who died four years ago – was suddenly beside me and she calmed me down."

Michelle stared at Sasha with her mouth open, struggling to take it all in.

"Then we ended up in what is kind of like heaven maybe. Oh, Michelle, I'm hearing myself telling you this and it sounds like I've made it up but I swear it's true."

"Don't worry – just tell me what it was like."

"Well, it was beautiful with colours I can't even describe and animals roaming around without any fear. Then we walked to some buildings and I met people who'd died. It was all so real. I visited my great-grandparents and saw two children. I was told about them and asked to come back and tell their parents they were okay."

"You're kidding me. So they're relatives of yours?"

"Yes. I didn't know them before – it's a bit of a long story – but I've actually already met up with them now; my mum drove us to a café and I told them everything I could. It wasn't easy, I can tell you."

"You met up with them? Did they believe you?"

Sasha wasn't sure whether Michelle herself believed what she was saying, let alone the others.

"Maybe? The children's grandad stormed out at first but I think the women accepted it."

"Gosh, I don't mean to be rude but I never thought you, of all people, would handle something like this."

"Me neither. But I've even passed on other messages too – and I haven't finished telling you about my NDE." Sasha paused to drink.

"My God, Sasha. This really is crazy. Keep going then."

"Oh, thank goodness you want to listen. I thought you might think I'm making it up and tell me to go see a shrink."

"Yeah, well, I still might – just tell me your damn story!"

"Okay. I talked to a woman at Henlow Spa and let her know her daughter hadn't committed suicide."

"No way!"

"I know. I also had a life review…"

"What, where you see everything that's happened to you since you were little?"

"Actually, I even got to see my parents getting together, the moment I was conceived – it didn't seem so yuck on the other side but now I think about it – eeoooh! And I saw lots of things that went wrong because of me."

"What do you mean – that went wrong?"

Sasha gave brief details of the main incidents.

"It must have been hard to watch."

"Yeah, although I had this sort-of-angel next to me and he was so lovely. Like he was really happy when I did good things but he didn't seem to judge me for the bad stuff."

"I like that."

"You know, I really didn't want to come back – it was so much better than I could ever describe. You don't have to worry about saying the wrong thing there – you just transmit your thoughts to each other and there are no misunderstandings. Talking seems so heavy and useless in comparison."

"What do you mean: you didn't want to come back?" Michelle asked, flicking her hair back from her face. Her deep brown eyes bored into Sasha's.

"It wasn't that I didn't love my babies or the rest of you," responded Sasha, sensing what Michelle was thinking. "But if you'd been there, you'd understand just how perfect the love and joy is on that side. Anyway, I was shown Noah reaching out for me and that made me come straight back. Oh, and I was told I had to accept a mission to help people."

"Jeez," said Michelle. "What a lot to take in."

"It doesn't even end there, though. When I was back, I could sense so much about anybody around me. I knew what the doctors' and nurses' problems were and I could see what people were thinking about and what they felt. I've actually seen Mark lusting after some bitch in his office – sorry, she's bringing out the worst in my language."

"You don't need to apologise," said Michelle.

"I don't think I can do it quite as easily now but I keep getting voices, like angels or people who've died, telling me stuff."

"This is major, isn't it? Start with what's going on with Mark and then what do you get about me?"

"With Mark I'm pretty certain nothing's happened yet but he's really tempted. He had lunch with the cow but he tries not to think about her. That must mean he's got some conscience. If he actually does have an affair, he's out the door. I may love the man but there's no way he'd ever be coming back into my bed."

"Gosh, Sasha. I've never seen you react so strongly to anything – but I do get it. I'd be just the same. Tell me to shut up if you want, but do you have any idea why he'd be thinking of an affair?"

Sasha shifted on her seat. "It's probably because we don't have sex any more. And that's because his laziness winds me up so much now. It's a real passion-killer when I've slogged myself out all day and evening and he just comes in, eats and watches telly."

"This has got pretty bad. Is it worth trying marriage counselling maybe?"

Sasha was glad to get the issue off her chest but she didn't want to face the confrontation that dealing with it would entail.

"I don't know, Michelle. Maybe it's best not to think about it at the moment. Anyway, let's talk about you. I knew you thought it was wrong of me, just earlier, not to want to come back to my children and felt a bit hurt as if I didn't value our friendship – which I do. The only thing I'm getting from you now is that you think it's Rob's fault you haven't conceived yet and you've finally decided you're going to ask him to go to the doctor's about it. I see you having IVF with a positive outcome in the end."

Sasha was also given an image of Michelle holding twin baby girls but she thought she'd save that surprise for Michelle and Rob to discover on their own.

"Ooh, it's like you've turned into a medium. How exciting!"

"Yeah, well, not really. If anything, I'm a bit worried about it all. It's such a lot to deal with and it's hard enough just coping with the children – and Mark – at the moment. I don't understand why this has happened to me. I'm never the person to get picked for anything."

"Hmmm, I've got an idea, but I don't know what you'll think of it. You could go to Saint Joseph's; it's a spiritual church. A friend of my mum's goes there every month – they do readings and stuff. Maybe they can reassure you. I can find out when the next date is."

"I'm not sure, Michelle. I'm not religious at all."

"That doesn't matter – they don't ram it down your throat. I went a while ago and it was a good evening out – quite entertaining in a gentle sort of way."

"Well, okay, but only if you'll go with me too," said Sasha.

"Of course," said Michelle, her eyes sparkling. "This is the most exciting thing to happen in ages."

There was a lot Sasha still hadn't told Michelle but it could wait until the next time. Whilst she would have loved to talk about the NDE all night long, she rather suspected Michelle's excitement might have its limits, so she decided to leave the subject on a high. Bernard would just have to continue waiting.

Rule Number One

I was having a lot of doubts myself now. I was pleased that Sasha had started to fulfil her mission, albeit with the odd prompt but I couldn't understand why she was letting her telepathic ability slip. She seemed to enjoy the psychic interactions and would tune in to others when it occurred to her but she hadn't made the connection between making a bit more effort to reap more reward. I don't think she realised she could stop it fading by being proactive and it was certainly something I wasn't allowed to prompt on.

In terms of my abilities, I worried how Hebron would be rating me. There were times when I slipped up regarding the rules and times when Hebron was right next to Sasha and me, taking over. Daziel, my wonderful soulmate, had made it look so easy, so why was I finding it so hard?

In actual fact, I was still questioning whether spirit guidance was my calling. Oswald could have gone on for another decade or two if I hadn't thought I'd known best. I'd made the mistake of not considering all the potential outcomes of my action – one of my shortcomings I was made aware of. In fact, Hebron continued to use my example as a warning to future spirit guides to this day.

With Sasha, I knew I was beginning to struggle with Rule Number One – staying emotionally detached. It had been much easier when she was growing up and in the early days of her marriage. But when she started to resent the imbalance in household chores and duties, I could really relate to her. Then, going through her NDE with her, I felt personally invested. Meeting each other in Soul Central had deepened our connection – from my perspective, at least. So being instructed to remain aloof was like telling the wind not to blow. I'd thought the job would be a breeze but, really, it was more like a gale-force ten.

I Don't Mean to be Rude, But Who Are You?

The replacement for Sasha's mangled heap had been delivered by Kevin and Steve and it was now sitting all shiny and bright on the driveway. Sasha kept walking to the window to look out at the silver car; she could almost hear it calling, "Ready when you are."

What if I have another accident though? Is it fair on the children?

Sasha felt Georgie rubbing against her leg, so she bent down and picked the cat up, placing him on her right shoulder. He nuzzled his jaw against Sasha's face; she nuzzled back and stroked his silky fur.

This is silly. Three weeks have passed and my leg is fine now. It should be safe.

"You think I'll be fine, don't you, Georgie?" said Sasha softly.

Georgie purred.

I was telling Sasha she had nothing to worry about but she seemed more interested in the cat's opinion than her spirit guide's. Maybe I should try purring. Instead, I urged the car keys, which were sat in a dish on the kitchen worktop, to tempt Sasha.

Her mobile phone pinged. It was a text from Mark:

Just remembered it's Uncle Bernard's birthday on Monday.

Any chance you can get a card? X

How rude! Someone else's prompt had got there before mine – I wondered whose.

A coincidence or Bernard again? thought Sasha. Well, Pagnell's got a nice little card shop, so I could pop in there and then go to the bakery. It's a Friday, so Ursula should be there, shouldn't she?

After lunch, Sasha put fresh drinks in the all-important changing bag, which was full of nappies, spare clothes, refreshments and so on.

"Come on, my beautiful babbies," she said to her brood, sounding much lighter than she was feeling inside. "We're going for a drive."

Sitting in the driver's seat with the children in their car seats in the back, Sasha inhaled the pine air freshener and residual odours of cleaning products. They prickled the back of her nostrils but at least they weren't doggy or cigarette smells. Her fingernails tapped on the steering wheel before she adjusted the seat and mirrors and familiarised herself with the controls. Turning to examine the children for any concerns, she drew a blank. They'd been in and out of cars since the fateful day and didn't seem to be the slightest bit concerned at having their mum in control.

So it's just me. The chances of it happening again have got to be tiny. Lightning's not supposed to strike twice, is it? Come on, stop putting it off.

Clenching her jaw, Sasha started the engine and cautiously inched down the driveway onto the empty road. Off she set, getting used to the feel of the car. Soon she was smiling and chattering away to the children as she drove the short distance to Newport Pagnell.

After buying a suitable card for Mark's uncle, they entered Bernard's Bakery. A bell tinkled with the opening of the shop door and Sasha wondered what she was going to say to Ursula. Another customer was being served, so Sasha squatted down to tell Rosie and Noah they could have gingerbread men if they were really good and quiet while Mummy was talking to the lady. It was an easy sell.

She studied the dumpy woman with short greying hair whom she presumed was Ursula. She paid for the gingerbread men and handed one each to the children. Then she launched straight in before she could change her mind.

"Um, you're Ursula, aren't you?"

"Yes. Have we met before?" Ursula smiled welcomingly.

"No, but I sort of know Bernard. He sent me to talk to you."

"Bernard sent you to talk to me?" Ursula's smile melted away as she crossed her arms over her chest. "I don't mean to be rude, but who are you?"

Bernard had been a very chatty man and would happily speak to anyone, but Ursula was sure she'd never seen this younger woman or her children before. It was a struggle to control her emotions whenever Bernard was mentioned – his death had been so unexpected as he'd only gone into hospital to have a hernia operation and, yes, she was coping but the loss was still raw.

I sent Ursula some healing as I wondered how Sasha would gain her confidence.

"Sorry, I'm Sasha Denning. I came across Bernard when I had an accident. He tried to speak to me but didn't get a chance to and then he did actually manage it when I was in hospital."

Ursula's eyebrows raised quizzically. "Were you in the same ward as Bernard? I don't remember seeing you there."

"Well, yes, but not at the same time. You see, when I had my accident, I had a near-death experience. After that I could see people who had died and Bernard came to talk to me one night…"

Ursula turned a guffaw into a cough.

"He told me he'd discovered Clive, your office manager, is taking money from the shop. Bernard wanted me to tell you so you can get rid of him and get someone trustworthy in. He'd really like to get Clive prosecuted."

"I think you must be mistaken – Sasha," said Ursula, tightening her arms across her ample bosom. "We've always trusted Clive; he does a very good job. Why would Bernard ask you to help, anyway, when we've never met before?"

"I don't know. In fact, I don't think he was actually supposed to ask me – I remember another spirit saying to him, 'Not this young lady.' It is strange how he later came to talk to me."

"Well, you seem to be as confused about this as I am. I'm sure the accounts are in good order; we've never had any problems as far as I'm aware. Thank you for, err, the message anyway."

"Wait – he said you should look on top of the office cupboard. There's an envelope with fifty pounds in it, which he put there as emergency money after the card shop got broken into about five years ago."

Ursula stared at Sasha, her eyes narrowing. As if she was about to go get the step ladder to check while this stranger was in the shop.

"Well, if you don't want to do that, he said his first dog's name was Blackie and you have a photo from your wedding day on your bedside table. You kiss the photo and say 'goodnight, darling' when you go to bed. And I hope you don't think I'm rude but I thought Bernard looked like Winston Churchill and one nurse thought he looked like a British bulldog. They said they missed him – he was a very kind and appreciative man."

Ursula still had her defences up but all the facts about Bernard stacked up. The chances of Sasha getting them all right by guesswork were slim. Just the other day, Ursula and her good friend Catharine had been discussing the possibility of visiting a medium to see if they could "contact" Bernard. What was happening right now wasn't so different.

"Maybe you could talk to a friend," Sasha continued as she tried to process Ursula's reactions. "That's what I like to do when I'm not sure about something. Bernard said the evidence was in the last five years of bank statements and he keeps – I mean kept – paper copies. Perhaps you could look through them."

"What for? I wouldn't have a clue." Ursula's voice was still sharp and defensive.

"I did try to ask him but a nurse poked her head round the curtain at that point and Bernard disappeared. I haven't seen him since, though I've kept getting reminders of him. Oh – wait! My husband, Mark, is an accountant. Maybe I could ask him to look through the paperwork for you."

What an idiot, Sasha said to herself. How on earth would she persuade him? He'd already poo-pooed NDEs, so she could hardly tell him the truth. *Ignore that, Ursula,* she pleaded silently.

"Hmmm," said Ursula, keeping her options open. "I'll have a think about it. How much would your husband charge?"

Sasha cursed silently. Out loud, she said, "Oh no, we wouldn't want any money. This is just to help you out – it wouldn't be right for you to pay him."

Not for the first time, I swelled with pride for Sasha. There's nothing better than an altruistic human and this made up for many of her faults (such as ignoring me).

However, Sasha was kicking herself so hard she should have been covered in bruises. Sure, she didn't want Ursula's money but it would have been a darned sight easier to persuade Mark if there was something in it for him. Idiot, idiot, idiot. But she couldn't back away now.

"I'll give you our phone numbers and address. Either Mark and I could come here or you could come to our house with the bank statements so you can see where we live and know we're not taking you for a ride. It does seem quite a lot for you to trust us with your paperwork but I'm sure Bernard wouldn't have come to me if he thought I was dodgy too. I reckon we could give you a legal letter to promise we will keep the information confidential and not make anything from helping you."

"Yes, it is a lot, and I'm not committing to anything. I'll have a think about it."

As Sasha and the children walked out, the shop door banged sharply shut behind her and she jumped. A shockwave of uneasiness vibrated down her spine and it wasn't just to do with the door.

When I tried to look ahead to see whether her apprehension had any substance, I was blocked again without any reason being provided. I didn't get it.

***

When Ursula shut up shop for the day, she went straight for the ladder in the office-cum-storage room at the back of the building. She opened it out in front of the office cupboard by the desk. Climbing up, she could see on top of the very dusty unit. At the back, under a thinner layer of dust, was a long white envelope. Ursula wiped it as clean as it would go and peeled it open to reveal two twenty-pound notes and an old-style tenner.

I don't believe it, she said to herself, in a passable Victor Meldrew tone.

She stayed on the top step, thumbing through the notes as if they might change amount and she could then say

Jay Jacobs

that Sasha had been wrong. But that didn't happen and, anyway, the other facts had all been right. But how? There were lots of accomplished magicians around who could make the impossible seem possible. Not that this Sasha woman seemed remotely like an accomplished magician.

Ursula decided to call Catharine after dinner and see what she thought about it all.

She unlocked the filing cabinet in the office and slid out the drawer that contained the paperwork. Everything was neatly organised with separate tabs labelling corresponding years. Yet again, she was impressed with Clive's efficiency and she really didn't want to believe he could be swindling them. He'd worked mornings for them for the last four years after Patricia retired. They'd never thought anyone could be as good as Patricia but Clive soon proved otherwise and he was such a polite, quiet man. It was a bonus he was also a qualified accountant and experienced auditor, so he was able to cover all the finance as well as the admin. He'd actually saved them money. Would someone who was stealing do that? Of course not.

Ursula took out the bank statements for the last three months. She started looking through the line items but couldn't see anything amiss. What exactly should she be looking for anyway? Not really concentrating, she put the paperwork down on top of the in-tray. She just wanted to get home to eat and call Catharine.

The Job's a Good'un

Clive was a little whippet-like man dressed in a suit and tie. He despised suits but wore them for the professional façade. He kept his thinning hair trimmed short, shaved his jagged jawbone every weekday and applied inexpensive aftershave. Clive had the conscientious employee down to a tee. Externally he was pleasantness personified; internally, he was critical and coarse.

Monday morning, he arrived at the bakery at his usual time of 8.45am and made himself a coffee. As he hung his suit jacket over the back of his chair, his eyes locked onto the bank statements in the in-tray. Who had put them there? It certainly wasn't him.

"Ursula, can I borrow you for a moment, please?" he called through to the front where she was chatting to her assistant, Felicity.

"Of course," she replied, her face rising in temperature as she recalled yesterday's conversation.

"I was just wondering why these bank statements are here," he said, pointing at them.

"Oh," said Ursula, certain her cheeks were now as bright as poppies. "Um, I just thought I'd have a look through to see whether our profits have changed."

"Ah, well, it's not bank statements you need; it's the profit-and-loss accounts. Here – in this drawer."

"Oh, of course. I'll just put these away then and get back to Felicity – ah, I was just explaining something to her."

"Don't you want to look at the profits?"

"Oh, another time is fine now, thanks."

Clive assessed Ursula through narrowing eyes as he watched her put the bank statements back in the filing cabinet. Her face was flushed and she was prattling on about today's deliveries – as if he'd be interested. Something was off.

He liked this job. He liked it very much. The Walkers were easy-going people who let him get on with his work without peering over his shoulder. They trusted him and he kept their office in good order, taking great pride in his own efficiency. Which was always best when adding another layer to the accounts. Another rather lucrative layer, thank you very much. It also helped that Bernard hadn't been the most financially astute boss and he was hoping Ursula would be much the same. She hadn't asked to look at any of the figures – until now, that was.

Clive liked his job title too. Clive Jones, Office Manager. He didn't actually manage anybody but it sounded good when he told people. Besides, it was as easy to him as drowning a newborn kitten to conjure up imaginary staff if he felt the need to impress. Sometimes, he'd say he was an accountant. The Walkers had believed it when he provided bogus references and forged qualifications. It was pathetic how gullible they were. But he had to keep Ursula sweet and be extra vigilant from now on. He knew how to procure phone tapping devices to install on Ursula's mobile and the business landline, with next-day delivery.

I almost went running straight to Hebron for advice. Was this something I should be dealing with? But I was due to qualify soon and thought I'd better look like I was in control. I poured over my tablet and read The Spirit Guidance Rule Book from start to finish. Fat lot of use that was.

More Tea, Vicar

Mark pressed his advantage after Sasha had her evening out with Michelle and arranged to go down the pub with Phil the next weekend. They had met playing pool soon after Mark had moved to Milton Keynes and always had a good laugh together. To be fair, Phil had a good laugh with just about anybody but he and Mark did get on especially well. They used to go out as a foursome when Phil was engaged to Kathy, one of Sasha's friends from high school, but that came to an end after Kathy found out Phil had been unfaithful. He was a self-employed carpenter and he'd been caught helping Mrs Hendry test out her new dressing room in more ways than were strictly professional – or advisable.

Phil drove over Saturday evening and he and Mark walked to The Greyhound, which was only down the road, arriving early enough for the pool table to be free. Mark got their first pints of beer in, and Phil set up the pool balls. When they were onto their third game and at least as many pints, one of the regulars came over and put some money down on the pool table. Mark and Phil made their excuses, ordered a couple of whiskies and meandered over to a table.

"You seeing anyone?" Mark asked Phil with a burp.

"More tea, Vicar! Nah, mate," replied Phil. "Though the woman at the house where I'm putting in a new kitchen is a bit of all right. She keeps bringing me bacon butties and then hangs around, playing with her hair and stuff. I reckon she's well up for it."

"Is she married though?" asked Mark.

"Yeah, but I never see her husband. I reckon she doesn't see much of him either. If she wants a shag, who am I to say no? Tough job but someone's got to do it."

"What if the husband catches you?"

"I wouldn't risk it unless she's sure he's away."

"Hmmm," said Mark. His first thought was that Phil shouldn't do it but then he thought about Natalie. Now he could relate to the temptation.

"What would you do if you didn't have her house to have sex in?" he asked.

"You what? We do, so it's not a problem. Why are you asking all these questions?"

"No reason; I was just wondering."

"Wondering, my arse. What are you up to?"

Mark sighed. He knew he should keep quiet and definitely not tell Phil but the lager and whisky were playing havoc with his reasoning powers.

"Well, there's this girl at work. She's made it obvious that she's keen on me. And she's really hot. And I can't remember the last time Sasha was up for it, so…" He trailed off.

Phil grinned for a minute, then frowned. "Tell me to mind my own business if you want but have you asked Sasha why she's, err, not keen?"

"Twice. First time she said I should be able to work it out and refused to say any more. Second time she said something about seeing things from her point of view and stormed off. I haven't got a clue."

"Does she think you've done something wrong?"

"I dunno. Oh, she got cross with me when I thought I'd surprise her by doing some ironing. I did surprise her – by burning one of her favourite tops. I haven't done that again."

"Hmmm. Women. Though out of everybody, mate, I never thought you'd do the dirty."

"And I shouldn't," slurred Mark. "I wouldn't look twice at Natalie if Sasha and I had a sex-life, but Sasha won't come near me anymore. Natalie's always making it obvious that she wants me."

"Doesn't this Natalie have her own place?" Phil asked.

"No, I'm sure she lives with her folks, and anyway, I haven't definitely decided to," said Mark, as shame and self-loathing chomped at his conscience.

"Well, I dunno. Maybe find out when her folks are away or would she be up for a quickie in the car? Whatever you do, just don't get caught. Sasha's a diamond."

Mark downed his whisky and headed off to the bar for another round. He could hear a local, called Colin, talking about a recent accident in which he'd thought his time was up and how he now appreciated his wife and girls so much more.

That's a coincidence, thought Mark, failing to compute that Colin was the van driver who'd been involved in Sasha's accident and forgetting how he'd felt when he'd contemplated losing Sasha.

I can only go so far with creating opportunities, especially when they aren't directly for Sasha. As I said before, people have free will for how they deal with events.

When he got back to the table with the drinks, he talked about football, and soon enough, it was kicking-out time. They staggered back to the house and drank strong coffee in the kitchen, trying with minimal success to keep quiet. Sasha was already in bed, and Mark invited Phil to stay over on the sofa rather than get a taxi home and then have the fuss of retrieving his car the next day.

They ricocheted like steel balls in a pinball machine from wall to furniture and back again, ineffectively stifling loud chortles. The children didn't stir but Sasha huffed and jammed her pillow over her ears.

Mark reeled into the bedroom, apologising repeatedly in a loud hiccuppy whisper. His T-shirt got stuck over his face as he undressed and he capsized off the bed. Then he crashed into the wardrobe whilst attempting to peel his jeans off. Eventually he collapsed on his side of the bed and was snoring within seconds.

Sasha couldn't have been more unimpressed but Mark had me creased up laughing. However, I was concerned for Sasha. I'd really hoped she might have started discussing her issues with Mark by now but neither of them was making any effort to bridge the ever-increasing chasm between them. I know communication is made much harder in the human form than it is in my dimension, but honestly, not even to try? The fact they could solve their issues so easily just by talking about what was wrong was so obvious to me; why couldn't they see it too?

***

Sasha was the first to rise, to attend to Violet. She tiptoed round where one side of Phil was hanging off the sofa like he'd been dreaming of star jumps, not that she'd ever put Phil and star jumps together.

When Noah and Rosie woke up and bounced into the sitting room like Tigger and Roo, they soon had Phil sitting up, rubbing his eyes and groaning but willing to entertain in return for coffee and breakfast. Mark was roused by the waft of toast and crawled out of bed like a sedated sloth. His head was throbbing with a heavy hangover and the horror of the last night's conversation.

As the day went on, Mark kept a wary distance from Sasha, but she wasn't inclined to make an argument. She didn't even want to be near Mark at this point in time, let alone engage in conversation with him. Instead, she contemplated Michelle's suggestion of going to Saint Joseph's.

Sasha had a look online and found it held regular Sunday services from 6.30pm. It looked pleasant enough on its website so she sent Michelle a text to ask her if she would like to go that evening, hoping again it wasn't too short notice. This was becoming a habit – asking Michelle to drop everything for her. Thankfully, she was perfectly happy to go and Rob didn't mind. Michelle was more cheerful and loving towards him after her last evening out with Sasha, so he was all for more of that.

Once Phil had left, Sasha informed Mark she'd be going to the spiritualist church that evening.

Blimey, he thought. *That's got to be an over-reaction, right?*

"Michelle and I are just curious," said Sasha. "They have mediums there who give you messages from loved ones. It could be quite interesting."

"If you're gullible enough to believe it," replied Mark.

"Well, whatever," said Sasha, frost crisping her words. "I knew it wouldn't be your thing."

Top of the World

On the way to the church, Sasha asked Michelle, "Are you sure they won't ask what church we normally go to and that sort of thing?"

"I doubt it."

"They might be really stern and serious."

"No, they won't."

"I bet it would feel awkward to leave if we wanted to."

"Honestly, Sasha, chill. I'm sure you'll like it."

They approached an unassuming brick-built church. There was a car park at the side from which they could see another nondescript building attached behind the main one.

They parked up, walked cautiously into the church and slipped into a pew at the back. Sasha counted thirty other people sitting in small clusters along the smooth wooden pews. Many of them chatted quietly, with tinkles of laughter breaking out here and there, whilst others sat in silence. A medium walked up to the lectern in front of the congregation.

"Welcome to Saint Joseph's," said the tall, graceful lady wearing wire-rimmed glasses. With a clear, friendly voice, she introduced herself as Evelyn.

"Haven't we been blessed with a beautiful day today?" she said. "I do hope you've all had a chance to enjoy it. I'd like to extend a warm welcome to our newcomers and hope you will feel right at home here."

She gave a mild sermon and invited the congregation to sing "Top of the World". Michelle and Sasha were pleasantly surprised with this alternative to boring old English hymns and joined in, trying (not altogether successfully) to keep in tune on the high notes.

Evelyn then talked for a while about the week she'd had and gave some examples of the ways in which she had witnessed minor miracles, such as the magnificent oak tree she passed every day, brimming with budding green acorns that would sustain many creatures in the winter, and seeing a young teenager stop to help a frail elderly woman across the road, even though he was laden down with a bulging rucksack. She encouraged everyone to try to do a good deed every day.

Next, she announced it was time to invite loved ones from the spirit world to bless the congregation with their presence and she would do her best to pass on their messages. She asked everyone to open their hearts and to let her know if they thought a message was meant for them. She was drawn initially to the front left of the room, saying, "I want to come to you, the lady in a blue top, please."

As they craned their necks to see who the lady was, Sasha felt her heart beating faster.

Evelyn went on to describe a gentleman she could see on the other side. "I have a tall, rather imposing man here. He is wearing what looks like a farmer's smock and has a battered old hat on his head – I think made of felt. He's standing with his arms folded across his chest and his shoulders back as if he's assessing his flock."

The-blue-top-lady nodded.

"I'm getting a father figure – perhaps a grandfather."

"Yes, that's my grandpa," said the lady, surreptitiously taking a crumpled tissue out of her pocket.

"He's now lifting his hat and, oh, he's showing me a great wound to his head – that's how he died. I understand it was an accident at the farm."

The lady nodded again, her eyes moist with emotion.

"He's very proud of you and your son. He says it doesn't matter that your son doesn't want to follow in the family footsteps. He should be supported in whatever he chooses to do. The gentleman is now showing me a trophy, so I take that to show your son will be successful in his own field. He's asking me to look more closely at the trophy – oh, it has a man swinging a golf club on it. Is your son a golfer?"

"He's trying to be. But we haven't taken much notice of it, what with all the work to do."

"Well, this gentleman is saying give him the time he needs. If he keeps practising and working hard, he'll go far. He's now pointing to you and holding his hands to his right side. He's saying, 'Go to a doctor to get yourself looked at.'"

"Yes, I have been having pains."

"He's saying it's nothing to worry about but you need to get it sorted. He's not normally one for expressing emotion, he tells me, but he sends you his love. Can I leave that with you?"

"Yes, thank you very much," said the woman, smiling through tears of joy.

Then Evelyn pointed in the direction of Sasha. "I have a lady with me who's looking ever so proud, with bright blue eyes. She's saying, 'That's my girl', but I'm seeing her as a grandmother rather than a mother. Can you take this?"

"Yes," replied a rather shocked Sasha, who'd hoped to observe rather than participate.

"Now, I'm a bit confused because she's telling me she passed a while ago – she's showing me chest or heart problems – but she's also saying it was so good to be with you recently. She made sure she would be the one to come for you. Sorry – that doesn't make much sense."

"Actually it does. I had a serious accident and she came to take me over," said Sasha. "But obviously I didn't actually die."

There was a light ripple of laughter within the pews before the medium continued.

"Well, she's also telling me you are doing well – she's watching you and your children all the time – but you haven't finished helping. And she says you now have the gift of healing; she watched you with your mother. She says you have a good husband. And just have faith and ask for help when you need it. I'll leave that with you."

"Thank you so much," said Sasha, who couldn't control her broad smile.

"Well, that proves what you told me really happened, doesn't it?" whispered Michelle.

"Yes," replied Sasha quietly. "Sometimes, even though it was more vivid and real than anything else I've done, I've wondered whether it really could have happened."

I approached Sasha's grandmother before she disappeared to thank her for her communication. She seemed to be doing a better job at guiding than me, and I was grateful she reminded Sasha to ask for help. If only Sasha would call on me, I could do so much more for her.

In the church, there were several more connections followed by a prayer of thanks and a cheerful rendition of "Bring Me Sunshine". As Michelle and Sasha were leaving the room, Evelyn approached them.

She said to Sasha, "I don't often retain the messages I give, but I remember that you were told you have the gift of healing. Is it the first time anyone's said that?"

"Yes, and it's all very new," said Sasha. "This started after I had a near-death experience at the end of June. I'm still getting used to everything."

"Oh, are there other changes too, then – if you don't mind me asking?" Evelyn smiled invitingly.

"Well, yes. I could seem to read people's minds after the accident but that doesn't happen very much now. And sometimes I get voices. I've been able to pass on information to a couple of people. Oh, and one spirit came and sat on the end of my bed to ask me to help his wife. I think my grandmother was telling me I have to find the others that were to do with what I saw on the other side and help them somehow."

"That certainly does sound like a lot to get used to. You're always very welcome to come back any time, if you would like some guidance and a shoulder to lean on. Did you know we also hold healing evenings every Thursday from 7pm to 9pm in the church hall? You could have some healing yourself to see what it's like. We have workshops for developing healing and mediumship, both of which I think would be perfect for you. It would be lovely to see you back again," she said, including Michelle in her gaze.

"Thank you very much," they replied in unison and made their way out.

In the car going home, Sasha asked Michelle in for a coffee so they could talk over the evening's events.

Mark had put the children to bed and was slumped on the sofa in front of the television, with Georgie on his lap, when they got back. Michelle said hello and then the women sat at the kitchen table, hot mugs of coffee in hand.

"Well, what do you make of that?" started off Michelle.

"It was mad, wasn't it?" replied Sasha, quietly enough that Mark wouldn't overhear. "I can't believe my gran came through and told me I still have more work to do. I'm busy enough with just the kids and stuff."

"I wouldn't say 'just'. Three children under the age of five must be exhausting. I think I'll settle for one or two, thanks. How many others have you got to deal with? Dead people, not children, I mean."

Sasha laughed. "Let's see… the first person I saw was a guy with a wife called Anita. I think I need to explain to her what really happened, if I ever find her. There was the lady who had the horse-riding accident, a girl from school and Mr Taylor, who I mentioned before. I've no idea how I can help him now. And, anyway, how am I even supposed to find these people?"

"I don't know, Sasha. I'm not really big on religion, but maybe you could pray for answers?" Michelle squirmed as she said this, knowing Sasha wasn't religious either. "And your grandmother said you can always ask for help."

Sasha squirmed too, but not because of praying, which went in one ear and out the other. "Ask for help" was the suggestion she took objection to. The only way she might do so was for someone else's sake, like her mother, but not for anything that she needed herself. She couldn't just ask for the mission to be made easy.

"Hmmm. I'll think about it," she said, avoiding Michelle's eyes.

Sasha's lack of religious inclination wasn't an issue for me. In the spirit world, we're interested in compassion rather than doctrines. If someone were to pray, great, but it didn't always make them a kinder person. My only issue was her childhood vow, or rather, childish vow. She did actually ask for some things without thinking about it so maybe there were some double standards going on. Still, that hardly mattered if she didn't realise it. How are we ever going to get over this hurdle? I wondered. Yet again, there was nothing in The Spirit Guidance Rule Book to help me here.

Sasha told Michelle, in much greater detail, about her life review, and they talked about choices and consequences. Before they knew it, it was getting late, and Mark came into the kitchen to say he was going to bed.

Michelle left, and Sasha got ready for bed and slipped in beside her husband, who was already breathing heavily. She lay there, wondering how on earth she was going to fulfil all these new responsibilities and why her gran had said Mark was a good man. Perhaps it was because she was having serious doubts at the moment.

Quite the Opposite

Sasha woke the next day, hoping to find she'd received some inspiration in her sleep but no such luck. There were three weeks before their holiday, so she did need to start thinking about checking their clothes, sun cream and so on, then buying whatever was lacking, but she was struggling to concentrate. There was a restlessness inside her that wouldn't go away and she felt like she had to get out and just get away – anywhere. Sasha didn't consciously have a place to go in mind but the desire to get in the car and drive wouldn't leave her alone, so she got the children ready and told them they would go for a mystery drive.

Okay, so I was responsible for this "urge". I'd like to say I had been behaving myself for ages but it was so, so hard. Today, I was frustrated with Sasha's inertia, and I hoped this little urge-giving could be overlooked. I think it was less than a nudge.

With no destination in mind, Sasha let Rosie and Noah call out "left" or "right", and she would then change direction at the next side road or junction according to their spontaneous instructions. That way, it was fun for all of them. Rosie seemed to understand the directions quite well but Sasha was greatly amused by Noah. He almost certainly had no idea what he was doing but he enthusiastically called out "leff" or "wight" whenever it was his turn, giggling and bouncing against his car seat straps. Violet added her undecipherable noises to the effervescent atmosphere.

Before long, Sasha saw the library ahead and her mind flitted to the horse-riding lady in her NDE who'd found a job in a library. *Could it be this library? Could she still be there over thirty years later? Unlikely, but might as well look…*

She drove into the last free parking space in the library car park. As she pulled up the handbrake, the relevant part of her NDE replayed before her:

Sasha was a toddler, enjoying a picnic with her mother in a lovely wooded park. She waddled off to chase a butterfly, picking up speed and tumbling over on the path just as a pair of horse riders came trotting around the corner. The lead rider jerked the reins heavy-handedly and her horse reared up, losing its footing in slippery mud and falling onto the rider whose boot had caught in a stirrup. Pauline ran to the scene, secured the horse and tended to the woman as best she could – whilst now keeping an eye on Sasha – and the other rider raced off to call for help.

The scene segued into the lifeline of the rider, a twenty-year-old who had recently finished her second year of studying English Literature at University College London. The worst injury from the fall was the spinal cord damage, causing near-total paralysis from the waist down, with all the complications that were a package of such an injury. She abandoned her course and moved back to her parents. Some years later, she took on part-time work in her local library, where they were understanding of her medical needs.

Sasha took a deep breath to ground herself back in the present and turned to her children.

"Shall we go look at some books?" she asked, and they gave varying sounds of approval. She placed Violet in the buggy, put reins on Noah and asked Rosie to hold Noah's hand too. As they walked into the entrance lobby of the library, Sasha was drawn to a stand containing rows of leaflets that advertised local courses, events and places of interest.

I persuaded her to pick up leaflets on pottery and watercolour courses, plus a couple of leaflets about Saint Joseph's Church and their healing evenings. She put these in the changing bag and on they strolled into the library.

As they walked through to the children's corner, where there were small brightly coloured stools and cushions surrounding an alphabet rug, Sasha tried to take a surreptitious look at the library staff. It wasn't exactly hard to spot the lady in a wheelchair, sitting behind a desk with a monitor on it and a plaque at the front stating Information Desk.

Oh my goodness, thought Sasha. *This is too good to be true. But it must be her; why would she change jobs if the staff were caring and she were happy here? I certainly wouldn't.*

Sasha parked Violet, got a couple of books and perched on a green pouffe facing the desk, gathering her children around her. As she read the story, mostly on autopilot since it was one she had read over and over again, she examined the lady.

She looked to be in her late fifties. Oval glasses rested on her Roman nose and her lips were pursed together as she concentrated on the computer screen. There were creases and lines on her forehead, around her eyes and mouth, but her fluffy beige cardigan softened the image. Sasha wondered how approachable she would be. What on earth could she say to the woman without sounding completely ga-ga?

She picked another book the children enjoyed listening to and started reading it. Then an idea came to her: She could approach the librarian to ask what else there might be by that author. As soon as she finished the book, she put it back in the box, picked up Violet and led the other two to the information desk.

"Excuse me, please," said Sasha, "I was wondering whether you have any more books by Jez Alborough. You've got *Duck in the Truck* already; I've just read it to my children."

"I'll have a look for you," the lady replied, barely glancing up. Sasha read "Heather" on her name badge, whilst Heather tapped away at the computer.

"Ah, there are quite a few books to choose from. There are two more in the Duck series and also two about a boy called Freddy who has a teddy. We should definitely have the Freddy books on the shelves; shall I help you find them?"

"That would be lovely, thank you," said Sasha.

Heather reversed out from behind the desk and wheeled herself past adult fiction A-J. Sasha and her brood followed behind.

As Heather leant over to thumb through the books in one of the large boxes, she winced with pain and apologised.

"Oh, there's really no need to apologise," exclaimed Sasha. "Quite the opposite!"

"Oh?" queried Heather, being far too reserved to directly ask what was meant by "quite the opposite".

Sasha gave a shuddering sigh at the prospect of telling Heather what she knew. She sat down on one of the children's chairs near to the box and directed Rosie and Noah back to another book box; Violet had nodded off to sleep, so Sasha slipped her back into the buggy, head lolling to one side. With no more ways to put off the inevitable, Sasha launched into her explanation.

"You're probably going to think I'm a complete nutcase but here goes. Over a month ago, I was in a serious car crash and it would seem I almost died. I was taken up to – for want of a better word – heaven, where I saw everything that has happened in my life up to that point."

Sasha glanced at the librarian but she couldn't gauge a reaction, so she carried on cautiously.

"Well, one of the things I saw was me, as a toddler, falling over in front of two horse riders. You were the one at the front, whose horse reared up and fell back. Your left foot was caught in the stirrup, so you couldn't get out of the way and the horse landed on you. My mother, who's a nurse, looked after you while your companion raced off to get help. I know that's why you're in a wheelchair now and I'm so sorry it happened. It's me who should be doing the apologies for causing you pain. Err, my name is Sasha, by the way."

With a sharp intake of breath, Heather turned her wheelchair abruptly away from Sasha.

How on earth does this woman know exactly what happened to me, she thought, *let alone claim it's her fault?*

She wanted to shout, "How dare you be unaffected by the accident while my life is all restriction, pain and the constant fear of complications?" but that wasn't Christian, so of course she wouldn't.

"I was told I can help you in some way," continued Sasha, trying to peer round at Heather's face. "I couldn't think how I possibly could, but last night I went to a spiritualist church for the first time and found out they do healing every Thursday evening. I'd be happy to take you there, if you like. I know it won't undo what's happened – if only I could manage that – but maybe it can help with the pain?"

Heather clenched her hands into tight fists. How ignorant to suggest a healing session would magically fix everything. Her church members had prayed for her time and time again to no avail. Heather concentrated on her breathing – in, out, in, out, keep control.

"That's highly unlikely," she said icily, studying her white knuckles.

"Well, you don't need to say yes or no now," said Sasha. "I'll, um, pop in again on Thursday and see what you think then. And I'll give you my phone number and email so you can contact me if you want." Sasha found a little notepad in her bag and wrote her details down on the first page that wasn't scribbled all over. She tore it out and handed it over to Heather. When she put the notepad back, Sasha noticed the leaflets in her bag and took out one of the Saint Joseph's ones.

"This is the place I'm talking about," Sasha said as she offered Heather the leaflet too.

Resisting the urge to screw the paper up into a ball and lob it at Sasha, Heather tucked it together with Sasha's details between the seat and the side of the wheelchair, saying nothing further. She resumed flicking through the books until she found what she was looking for.

"Here's *Where's My Teddy?* Would you like to take it out?" she said indifferently.

"Yes, please," murmured Sasha.

As soon as they had exited the library, she turned to her children. "You were wonderfully quiet while I talked with the lady. You're the best in the world." She pulled them close for a reassuringly warm hug.

Well done, Sasha, I was thinking. Even though it had taken a bit to get her there, she had stepped up to the challenge, which hadn't been an easy one, and was ticking off another one of her missions.

A Cat's Life

Sasha drove the children home, fed and changed Violet and played with them all for a while. She then put CBeebies on the television for the older two and put Violet in a baby walker. This left her free to get on with washing up and making dinner. And to dwell on things.

This mission stuff isn't for me. Apart from that lady in the changing room, nobody seems to believe me – I bet Nancy and Tanya were just humouring me too. And Mum does. I don't want to do it any more.

What? She was doing so well.

Violet trundled in, rebounding from wall to wall. Sasha burst out laughing and went over to her to plant a flurry of kisses on Violet's velvety forehead.

"Dinner's almost ready," she declared in an excited voice. "Are you hungry? It's going to be yummy! Yummy in your tummy!"

Suddenly, Sasha heard a harrowing yowl mixed with screams from Noah and Rosie. She ran out of the kitchen, followed the sounds upstairs and threw open the bathroom door.

Georgie burst out and flashed down the stairs. The children were sitting on the bathroom floor, sobbing, with Rosie clutching a bleeding right arm. The bath was half-full with water and bubbles.

"What's going on?" Sasha asked Rosie.

"Wanted to give Georgie a bath," hiccupped Rosie through her sobs.

"Georgie no want!" joined in Noah.

"No, I don't suppose Georgie did want," replied Sasha. "Cats don't like water. They keep clean by licking their fur. Let me look at your arm, Rosie. Did Georgie scratch you?"

"Yesssss!" she sobbed.

Sasha gently peeled Rosie's left hand away and looked at the damage.

"It's not too bad, sweetheart, but we'll give it a good clean to make sure there are no germs in it. You'll be fine."

She got Rosie to stand on the bathroom stool in front of the basin and washed the grazes on her arm thoroughly with soapy water.

"I'll put a couple of plasters on you and you'll be all better. And I don't want either of you playing with water in the bath again. Do you understand?"

The children looked up earnestly and nodded. Sasha pulled the plug out of the bathtub, wiped their faces dry and took them downstairs for their dinner. She couldn't see Georgie anywhere and was very concerned for him. Instantly, she was back in her near-death experience, immersed in the scene of Georgie's rescue at Willen Park:

The cat was picking its way along a muddy path on the edge of the lake, where there were abundant patches of tall reedy grasses and bushy undergrowth. Initially, it was unaware of the three preadolescent lads who were creeping up behind. Sasha felt the cat's sudden spike of fear as a boy swooped down and seized it by one hind leg before it could sprint away. Then it was spiralling through the air towards one of the other boys. That boy yelped and recoiled instead of catching the cat, which resulted in it slamming into his torso and slumping down to the cold ground at the boy's feet. The boy kicked out, striking the cat's leg; the second kick struck its ribs, then somehow his trainer slid under its belly making the cat fly, hind legs and tail uppermost, through the air, flipping over and landing face-first in the water. The panic-stricken creature came up gasping for air and scrabbled to the bank.

Sasha wanted to scream at the boys, halt their callous laughter and make them suffer like the cat but all she could do was watch helplessly.

Just then, there was the thud, thud of heavy footsteps. The boys turned to see a glowering man striding purposefully towards them. They scurried away.

It took a few minutes before George, the dad of Sasha's supervisor at work, found the bedraggled, shivering feline camouflaged amidst the undergrowth. Sasha could tell that on first appearances he thought it was dead but he bent closer and saw the ribcage rising and falling. Tenderly, he picked the cat up and carried it back to his car. He placed it gently on the blanket he always kept in the boot and drove very carefully to the nearest vets.

A Miss Casey examined the cat, an attractive silver tabby with a white bib and paws. It was a young unneutered male, no more than a year old. She used a scanner to check for a micro-chip, which would give an owner's details, but none could be detected, leaving them unclear whether this was a pet or a stray. Its matted fur was starting to dry out but Miss Casey deduced it had been in water, presumably the lake. She listened to its chest and was satisfied with its pulse and breathing. She felt the cat over and it mewed piteously when touched round the mouth, the ribcage and on its left hind leg. The mouth was swollen and bloodied on one side of the jaw but there were no other injuries visible and no apparent broken bones although its temperature was below normal. The prognosis was largely good. The receptionist checked the journal of missing animals in case it had been reported but none matched, so she added it to the list.

As there wasn't room to keep the cat at the veterinary surgery, George, somewhat reluctantly, agreed to take it home as a temporary measure. Spirit Sasha smiled wryly as she could tell he was more of a dog than a cat man, but he was far too kind to abandon any animal in distress. Three weeks later, her supervisor was asking whether anyone in the office wanted a cat. Sasha said yes as she and Mark had talked about getting one and they'd named the cat after George.

Sasha emerged from her flashback, realising Rosie trying to plunge Georgie into a bath of water would have seemed like a repeat dose of torture. She really wanted to go comfort him but the children's needs took priority.

Sasha cleared the table of the dirty plates and cutlery before ushering the children back to the sitting room to play with their toys. When Mark got home, Georgie was still in hiding. Mark swept Violet up to give her a cuddle whilst Sasha dished up the adults' dinner. They all joined Noah and Rosie in the sitting room; Violet was put on a blanket with her activities and Mark and Sasha sat down on the sofa to try to eat their dinner without too much interruption. Mark flicked through the TV channels until he found a quiz show to watch at the same time. Sasha ate quickly, desperately wanting to find Georgie but accepting it would be best to get the chores out of the way so he could then get her undivided attention.

As soon as the children were all in bed and the washing up was done, Sasha searched the house for Georgie. When she told Mark about the incident, he said, "You don't need to worry. He'll appear when he's good and ready."

But Sasha wasn't having that and she started to panic when she couldn't see the cat anywhere. Wondering if he'd run away, she remembered where he'd hidden on the first day they had got him, all those years ago.

That was a little prompt I could do that was in the rules for once. I wasn't doing anything to change the outcome of a situation; it just eased it a little.

Sasha peered behind the sofa and, sure enough, there was Georgie, crouched down low, staring up with wide, wide eyes. It really was like déjà vu and Sasha suspected he hadn't moved at all since escaping from the bathroom.

She was right of course.

Once she'd persuaded Mark to get off the sofa so she

could pull it away from the wall, Sasha slowly approached Georgie, picked him up and sat down with him on her lap on one of the armchairs. She stroked him repeatedly, to soothe away his shivers.

Hmmm. The medium said I had the gift of healing; I wonder whether it works on animals too? Maybe I can try it on Georgie, but how do you do healing?

"Have faith, Sasha," she heard in her head. "You can work it out."

Yeah right! Some actual instructions were more like what I had in mind, she thought. But the voice had gone and Sasha was left to her own devices.

I had copied Hebron for the voice and didn't dare do any more. I just hoped it was enough (and not too much – I'm sure imitating your superior was not encouraged).

Sasha closed her eyes and relaxed her breathing. Then she tried to imagine sparkles of healing light falling over Georgie. Sasha opened her eyes just enough to see Georgie's outline on her lap and gently held her hands over his body without actually touching him. This felt like the right thing to do, so she continued. She started at his head, then slowly worked her way down his body to his tail and back up again, spending the most time over his head. She also spoke silently to the cat, telling him she understood the fear and pain from his lakeside encounter and the recurrence of that fear today. She told him she would do her best to protect him and ensure nothing else would hurt him, that she loved him completely and would always look after him. The logical part of her brain told her how silly this was – cats didn't understand English, and how would he hear her anyway – but she carried on. She became aware of a peculiar prickly sensation as if energy were flowing from her hands, very similar to what she'd felt sitting next to her mother.

Finally, she stroked Georgie reassuringly and murmured sweet platitudes to him. The cat started purring, very quietly at first, then progressively building to his normal rumble, and Sasha sighed with relief. She would talk to the children tomorrow to instruct them on how to behave with cats – and other animals, for that matter.

A Healing Hand

Sasha hadn't seen as much of her parents as usual since her mum had started the chemotherapy. With the second week following the same pattern as the first, Pauline had resigned herself to writing off the Monday and Tuesday of each week, whilst gradually trying to get back to normal the rest of the time.

Sasha called, and Kevin answered the phone.

"Hi, Dad! I've started driving the new car now, so the kids and I can come over without needing Mark."

"Hello, sweetheart. The thing is, Mum's finding the chemotherapy a bit tiring at the moment, so I think the children might be a bit much for her."

"Well, I've got an idea. If I bring things round for them to play with and you don't mind keeping them occupied, maybe out in the garden, I can just sit quietly with Mum. It would be really good to see her."

"Hmmm, I suppose that sounds reasonable. I'll have a word with her. If I don't call back to say otherwise, how about coming over on Friday, after 2pm?"

***

That Friday morning, Sasha made some flapjacks to take round, with Rosie and Noah joining in and Violet getting excited from her baby walker. She also called Meena and arranged to meet her at the park the following Tuesday for the promised picnic.

After lunch, Sasha gathered some bits and pieces for the children's entertainment. Their current play involved pushing round a doll's pram and pushchair, and Violet had a stroller to follow along with – she was very close to being able to walk independently now. Sasha crammed them all into the boot of her car.

When they arrived, Kevin opened the front door and helped his daughter bring the children and the playthings into the house.

"Good grief! Are you moving in?" he joked with his arms full.

"Well, if that's all right with you, Dad," replied Sasha. It was a tempting thought though she couldn't imagine her parents being so happy about it.

They walked through to the lounge where Pauline was resting in one of the comfy armchairs.

She smiled wanly at Sasha and the children, bending forward gingerly to give them each a hug.

"How are you feeling, Mum?" enquired Sasha gently.

"Oh, I've known better days," Pauline replied, not quite managing the joviality she'd been aiming for. "Mustn't complain though; there's worse off than me."

"Maybe, Mum, but you don't look great – no offence!"

"Thanks very much," replied Pauline, with more of a smile this time. "I have to say, it's hit me harder than I'd expected. I thought I'd be feeling better than I am today but I'm trying not to worry or let it get me down."

"You're not fooling me, Mum. You are worried about it, aren't you?"

Pauline sighed. "Yes, I suppose I am. But what can I do? Sometimes it seems like it's never going to end."

Sasha had a tentative idea. She gently asked her dad whether he'd take the children into the garden to play. As they were leaving the room, she turned back to her mother.

"Mum…"

"Go on, you can do it," I encouraged. It was impossible to tell whether she'd heard me or not.

"…I went to a spiritualist church on Sunday with Michelle. I got a message from Gran and was told I have the gift of healing. Gran said I should start with you."

"Really, Sasha; are you sure?" asked Pauline, whilst thinking, *First a near-death experience and now she thinks she's a healer,* but it was hard enough just keeping her eyes open and listening to Sasha. She wasn't sure she wanted to be Sasha's guinea pig and wondered whether it would be very rude to ask her daughter to leave right now.

"Well, yes, I am sure Gran came through to me, but I'm not so sure about the healing bit. Although…"

She paused as she remembered the tingling heat when sitting next to her mum and with Georgie. Perhaps she should have more faith in herself, like the angels suggested.

"Like I suggested, Sasha, but you seem to have forgotten about me." There was no reaction, so she definitely wasn't tuned into me. I reminded myself not to take it personally.

"There'd be no harm in me trying it, though, if you don't mind. What do you reckon?"

"What does it entail then?" Pauline asked with a sigh.

"I think I just ask you to relax – you can stay in that chair – and I'll hold my hands above you – not touching you – while I try to let the healing powers come down through me. The way I see it, it's not me doing it so much as a power through me, if that makes sense."

"Whatever you say, Sasha. Sounds like it's not going to kill me." Pauline was trying to make a joke but it didn't come out that way.

Sasha kept her face as neutral as possible to stop her concern showing.

"Right then, Mum. Are you sitting comfortably?"

"Yes, dear."

"Then let us begin. Take long, gentle breaths in… and out… in… and out… and close your eyes if you feel like it." *I do hope this is right – at least let me know if it isn't, please, Gran.*

There she went again. Gran, this. Angels, that. "My name's Zinnia; I'm the actual one assigned to you, Sasha." Oh dear, Hebron would be having words with me again at this rate.

Not sensing any response, Sasha continued, trying to sound like she knew what she was talking about. She roughly followed a relaxation technique she'd heard about ages ago.

"Start relaxing from your toes upwards. Give your

toes a little wiggle, then relax them and repeat; do the same with your feet... then your calf muscles... and your knees. Squeeze your thigh muscles and relax... then your backside. Come up your back and feel your tummy relax too. Wiggle your arms and fingers, then let them fall. Rotate your head one way and then the other. Give a big smile and let your smile relax away gently. Now I'm going to place my hands above your head and slowly work my way down your body. Then I'll come back to your chest. Just keep breathing nice and gently and try to stay relaxed."

My mood improved, watching Sasha's intuitive actions. She didn't actually need to start with the relaxation exercises but, otherwise, she was a natural. And, even better, her confidence was growing appreciably – even if she didn't realise it yet.

Sasha held her hands over her mother's head, several inches away. She relaxed her own breathing and asked angels to heal her mum. As she slowly worked her way down Pauline's body, Sasha felt the now-familiar warm and tingly sensation through her hands. She knelt down in front of Pauline as she reached her legs and feet before working her way back up again. She concentrated the most over the chest area and her hands felt very hot indeed by now.

Is this really working or am I just imagining it? she wondered. *I don't think I could feel like this unless it was real.*

When she believed she'd done enough, Sasha stepped back and asked her mother to wiggle her fingers and toes again, take deep breaths and open her eyes. Sasha then sat down next to her.

"How do you feel?" she asked.

"Well, very relaxed; I almost dropped off. And possibly not as exhausted as before. Thank you, Sasha, that was very pleasant indeed." Pauline didn't think any healing had actually happened, just a bit of relaxation.

"Did you feel any heat?" asked Sasha.

"I can't say I was aware of any. Why? Did you?"

"Yes. It was really strange. My hands were hot and tingling by the end of it in a way that's never happened before." *Well, apart from the cat, but I can't see you accepting that.* "Maybe we could do this again, as I'm sure just once won't make that much difference. It probably ought to be a regular thing."

"That's fine with me," agreed Pauline, more to appease her daughter than because she had any faith in the process. In any case, she did enjoy her daughter's attention. "Let's see how your dad and the children are getting on, shall we?" and she got up, forgetting how delicate she'd been feeling earlier.

***

Kevin stared in disbelief as Pauline and Sasha walked through the patio doors into the back garden with a jug of iced orange squash, a stack of picnic glasses, a plate of flapjacks and big smiles on their faces. Pauline might not have been impressed with the healing but Kevin was blown away by the transformation in his wife.

When the children led Pauline further down the garden, Kevin said quietly to Sasha, "What on earth have you two been up to? I hadn't been sure I was doing the right thing, having all of you come over, the way your mum's been this week, but you seem to have cast a magic spell over her."

"Oh, really? That's brilliant!" beamed Sasha. "I've been trying healing on Mum, but I didn't really expect much. I can come back and do it again next week, if you think it's helping."

"You certainly can. Healing, you say?" pondered Kevin. "Well, whatever it is, she seems better than she's been all week. Since the accident, you've been full of surprises, Sasha," he added, scratching an itch just above his right ear. It was as if there was something he should be able to comprehend but it was just out of reach, beyond his grasp.

Not to worry, he thought, turning to admire the woman he adored as she played with her grandchildren.

Back For Good

When Sasha got home with the children, she was bursting to tell Michelle about the healing but she had to prepare dinner. As soon as she got a moment, she texted Michelle:

> Got lots to tell you about. When are you free? x

> Tomorrow night is okay

> Okay, I can drive this time. 8pm?

> Great! Looking forward to it ☺

I haven't even checked with Mark, fretted Sasha. *And this is getting into a habit, me going out with Michelle and him going out with Phil. It's not very good, is it?*

She'd have been disappointed (again) if she'd hoped for any answers – I wasn't allowed to offer my opinion since she hadn't asked me directly, and it's unlikely she would have heard anyway. She hadn't taken on board the suggestion to communicate with me whatsoever.

***

Once the children were in bed, Sasha asked Mark if he was okay with her seeing Michelle again. He agreed, though somewhat distractedly. Luckily for him, Sasha didn't notice; she was just relieved. Not so long ago, she would have been excited to tell all her news to her husband but times had changed.

The next evening, Sasha drove round to Michelle's house and they went to their old regular.

"So, how's it going?" asked Michelle once they'd sat down at the corner table with their drinks. "Is Mark doing any more to help and have you done any of your good deeds yet?"

"Mark's still bloody useless. You know, I used to put up with it because he's considerate in other ways and so good with the kids. Now all I notice is everything he doesn't do and it's driving me mad. Anyway – that's not what I wanted to talk about; I have actually done some healing – on Mum and Georgie," replied Sasha.

"You're kidding me! What are you – Doctor Doolittle now? I'm sure the cat wouldn't need persuading but how did you get away with your mum?"

Sasha explained all about it.

"Do you think it worked?" Michelle asked at the end.

"Well, the funny thing is, she didn't feel any different afterwards, but then she went outside and played with the children like she would have done before the chemo started. Dad was blown away by that. So I reckon the healing must have helped, don't you?"

"It does sound like it. Are you going to do it again?"

"Hopefully. What I really want is for the healing to get rid of the cancer."

"That would be amazing," said Michelle. She hoped so too as she was very fond of Pauline. "And how's the mission going?"

"Oh, don't ask." Sasha took a swig of her Coke.

"Why? I thought you were getting into it."

"Not very well. I found the horse rider and spoke to the wife of that spirit, Bernard. It wasn't very nice with either of them."

"Oh dear. Tell me about the horse rider first."

Sasha explained about turning up at the library.

"Wow!" exclaimed Michelle. "What are the chances?"

If you knew anything about spirit guides, you wouldn't ask that question, I would have loved to say to her.

"I know," said Sasha. "I basically told her I was the kid who'd wrecked her life and apologised. Then I suggested the healing nights at Saint Joseph's and said I could take her there. I could see she was seething underneath but somehow I managed to give her my contact details and say I'd call in again to see if she wanted to go. I should have gone back on Thursday but I chickened out."

"I'm not surprised but I can't believe you did all this. Well, she didn't tell you to piss off, so there's a chance she'll go along once she's had time to think it over. Imagine what it must be like to come face-to-face with somebody you've probably resented big time – even hated. It must be a big shock really."

"Oh, don't! She probably does hate me. And it was

pathetic to suggest healing as if it would be some miracle cure." Sasha picked at the edges of a beer mat.

"No point worrying about it now. What happened with the other woman?"

"Ursula. I told her what Bernard had said, and she was really cold and defensive. But at the end, she said she might let Mark look over the accounts – which I was dumb enough to offer. God knows how I'd persuade him to do that. I'm rubbish at this."

"No, you're not, Sasha. It's a lot to take on – for anybody. And I suppose you have to finish the mission?"

"Probably. What might happen if I don't?" Sasha picked up her glass and gulped her drink down. "I'm scared to carry on and I'm scared not to. Why did it have to happen to me?"

Michelle reached over and gave Sasha a big hug.

"You're doing brilliantly, Sash. I'm here if you need me and just remember – you've done loads more than you'd ever have imagined. To be honest, I never thought you had it in you to do this much."

Sasha gave a wobbly smile. "Rude! But I suppose you're right."

"And you know what else? You came back from dying to do good things. You know – back for good, just like the Take That song. I bet Gary Barlow would be well proud of you."

Sasha laughed as a tear plopped onto her cheek. "You just want him to *Relight My Fire*, don't you? You're the best friend ever, Michelle. Thank you."

One in a Million

I thought it would be a good idea to see what Mark was doing whilst Sasha and Michelle were catching up. It was a good example of one of my poorer decisions.

He was bored and feeling left out. He and Sasha used to ask Kevin and Pauline to babysit at least once a month so they could go out or visit friends but now Pauline was having chemotherapy, they'd stopped asking. At least, that was the only reason Mark was aware of.

He lay on the sofa with the television on and the cat curled up next to him. He wasn't particularly interested in the programmes that were on and his mind kept drifting. He replayed his conversation with Phil regarding being unfaithful. He thought about Natalie and how she was still coming on to him even though he did his best to avoid her.

He now imagined being alone with her, kissing her lips softly, teasingly at first, and then passionately, intently, tongues exploring. Natalie groaning as he kissed his way down the side of her throat to her generous cleavage. Him reaching round her back, up her top and effortlessly unclasping her bra. Then he'd run his fingers down her arms, tickling the inside of her elbows as she trembled with excitement. Sasha had always loved that. He'd take hold of her hands and raise them over her head so he could lift her top and bra up and off her in one deft movement. Bringing her in close for more passionate kisses, he'd resume his downward journey to her lusciously full, upturned breasts, where he would lick and suck her pert pink nipples.

A loud advertisement with a very annoying jingle jolted him back to reality. What if he really did take Natalie out? His urge to relieve his hard-on was overpowering and he unzipped his jeans, pushed them down just low enough to slip his right hand under his trunks. It would be so fucking amazing! He resumed his fantasy and released his pent-up frustration.

That's it, he decided. *I'll see if Phil will cover for me next Saturday.*

The car didn't seem such an inferior proposition now he'd made up his mind to go for it. Any option was better than nothing. He called Phil.

"You go for it, my son," Phil said with what Mark could imagine was the dirtiest grin on his face. "Just remember—"

"I know," interrupted Mark. "Don't get caught."

"Too right," replied Phil. "Sasha's one in a million; you'd be a fool to lose her."

"Yeah, well, I'm going to have to take the risk or I'll go crazy. Keep your fingers crossed for me, mate," he said, frowning. He knew he was being a massive tool. The stakes were high but his desire sat higher.

The Usual Shtick

Michelle had bolstered Sasha's confidence and given her the encouragement to have one more try at the mission but she could have done without it being Mr Taylor – her least favourite person. She steeled herself for the flashback of when she was a twelve-year-old, playing with an old cricket ball in her friend Ryan's front garden:

Ryan threw the ball carelessly to Sasha. She missed the catch and the hard red ball struck her quite sharply on her left shoulder. She picked it up and hurled it back at Ryan, who skipped impressively out of the way. The ball sailed straight over the low brick wall and thwacked right into the brittle rear lights of the neighbour's parked car, sending bits flying. Sasha and Ryan gasped and sprinted indoors. They didn't dare go back to take a look at the damage and certainly weren't confident enough to confess to Ryan's mother or to their neighbour.

Adult Sasha watched Mr Taylor walking out of the house the next morning, wearing a smartly pressed suit and polished shoes. His glasses were glinting with the extra buffing Mrs Taylor had given them, as she wished her husband the best of luck. He set off in his green Toyota, practising answers to potential questions in his head as he was on his way to his first job interview in ten years.

Every time he applied his brakes, only the offside lights came on and the nearside indicator light didn't work at all. With unfortunate timing, a pair of traffic police happened to drive along behind. They pulled him over. He waited nervously as they inspected his car, though the only issue was the broken light fitting. Mr Taylor's relief was short-lived, however, as he was told he couldn't drive the car until the fault was rectified. He pleaded with them to make an exception, explaining about the interview, but there was no trace of compassion or leniency.

"The law's the law," was all he got.

Time raced by as Mr Taylor searched for a public phone booth, called a taxi, rang the company to explain his predicament and eventually arrived at the building. They granted him a later interview but it was no great surprise he didn't make it to the short list. Reliability and attention to detail were a key part of a financial officer's role. If it hadn't been for the broken light fitting, he thought, he'd have been offered the job, with a substantial pay increase and improved career prospects. Instead, Mr Taylor stayed in his dreary-but-safe job in a dreary-but-safe manufacturing company. Spirit Sasha could see him becoming more and more bitter and withdrawn, finding fault with all and sundry in his dreary-but-safe existence.

She resurfaced from the vision and futilely wished she'd been a brave enough child to tell the Taylors what had happened at the time. She asked Meena to babysit. Meena assumed it was for a hospital check-up and brought Jake round after lunch. Violet was having a nap, so Sasha suggested she could go out first, so there would be one less child to keep an eye on, and then she could explain about things when she got back. She also had to tell Meena she might be very quick, if the person she was going to see wasn't home, or it might be a little longer – but still probably under an hour.

I could see that Meena was most intrigued, as this didn't seem like a medical issue.

Sasha sorted refreshments, pointed out things for the children to play with and left Meena to it. Just before setting off, she had a sudden impulse to open the changing bag, where she saw the pamphlets she'd picked up at the library.

I still gave the occasional thought placement when prudent. With Sasha's lack of experience in things metaphysical, I couldn't expect her to have the same forethought. She dutifully took out the one to do with Saint Joseph's Church, folded it and put it in her handbag.

Once she was driving, she regretted not letting Meena know where she was going. Michelle was the only person who knew about Mr Taylor, but she didn't know Sasha was off to see him now or where he lived. Her stomach prickled.

Before long, she turned right into Maple Close and slowed the car to a crawl. Most of the residents had paved their front gardens and it was hard to recognise the place. After all, the cricket ball fiasco had been twenty-six years ago and Sasha hadn't been round much after that.

There were cars dotted sporadically along the left side of the road and Sasha squinted for house number thirty-three as she inched along. She pulled up outside and sat there for a moment. That was Ryan's house, so she needed the one to the right of it.

The house that may or may not still be Mr Taylor's was constructed of honey-coloured bricks, with a red brick pattern arched over the lounge window. The old front door was standard PVC, discolouring at the edges and lichen, or some other plant growth, had turned it green in places. The window frames looked equally neglected. There was a scruffy lawn at the front of this property and shaggy bushes in each corner. At some houses, it could be seen the owners had a great sense of pride in their property but this was definitely not one of those.

Okay, here goes, said Sasha to herself as she stepped out of her car.

A sudden gust of wind blew sharply, knocking her back as the sun disappeared behind a dark cloud. Reluctantly, she walked up the path, knocked and waited. It didn't seem like anybody was in, so she turned back to her car. As she was contemplating whether to be relieved or disappointed, Sasha jumped at the sound of a door creaking opened behind her.

A diminutive lady with frizzy white hair and glasses peered around the slither of the open doorway. Sasha reckoned this must surely be Mrs Taylor and quickly reversed, tripping over a stray stone and just managing to stay upright.

"Oops, sorry – I'm Sasha Denning. I'd like to speak

to Mr Taylor, if he's here, please," she said, sounding as flustered as she felt.

"What do you want?" asked the lady suspiciously. Sasha could see her eyes darting up and down, assessing her, a stranger on the doorstep.

"Well, when I was twelve, I used to be friends with Ryan, who lived next door and I have some information to give Mr Taylor to do with something that happened back then. Something I'd like to apologise for."

"I see," said Mrs Taylor, though she didn't see at all. "Wait there and I'll go check."

She all but closed the door on Sasha, leaving an even smaller gap than before.

Sasha tried to second-guess the conversation that might be going on inside the house.

She couldn't hear but I could and it went:

"There's a woman who wants—"

"I know; I heard her. You take the phone and stay out of sight but listen in case I need backup. Now move out of my way."

A man who had once been tall but now stooped as if defeated shuffled to the door and opened it. He had a comb-over of waxy hair, slug-like bags of loose skin under his lined, washed-out eyes and a down-turned mouth. Melancholy oozed towards Sasha.

"What do you want?" said Mr Taylor, echoing his wife's words.

"I was recently shown some information – something that happened a long time ago – which I think I should tell you about and apologise for. It was when I was a young girl playing next door with a boy called Ryan. My name is Sasha. Um, would it be okay to talk to you inside, please?"

Mr Taylor was weighing up whether this stranger was a door-to-door salesperson or a Jehovah's Witness. In either case, he wouldn't hesitate to direct her straight back out the way she came in. And he had his wife ready to call the police if needs be. Should be safe enough.

After Mr Taylor growled, "Come in", Sasha followed him through a dingy hallway where she could almost taste the dank mouldiness lining the walls, into a living room which appeared to be stuck in the twentieth century. Green and cream Regency striped wallpaper rose from the floor up to hip-height where a border consisting of paisley swirls joined a cream wallpaper with a diamond-shaped fleck pattern. A lumpy green sofa and two armchairs faced a mahogany coffee table and matching corner unit upon which a large television squatted. Valanced floor-length curtains enshrouded the net-curtained window.

Mr Taylor slumped into the armchair nearest to the door they'd walked through and Sasha perched herself on the sofa. She wondered where his wife was.

Mr Taylor sat silently, his eyes boring into Sasha. He wasn't planning on making this easy for her, whatever it was about.

Sasha took a deep breath before launching into what was becoming a regular spiel. She sensed she'd have to approach it with great caution this time.

"I'm not sure you're going to think highly about what I have to say, so I'm just asking you to hear me out before you pass judgement, please. I had a car accident in June and I nearly died."

Sasha couldn't hear his internal response, which was, *My heart bleeds for you. So what's this got to do with me?*

Noting his narrowing eyes and stubborn silence, Sasha thought, *Oh boy, another Arthur.* She pressed on reluctantly. "I don't know if you've heard of near-death experiences..."

Mr Taylor crossed his arms, his hands balled into fists. *Sounds like new-fangled, new-age mumbo-jumbo to me,* he thought.

"...but I think that's the term you'd use for what happened to me. I was transported into a different space, a beautiful loving place, where I was shown a review of my whole life to date, in incredible detail."

I suppose your life flashed before your eyes, did it? The usual shtick!

"One of the scenes was when I was twelve and I'd come over to my friend Ryan's house next door to you here. Ryan and I were bored, waiting for lunch, and we were playing catch with a cricket ball out the front. On one of my goes, I threw the ball as hard as I could. It flew over the garden wall and smacked into the back of a car..."

What, my car?

"...We heard a crack and realised something had broken. I was so ashamed and scared we ran indoors and never told anyone. I'm afraid it was your car..."

I knew it! I bloody knew it.

"...and it was the next day when you went to an

interview and got stopped by the police for the broken tail-light. I'm really sorry."

You little bitch! And you thought you'd come and tell me this now? For what? If you expect me to say I forgive you, you can forget it straight away.

Mr Taylor sat there fuming, his lips still glued together. His face had turned a mottled mixture of burgundy and white, his breathing erratic.

Oh my God! Is this all because of me? Sasha asked herself, wishing she could undo the last half hour.

"No," came a reassuring response in her head. "He was in charge of how he dealt with the situation." Hebron had dropped in on the encounter.

"I don't expect you to forgive me, Mr Taylor. I know things haven't worked out so well since that day. I wish there was something I could do to help, but I'm not sure there is anything."

"Of course there bloody isn't," he said out loud at last. "I don't know what you were thinking of, young lady, coming here to tell me this. You know very well you should have knocked at my door and confessed your crime when it happened. What's the point now, eh?"

"I know – you're right! If I could go back and change it, I would. I know it's pointless to keep saying it, but I really am truly sorry."

"Quite right it's pointless. This is a complete waste of my time."

Mr Taylor stood up to indicate it was time for Sasha to leave.

I quickly filled Sasha's mind with the image of the

church pamphlet.

"There's just one thing that maybe could be helpful," Sasha said hesitantly as she took the pamphlet out of her bag and held it out to Mr Taylor.

"I've been to a lovely spiritualist church called Saint Joseph's where they do readings and healing. The healing is every Thursday evening at 7pm, and I just thought maybe you'd be interested in going."

"So that's what this is all about, is it?" thundered Mr Taylor. "Coming in here with a fancy story just to convert me into some crazy religious cult?"

"Oh no! It's not like that at all!" exclaimed Sasha. She really hadn't seen that one coming. "They won't try to convert anybody, I'm sure. I'm not religious and I didn't feel under any pressure when I went there. I'm planning on going to the healing myself actually; I think it will be good."

"And I think you've said quite enough, young lady," growled Mr Taylor, pointing a twitching finger towards the hall. "The door's that way!"

Mr Taylor's hostility looked ready to erupt, and Sasha swallowed. She let the pamphlet fall onto the sofa and shrank past him into the hall, clutching her handbag to her chest. The moment she was outside, the front door slammed shut behind her.

Oh my God! she thought. *I'm never doing that again.*

***

Sasha drove back home, crying all the way. On the

driveway, she dried her eyes and blew her nose, hoping her face didn't look too bad.

"That's good timing," called Meena as she opened the door with a dopey Violet in her arms. "She's just woken up."

Violet reached out to her mummy who gave her a big hug and kiss before a nappy change and some mid-afternoon milk.

Noah and Jake were like bookends, having naps of their own on the sofa and Rosie was reading her picture books.

When Sasha had Violet settled on her lap, Meena sat down in the other armchair and studied Sasha's face. "So, erm, was your trip successful?" she asked hesitantly.

"Successful isn't the word I'd use," said Sasha, wondering how much to tell Meena. Probably the minimum. "I went to see a man because I recently discovered I'd accidentally broken his car lights when I was twelve, playing ball. I went to say sorry. Like twenty-six years too late."

"God, Sasha. I'm not sure I'd have done that and I can't believe you did. How did he react?"

"Um, like he wanted to murder me."

"Oh." Meena shuddered and shrunk into her seat.

Sensitive to Meena's reaction, Sasha changed the subject. "Well, at least going to the park tomorrow should be a lot better."

I shimmered in delight at the prospect.

Sugar Lumps

Sasha woke up with her mind made up: no more stupid mission. What she'd done just had to be enough.

I was gutted, as you'd say. If she stopped now, was she ever going to think about her vow? I scrolled through my tablet for inspiration on how to reignite her confidence. There was a chapter on placing items such as feathers, birds and butterflies in front of one's human for association but I didn't see how that was relevant. And there were lots of rules about what I couldn't do. I cast the tablet aside and watched Sasha prepare for the park, filling a picnic box and sticking a blanket, towels and sun cream in another bag.

She told herself to forget about the mission and get on with enjoying life. Lastly, she gathered Rosie, Noah and Violet and settled them in their car seats.

"This is going to be fun," she told the children as she got behind the wheel, looking forward to it herself.

***

Sasha turned down the lane that led to the park and waved at Meena and Jake, who were sitting on a wooden bench. She liked this park because it wasn't just the average playground/playing field combo. There were mature trees all around, including rhododendron and camellia bushes. Even though the trees no longer had pretty blossom on them, there were lots of colourful flower-beds. With plenty of paths to run around between the foliage, it was great fun for the children and a refreshing escape from pavements and houses.

She got out of the car, removing children, bags and more bags.

"You'd think we were setting up camp with this lot." Sasha grinned.

"I know," replied Meena, "I don't know how you manage."

"Oh, you get used to it," said Sasha as she strapped Violet into her pushchair and wondered whether all her friends thought she was crazy having three young children.

They walked into the play area, which was enclosed by a low fence, and laid out their picnic blankets side-by-side under the speckled shade of a horse chestnut tree. The children were too excited by the swings and slides to sit down to eat, so Sasha and Meena let them play on the equipment, assisting as necessary. Sasha held Violet's hand as she investigated the smaller slides, see-saws and baby swings; Meena kept an eye on the other three. It was good to see them laughing and giggling, racing around and tumbling safely.

At last, the children tired and they returned to the

picnic blankets. Sasha laid out food, then spooned puréed shepherd's pie and broccoli into Violet's mouth. Meena had sandwiches and crisps for Jake and herself and they all settled down to eat and chat.

They both saw a young woman walking straight towards them. She looked remarkably similar to Meena: the same slight build and long, dark hair. She walked with shoulders rounded forward and head tipped down, hands thrust into jeans pockets and intermittently stumbling. Her purple top was creased and her monkey boots were grey with dust and dirt.

"Oh no," groaned Meena.

"Hiya, Sis!" the girl called out.

She glanced quickly at Sasha and smiled uncertainly at Meena. "You said you were going to the park, so… can you lend us twenty quid? Only I don't get paid till Friday and I've got nothing for dinner. Please?"

Meena said to Sasha, "This is my sister Anita." Turning to her sister, she said, "You never make your money last. What have you spent it on this time?"

"Oh, I don't know. Everything's so expensive nowadays."

Sasha could tell that Meena was thinking, *you mean booze and fags are.*

Meena worried about her younger sister, but she was also fed up with bailing her out. She wasn't made of money.

"I can only give you a tenner," she said. "Buy some sensible food and make it last."

"Of course, Sis," said Anita.

I can tell you she was wondering what special offers

there might be on wine at her local Co-op rather than contemplating sensible food.

Whilst the sisters were talking, Sasha was staring at Anita, thinking: *Anita. I'm certain I know that name. Where from?*

Suddenly, despite Sasha's insistence that she was done with the mission, she was deep within a flashback of her NDE, listening to the man with the caterpillar eyebrows talking about his wife:

"I should never've left her. I could tell she was upset but I wanted to shake Dave until he begged me to stop. He was manipulating Anita and she had no fucking idea. He didn't care about her. He was just using her to get at me, to get revenge because his first-ever pathetic little girlfriend left him for me. We were only sixteen, for God's sake."

Spirit Sasha felt compelled to say, "Do you want to tell me about Anita?"

"I knew she was the one as soon as I saw her. She's amazing! Giggling when I tell her I love her, then kissing the end of my nose saying, 'Love you too, Sugar Lumps'."

A flush of embarrassment crept up his face and Sasha could hear him pause to consider how odd it was he was telling these strangers such intimate details about himself; he wasn't a talker. That thought came and went like a spark of static as he carried on, rather more calmly now.

"We got married two years ago. Things got tough: she had a miscarriage and I lost my job. She took on the pub job – where Dave worked, as it turned out. When he realised she was married to me, he started playing her. Telling her how beautiful she was, that she could do better than me, telling her he could give her a better life. Mickey heard it all and told me – he's the bar manager.

"I had it out with Anita. I lost the plot and she started crying. I told her she could have Dave if she wanted him and stormed off on my bike. I was going to go find Dave and make him pay for what he did. The bastard! I wasn't thinking straight, I was going too fast and went through a red light. I got hit and went flying. My crash helmet wasn't done up and it came off before my head hit the post. That was me done for. Now I'm here and I don't know what to do. I only want to be with Anita. I thought she didn't love me anymore but now I know that's not true. I ruined everything and she hasn't stopped crying and she can't hear me tell her I love her. She doesn't see me. I'm an idiot and I fucked up. This should never have happened."

"Oh my God!" exclaimed Sasha as she surfaced from the flashback. The sisters' heads span round to face her.

"I've just realised who you are! You're Anita!"

"Yeeesss…"

Sasha heard Anita thinking, *my sister just told you that,* and realised that flashbacks gave her a temporary increase in psychic awareness. She also noticed Meena's suspicious look – the same as she'd worn when they'd met up at school after the accident.

"Oh gosh, I'm going to have to explain. If you're the Anita I think you are, this might be a bit upsetting, so I'll apologise in advance."

A bit upsetting? ran through her mind. *That hardly*

covers it. I wish I knew a better way to do this.

"I had an accident back in June. I almost died and I guess you could say I went to heaven and I saw other people who had passed over."

The colour was already draining from Anita's face, her eyes wide and fearful. She swayed and Meena ordered her to sit down on the blanket.

Sasha registered Anita's reaction and knew she'd got the right woman.

"The first person I saw – well, after my gran, that is – was a man who'd died from a motorbike accident. He hadn't been wearing his crash helmet properly and it came off when he hit a traffic light."

"Oh my God!" said Anita, closing her eyes in a vain attempt to close down a picture of Chris striking the post.

"I can stop if this is too much, but I think your husband wanted me to tell you what he said. I've just realised; he didn't tell me his own name..."

"It's Chris," whispered Anita, barely audibly. "You can carry on."

Meena put her arm around Anita's shoulder, pulling her close.

"Well, he told me all about the guy called Dave, who'd been his friend at school but now hated your husband. Apparently, a girlfriend of Dave's left him for Chris when they were sixteen. Dave held a massive grudge. When he met you at the pub where you started working because Chris lost his job, he used you for revenge. That's why he chatted you up and tried to break up your marriage."

It was a good thing the children were behaving

themselves because Anita and Meena were glued to every word Sasha spoke. It fitted so well to what they knew about Chris and Dave even if they couldn't get their heads around how she could know.

"When Chris found out," Sasha continued, "he was furious; he argued with you and stormed out. He told me he hadn't meant it when he told you to go off with Dave and he should never have got on his bike. I remember him saying how he loved the way you'd giggle when he said, 'I love you', and you'd kiss the end of his nose and say, 'Love you too, Sugar Lumps.' He'd thought you'd stopped loving him but he watches you now and knows that wasn't true."

Tears were streaming down Anita's face, and Meena was trying hard to hold herself together, to be the good protective sister.

Sasha was drained and turned momentarily to check on Violet and the others.

"Thank you," said Anita after blowing her nose. "I don't know how you could know, but it's all true. I miss him so much and I never stopped loving him."

"I know," said Sasha gently. "The way he spoke to me, I don't think he'd really accepted he'd died. I would have stayed and listened some more but my gran made me move on – I know this doesn't make much sense, but it was all new and strange to me, so I just did as I was told. I could see Chris really missed you too and was upset at himself for making everything go wrong. I'm positive he would just want the best for you now though." Sasha paused, wondering if this last bit really was true.

Hebron had appeared next to me and actually told me

to step in to confirm, making sure Sasha could hear me. I said, "Yes, it's true. He is being healed now and will be happy for Anita by the time she falls in love again and has a family. He will watch and love them too, as if they are all a part of him. He will feel so proud. Tell her."

Sasha repeated this to Anita, word for word.

"Blimey, Sasha," exclaimed Meena. "I didn't know you were psychic!"

"Me neither," agreed Sasha, also feeling a little shocked. "Everything's changed since the car crash. It's really weird."

"Well, I'll leave you both to it," said Anita, as it seemed Sasha had finished talking about Chris. She got up to go, wanting to be on her own for a while to mull over everything that had just been said and absorb it all. "Thanks again, Sasha. See ya, Sis."

She started walking away, turning to wave and give a little smile as she went. For the first time since Chris's death, it seemed like the claggy grey smog that persistently clung to her might finally let go.

Sasha and Meena turned their attention to the children, helping them to finish their picnic.

"Going back to what you were saying, Sasha, about seeing into other people's lives, err, could you by any chance have seen into mine?"

What do I tell her? asked Sasha in her head, worried how Meena might react if she let on how much she knew.

With a little less surprise this time, she heard me reply, copying the way I thought Hebron would. "Just tell her the truth. It will be good for her. You will see. Trust!"

Meena was also getting used to Sasha's pauses but she waited apprehensively.

"When we spoke at nursery before the summer holidays, I think you were aware I wasn't answering you properly. That was because I was being shown what you've been through. Oh, Meena, you are so strong! I can't imagine how you managed to cope with all the awful things that have happened to you."

Meena looked down at her hands and bit her bottom lip hard in an attempt to hold tears back. Usually, she was very good at keeping up an emotional wall but Sasha hadn't judged Anita. She looked up.

"Things are better now," she said quietly.

"Thank goodness. You deserve to be happy. You were groomed by Lance and you didn't get any choice in what he made you do. I could see how unhappy you were. It doesn't make you a bad person. You must believe that."

"I dunno. I don't reckon most people would see it that way."

"Well, anybody with a normal half-decent brain in their head would. Whoever says otherwise has problems, not you."

"Yeah, then there's a lot of people with problems. It's easier not telling people, believe me."

"I can understand that but always remember you have nothing to be ashamed about at all."

"Not even bunking off school, smoking and drinking? We used to nick the booze, you know."

"But, Meena, you hadn't exactly had it easy up to then, had you? Those girls were your friends, the closest to kindness you got, so don't be hard on yourself. You – and the other girls – were young and vulnerable then. Look at your life now. You're kind and caring, in spite of what you've been through."

Meena smiled at last. "You should be my PR. You make me sound real good!"

Sasha laughed and replied, "You are good, Meena, and don't you forget it!"

Other than Angela at the homeless charity and of course her partner Tom, Meena hadn't come across anyone as sympathetic as Sasha. Meena would have hugged her if hugs came naturally; instead she just kept smiling.

Lunch was demolished and the children were ready to play again. Sasha and Meena smoothed more sun cream over their children, cleared up, packed the bags and put everything except the changing bag with the towels stuffed in, into the boot of Sasha's car, ready to let the children run around the park and dip their feet in the paddling pool. The sun had come out from behind the intermittent clouds and Sasha was thankful that, for once, something to do with the bloody mission hadn't been horrible.

Issues

Ursula had visited her friend Catharine to talk about Sasha's visit. Catharine had been surprised and intrigued but she was very level-headed, asking Ursula to explain all her concerns.

Firstly, she might have been able to handle it if her best friend had done the telling but Sasha was a complete stranger. Sasha swore she hadn't known Bernard before he'd died, but what if that wasn't so? It was hardly likely that Ursula was justified in feeling jealous – Bernard was a very chatty man who enjoyed company, that was all – but it would have been better if she had known and trusted Sasha already. It would also have been much better if Bernard had already spoken to Ursula about the problem. And, of course, the issue of Sasha communicating with Bernard psychically was hard to swallow.

The other issue to overcome was even more of a dilemma – if that were possible. Ursula and Bernard had been mightily impressed with Clive from the day of his interview right up to the point where Sasha'd walked into the shop. The transition from Patricia to Clive had been practically seamless. He'd found them a cheaper computer support specialist and was a good negotiator with suppliers. It was so hard to contemplate he was anything other than a wonderful employee. Steal money from them? Clive? Never! And the thought of having to sack him and start again with somebody new – especially when Bernard wasn't there to deal with things…

What would Bernard have done? Of course, if Şasha were to be believed, then Bernard was actually telling her she should get rid of Clive. That wasn't what she wanted to hear.

In the end, Catharine and Ursula concluded that however deluded Sasha might be regarding the so-called psychic element, there would be no harm in having her husband look over the paperwork. There wasn't any top-secret information in the bank statements and it was all backed up on the computer if he didn't return them. Plus, she could type out a confidentiality agreement for the couple to sign. At the end of the day, there was a good chance Mark wouldn't find anything untoward. Perhaps Sasha just had a very active imagination and dreamt the whole thing up.

Ursula sat at the office desk in the bakery with the phone in her hand, having closed shop for the day. She tapped Sasha's phone number into the keypad.

"Hello, may I speak to Sasha, please?"

"Yes, speaking." Sasha recognised Ursula's voice straight away and she sat down with a thump.

"It's Ursula Walker here, from the bakery. I've decided to take you up on your offer, if that's still okay with you, of course. I could drive over with the bank statements whenever it suits you."

Sasha's internal language turned rather colourful, which was rare for her. She knew she was going to have a hard time persuading Mark to help out at the best of times, and currently, their relationship could hardly be described as "at the best of times". Maybe if she asked Mark when they were relaxing at Butlins, she'd stand a better chance. A few weeks' delay shouldn't be a problem for Ursula? It wasn't as if it were an emergency.

"Okay," replied Sasha. "Actually, we're going on holiday shortly so do you think it could wait until the start of September? And evenings would be better, then Mark will be here and you can meet him. He can ask you anything he might need to know before he starts. Maybe I can give you a ring after we get back?"

"Yes, of course. I don't want to put you to any trouble."

"I'm sure it will be fine," said Sasha, although she was far from sure. "Hopefully Mark can find the evidence for you."

"I hope so – or that he finds there's nothing wrong, which would be even better. Well, thank you, Sasha, and have a good holiday. Speak to you in September!"

Ursula was relieved she had finally made the call; it was a weight off her mind. She was also rather pleased it wouldn't happen immediately. She didn't want to think of the ramifications if Bernard's message was correct.

***

I turned straight to the office manager.

Every evening Clive had been checking the recordings of Ursula's phone usage and there hadn't been any unusual activity. He was beginning to hope she'd just picked up the bank statements innocently after all until hearing her call to Sasha. He hurled his coffee mug at the wall, shouting, "Fucking fuckwit!"

Violence was woven into Clive's past like twigs and bracken in a corvid's nest. He knew it was best avoided in theory but not always avoidable in practice. His physical education, nothing to do with the school gymnasium, had started at home when he was very young with his father as master. He treated Clive to shoves and slaps, whacks and kicks. Burns – from cigarettes, matches or even the cooker – were the worst. Before long, Clive was copying what his dad did on smaller children; it felt so much better to give than receive where pain was concerned.

Clive's attraction to violence had lain dormant since his release from Pentonville Prison but now butterflies of anticipation were dancing delightfully in his belly. A grin stole over his face as various scenarios sprung up in his mind.

Scenarios you really wouldn't want me to share. I was worried for Sasha and Ursula. They hadn't dealt with characters like Clive, and I can't say I had either.

What Annabel Thinks

Sasha's thoughts, meanwhile, were on the healing evening and she was unconsciously grimacing as she contemplated returning to Heather at the library. She really needed to turn up this week or never set foot in the library again. With her children's love of books, that wasn't an option, so she just had to ignore her pathetic excuses and get on with it.

Remembering Heather's wheelchair, Sasha rang the church to make sure there would be good access. The response was positive and inviting. She checked with Mark to see whether he was okay with her going out the next evening. He was surprised at her sudden interest in healing and assumed it was to do with her own injuries. He told her he didn't mind and he might go out for a drink with Phil at the weekend.

A flash of foreboding zipped through Sasha but she pushed it out of mind, as she did with most of her unsettling thoughts. The main thing was that Mark agreed to her going out to the healing evening.

Next morning, Sasha steeled herself to go speak to Heather.

Grrrr! I can do this. She growled at her reflection in the bedroom mirror, arms curled in a mock-strongman pose. She laughed out loud at herself, then glanced around quickly.

Nobody's looking – stop being such an idiot, she thought.

To be fair, Gran and I were looking – and laughing, but not in a bad way. Gran was more centred on Pauline at the moment but she popped in every now and then to see what her granddaughter was up to.

Sasha organised the children into the car and began reversing down the drive before it dawned on her she'd forgotten the library books to take back. She stopped and raced back into the house to get them.

At the library, Sasha zapped the books through the automated system, deposited Noah and Rosie in the children's corner to look for new books and steered Violet towards the information desk.

Sasha waited for Heather to raise her gaze from the computer screen in front of her. When she finally looked up, Sasha said, "Hi! I don't know whether you'll remember me…"

"Oh, hello," replied Heather as if she'd only just noticed Sasha's arrival. The weekend after Sasha had last been to the library, Heather had met up with her closest friend. She'd told Annabel about the encounter with the nutter in the children's section and had expected her to be wholly supportive but Annabel got caught up on Sasha's name. She knew someone with a daughter called Sasha and eventually worked out who it was. She told Heather how she used to work with a lovely lady called Pauline Carter when they were both nurses in the renal unit at the hospital. They'd had a laugh together and were familiar with each other's families.

"If they are the same, then I wouldn't think she's a nutter," Annabel had told Heather. "They're a good, solid family, so Sasha is likely to be genuine and well-meaning. Your religion tells you what she's said is wrong, but what if it isn't? I've never told you before but I've had things happen that make me believe in psychic stuff. And it's common knowledge that people have experienced their lives flashing before them when in mortal danger. Personally, I'd give her the benefit of the doubt, but the question is whether you want to get your hopes up again with the healing. If the doctors can't get rid of your pain, can a bunch of faith healers?"

Heather looked over the top of the screen at Sasha.

"I think I know someone who is friends with your mother. Is she a nurse called Pauline Carter?" Heather asked.

"Yes, she is – well, she was," said Sasha. She'd gone through possible responses from Heather in her mind but that definitely wasn't one of them. "She worked at Milton Keynes Hospital before she retired."

"Well, my friend Annabel Grayling thought very highly of her and passes on her regards then."

"Oh, thank you! That's really nice; I'll let Mum know. Annabel Grayling, you said?"

"Yes, apparently they worked in the renal unit together," replied Heather. She hadn't known whether to be pleased or disappointed when last Thursday passed without Sasha appearing. Now she'd had the endorsement from Annabel, it was easier to slip back to her charitable persona. Perhaps Sasha was lonely. If Heather didn't have any higher expectations for the healing evening than just having a pleasant, relaxing time, then there'd be nothing much to lose. And she did need to get out more often.

"Um, I was wondering whether you'd thought about going to the healing?" said Sasha. "I've checked there is wheelchair access and they've got a disabled loo." Her cheeks turned pink, then red.

"Actually, yes, I think I would like to go."

"Oh, really? That's great! Um, I can take you if you'd like."

"No need; I drive an adapted car. If we meet in the church car park, we could go inside together, if that's alright with you. It starts at 7pm, doesn't it?"

"Yeah. Do you know how to get there?"

"I checked online and it looks straightforward enough. Were you thinking of going tonight, then?"

"Definitely!" replied Sasha, beaming with delight. "Mark, my husband, can stay at home with the kids, so I won't have to worry about them. I've never been before, though, so I don't know what to expect."

"Same here but I'm sure it will be fine," said Heather, feeling a lot more comfortable with Sasha now.

Yay! Her spirit guide and I high-fived each other.

Is This Your First Time?

Sasha put on a comfy pair of navy leggings and a long white T-shirt, together with a hoodie and a pair of loafers. She tied her hair back and inserted her favourite dangly pair of earrings.

After saying goodnight to the children, she set off on the now-familiar route to Saint Joseph's Church. It was a clear, light start to the evening with very little traffic on the roads. She was surprised that she didn't feel quite as nervous as normal about going to a new thing.

Maybe it's because I've already had a go at healing with Georgie and Mum – though I'm not sure if Georgie counts. And Heather seems like a nice lady underneath all the frostiness.

Or maybe it's because your gran and I are showering you with love and positive energy, I said more to myself than to Sasha.

When she pulled into the car park, just before 7pm, she spotted a small white boxy vehicle she thought might belong to Heather and parked near to it. Sure enough,

Heather was sitting in the driver's seat. They smiled and waved at each other. Heather slid her door open, turned her seat and propelled the wheelchair out of the car from behind before manoeuvring into it.

That was slick, thought Sasha. *Now I see why it's easier for her to use her own car.*

The two women headed up to the function hall behind the church. Sunshine reflected off the shiny green door, which Sasha held open as Heather wheeled herself up the ramp. Inside, there was an entrance area to the main hall, a small kitchen and toilets. The double doors to the medium-sized hall were propped open and a number of people were already inside.

Sasha and Heather advanced cautiously. There were rows of chairs set out along either side, facing towards the centre of the room. Around a dozen people were sitting on these chairs, some chatting quietly and some on their own.

A gentleman with grey hair and glasses, dressed in beige chinos and a short-sleeved shirt, approached Heather and Sasha.

"Hello! My name's Graham," he said pleasantly. "I'm one of the regular healers. I haven't seen you here before; is this your first time?"

"Yes," they replied in unison. They laughed and told Graham their names.

"Pleased to meet you," he said. "You can see the chairs and therapy beds in the middle of the room; I think there's four of us healing tonight. Heather, you can stay in your wheelchair if that's best for you or we can help you onto a bed – your choice. Everyone who would like healing will get an opportunity and when you've had your turn, there are refreshments and biscuits. There's a collection bowl next to the tea urn, if you wouldn't mind contributing a small amount to cover costs. I think that's about all; it's very informal as you'll see. Any questions?"

"Not from me," said Heather.

"Nor me," said Sasha.

She sat down on a chair at the end of the left row so Heather could position herself alongside. The seats were filling up and they had a look round to see who else had come in whilst they were talking to Graham.

What the— exclaimed Sasha mentally. Sitting opposite them on the end of the other row of chairs were Mr and Mrs Taylor.

Mr Taylor was shuffling on his seat, head down, tap-tap-tapping his right heel, ready to sprint out of the room (although I knew he hadn't sprinted anywhere in the last decade or two). Mrs Taylor, on the other hand, was sitting as straight-backed as a ballerina, wearing a pastel floral dress and pale pink cardigan. She kept glancing around, a smile poised on her lips for anyone she could make eye contact with. She was talking quietly to Mr Taylor.

Sasha (and I) watched them as another healer, Joan, went over to give them the introductory spiel.

Five minutes later, the entrance doors were closed and Joan stood up at the far end of the hall.

"It's lovely to see our regulars as usual and also to welcome a number of others today. We hope you will enjoy your evening and do ask for help if you're unsure of anything at any time. We're a friendly bunch – we won't bite!" The lines around her eyes crinkled as she smiled.

"I'd like to thank the Lord for joining us tonight…" I noticed Mr Taylor rolling his eyes. "…and providing love, guidance and forgiveness. We can all do the same, including the most difficult part, which is being kind and forgiving to ourselves as well. There are few people who can look their reflection in the eye and say, 'I love you' or even 'I like you' but we do need to try. Instead of thinking about our faults and shortcomings, it's time to remember our strengths – which we have in all sorts of ways. Ponder on the positive! How's that for slogan of the week? Or love thy neighbour and love thyself."

Wow, thought Sasha. *This really is tailor-made for Mr Taylor.*

A broad grin spread across her face but thankfully everyone was looking at Joan.

"If you'd now like to close your eyes, try to picture the love and energy from above and all around us channelling itself into a column of healing energy in the centre of the room. You may then place anyone who cannot be here tonight into the column and we will pray they will receive help."

Sasha thought of her mum and concentrated all her efforts into imagining her standing in the middle of the column, getting help from the angels. She also tried to blank out the image of her elbowing for space with everyone else being put there. *Why does everything make me want to laugh?* she wondered.

I reckoned it was because she was nervous but I wasn't going to point that out to her.

There was a gentle silence for a minute or two before Joan concluded, "Thank you; you may open your eyes and we'll start this evening's healing."

People started going up to one of the chairs or treatment beds, where a healer was waiting. They would receive their healing, then vacate the space, ready for the next person.

When it was Heather's turn, she wheeled herself over to a chair and parked herself beside it. It wouldn't have been easy – or pretty, in Heather's mind – to get onto a bed. There was no way she was putting herself through that level of mortification on her first time.

I just said "first time", she thought in surprise and was further surprised that she didn't mind.

It wasn't just me listening to Heather; I saw Sasha startle and knew she had heard too.

Sasha was then wondering whether being in this environment had given her a perception boost. She'd guessed correctly. All the positive energy in the room, from both human and spirit, had that effect on her because of her increased sensitivity.

Silently, she sent out supplementary healing vibes to Heather.

Every little helps, she thought.

Then she saw Mrs Taylor virtually dragging her husband over to the other chair. Once the healer was talking to him and it looked like he wouldn't bolt away, Mrs Taylor sidled over and plonked herself on the empty chair beside Sasha.

"I bet you didn't expect to see us here," she said jauntily.

Has she just had a personality transplant? thought Sasha. Was this the same suspicious lady from three days ago? "Err, no, I didn't," she said.

"Well," said Mrs Taylor, "I was listening around the corner when you came over the other day. Malcolm is a stubborn man and everything has always been everybody else's fault, never his. It made a change for it to be yours, instead of mine, I have to say. I spotted the leaflet about the church after you'd gone and I figured it might be good for him, like you said, so I squirrelled it away. He's got all these sour thoughts going on in his head and it's not doing him or me any good. I really don't know how I put up with it, to be honest. Since healing might help fix the brain as much as the rest of the body and, actually, he does get bad headaches, which I think is all connected to his state of mind, I decided to get him here. I only managed by saying I wanted healing for my arthritis." Mrs Taylor glanced back at her husband sitting in the chair, the healer's hands hovering over his head. "I don't know how I got him to the healing chair – it's a miracle! I'd better go back now, before he's finished, as I don't think he'd be too impressed at seeing me fraternising with the enemy. Nice to see you, anyway, my dear." She patted Sasha's hand.

"And you," said Sasha, as she watched Mrs Taylor shimmy away. She actually seemed to be a very nice lady who clearly enjoyed an opportunity to socialise.

I do hope this will help them both, she thought. *For her sake as much as his.*

Heather's healing was complete and she returned with a tranquil smile.

Sasha could sense Heather's enjoyment at just being able to close her eyes and let go of everything for a while, whether it would help with pain or not. She tried to suppress her feelings of guilt and got Heather a cup of tea and a biscuit.

Soon after, there was another vacant healing position and Sasha took a turn. She took off her shoes, placed them neatly under the bed and laid herself down. The healer introduced herself as Daphne. She could have been in her seventies and was dressed in a knee-length pleated skirt and blouse. Sasha told Daphne her name too.

"So, Sasha, what would you like to get out of this?"

"Well, I broke my right femur in June and it gives the occasional twinge," she said, though she hadn't previously considered too deeply what she'd hoped to get out of the healing.

Probably, I'd like to know whether I am able to heal and whether I'm doing it right or not, she then thought but didn't feel confident enough to say out loud.

Daphne started by holding her hands above Sasha's head and moving them slowly around her crown and over her face. Sasha could feel the heat from Daphne's hands immediately and it almost felt like there were minuscule sparks of energy emanating forth. Daphne moved down and slowly, calmly, shifted her hands along the length of Sasha's body, always hovering just above, in the same way Sasha had done for her mother. Maybe she had instinctively known what to do after all. Daphne gradually reached Sasha's feet and worked her way back up the other side. When she approached the right femur, she paused for longer and did the same when she was at the right side of the chest. It reminded Sasha of the angels back in hospital.

After Daphne had finished, she asked Sasha to open her eyes and sit up when she felt ready. Sasha understood what Heather had been talking about; she too felt light and relaxed, as if all her cares had dissolved away.

"I'm intrigued by you, Sasha," said Daphne. "There was such a strong level of energy all around you. Are you by any chance a medium or a healer yourself?"

"No! Yes! No – not really," said Sasha. "But I came to a church meeting recently and I got a reading. My gran – on the other side – said I should start healing and I did try with my mum. I think it had an effect but I couldn't be sure."

"Right. I do think you've got the gift, Sasha. Joan runs healing development classes and it would be really good for you to come along. I think the next set will start in October. Once you've finished, we're always grateful for additional healers, if you'd be happy to join in. It's voluntary and you don't have to do it every week but you'll be surprised how it helps you feel better too."

"Well, I'll consider it," replied Sasha. "I've got young children, so I haven't thought about doing anything for myself, but I don't see why I shouldn't be able to." She was definitely warming to the idea. It would be doing something to help others rather than herself so that would be okay. "I'll have to talk to my husband about it, though, as he'd have to look after them, like tonight."

"Well, let me know next week how you get on," said Daphne.

"Okay," said Sasha, biting her lip. She really wasn't sure Mark would be too keen on the idea.

She got herself a cup of tea and a digestive biscuit, then walked back to Heather. She could see Mrs Taylor lying on the other bed.

"Isn't this a lovely thing?" Heather asked Sasha. "I was looking around as you were being treated, at the people in the middle and the others on the sides, and everybody seems so happy and smiley. Even if it doesn't help with physical problems, it's got to be good for our well-being."

"I agree. There is a lovely atmosphere here. I think I'd like to come on a regular basis but I don't know what Mark would say."

"Same here. Well, apart from the Mark concerns. Thank you for letting me know about it, Sasha."

"You're more than welcome, Heather, and I'm so pleased you've come. Did I tell you I was actually given a mission to help people when I had my NDE? I didn't want to know at first but I think I'm even starting to enjoy it. Did you ever watch a series called *My Name is Earl*?"

"No, I don't think so."

"Well, it's about a guy who felt it was down to karma he had a bad car accident, so to make things better, he has to find everyone who he's ever done something bad to and then help them. It was really funny! It's not the same for me because I'm not doing it to stop bad things happening but I was told in no uncertain terms I should now help people. Does that make any sense?"

"Sorry, I don't believe karma is doing things for the right reasons, though I do think good begets good and bad begets bad. But then there are powerful leaders who live in luxury while their people suffer dreadfully. So I just don't know. Maybe it's best not to question everything when you can't possibly know the answers."

"That's fair enough. Oh, I think Joan is about to wrap things up."

Everyone had finished with the healing and a few people were folding up the beds and moving the chairs back. Joan stood in the middle and thanked everyone for coming along.

As Sasha rose from her chair, she glanced over at the Taylors. Mr Taylor was pulling on his coat and straightening his collar. Mrs Taylor was speaking animatedly to Graham but turned quickly to look at Sasha. She smiled and gave a little wink. Sasha returned the smile.

Oh, I'm so happy, she said to herself, remembering her ghastly time inside the Taylors' house. *I can't believe they came along and I just know things will get better for them. Thank goodness it was worth it after all.*

And I was a very happy spirit guide at this point. If this could be the norm, everything would be so good. And it would be so much easier to pass my exams.

Validation

The next day was Friday, a week after Sasha and the children had visited her mum, and she was looking forward to another visit. Pauline had undergone three chemotherapy sessions now and Sasha wondered how she would look. Had the healing helped at all?

She took the children round after lunch, along with the usual paraphernalia. Chilly rain splattered down. Sasha tried to ignore the miserable weather and think positively about her mum.

Her dad opened the front door as Sasha reached for the doorbell and told the children to try to be quiet as Nanna was having a nap. They crept into the sitting room and Kevin said, "We knew it wouldn't be a walk in the park but we didn't realise just what an effort this would be. It doesn't help that her hair is falling out now."

"Oh, goodness. You should have called me and I'd have come over sooner."

"Sorry, love, but your mum didn't want to worry you. You know what she's like."

"I know, but maybe I could have helped. Please let me go see her. I won't wake her up; I'll just do the healing. It won't disturb her at all and might make her feel better. Remember how you thought I'd helped last Friday."

"I'm not so sure. I don't want you over-reacting when you take a look at her hair. It's very patchy now."

"I won't. I really should go in, Dad. I went to a healing evening with a friend last night and it was so positive and good. And one of the healers told me I had the gift. Please, Dad, it can't do any harm."

"I hope you do know what you're doing. If she doesn't want you in there, promise me you'll come straight out."

"I promise. If you're happy with the kids now, I'll just sneak right up."

Kevin sighed as he caved in. "Good luck then."

Sasha gave her dad a reassuring hug and crept up the thickly carpeted stairs, then tiptoed into her parents' bedroom. The curtains were drawn shut and the room was very dark. She stood still, waiting for her eyes to become accustomed. The air smelt unpleasant, perhaps made worse by the toxic chemotherapy chemicals. Even though the thought of her mother's suffering made her want to weep, she straightened her back and forced her frown away.

Pauline's breathing was slow and regular.

Thank goodness I haven't woken her, Sasha thought.

Once she could clearly make out the shape of her mother lying in the bed, she crept alongside. Copying the healers at the church, Sasha asked the angels to work their healing through her hands. She gently circled them above and around her mum's head, keeping away from the mouth and nose so that Pauline wouldn't be able to detect her there.

Sasha slowly worked her way down the body to the toes and back up again, spending extra time over the chest. When she had finished, she slowly, very carefully, turned and exited the bedroom. Once on the landing, she took a big breath and exhaled through her mouth. She was amazed she'd managed to stay in control and not make a noise. Now a few tears slipped down her cheeks. She paused to recalibrate once again, putting on a brave face for her dad's sake this time, then walked carefully back downstairs and re-entered the living room.

Kevin looked up anxiously.

"It's okay – I didn't wake her."

"Thank God. Let's hope you've done her some good, then."

"Fingers crossed, eh, Dad!"

Sasha picked up Violet and gave her a cuddle while her dad went to the kitchen to make coffee. She felt tired herself now.

If this does help, maybe I really should go to healing classes. It makes sense to develop the gift if I do have it.

That was good to hear, I can tell you. It was about time Sasha thought about developing her gifts, especially reaching out to me. If only she realised how much easier she could make her life if she did.

Kevin returned with a mug for Sasha and they played with the children for an hour or so before sitting down in front of the television.

Around four o'clock, Pauline walked into the living room and greeted her daughter and grandchildren, giving them all big hugs.

"How do you feel, Mum?" asked Sasha. "Dad said this week wasn't so good."

"That's true, love, but I feel much better now I've had a good rest. Can you see my hair? It's starting to drop out in clumps now."

Sasha hadn't spotted the patchy hair in the dim bedroom and she did her best to avoid showing her shock now.

"What a pain. I guess it must take some getting used to."

"You can say that again!"

When Pauline walked off to the kitchen, Kevin exclaimed to Sasha: "Well, I'll be darned. I thought she'd be sleeping until early evening, like yesterday, or even right through. How can she be up now? She's talking normally – not like it's a big effort. And she looks better; she looks like she's got the circulation back in her face. Whatever did you do, Sasha?"

Pauline walked back in, having heard the tail-end of the conversation.

"What's all this about, then?"

"When you were asleep, Mum, I came in and gave you some healing. Dad says you seem a lot better now."

"Well, when I come to think about it, I do feel quite a bit better. Thank you, darling!"

"I'm just glad the healing seems to do something. I can do it as often as you like."

"Why not, love? I'll be a new woman, swinging from the chandeliers with a bit of luck!"

It felt good to Sasha to get validation from her parents. It helped too to keep her mind off matters closer to home. She was feeling more and more unsettled by the growing rift between Mark and herself, and perhaps she was sensing a marital storm brewing on the horizon.

Past Caring

Whilst Sasha was at her parents', Mark was in the office as usual.

I watched with growing apprehension.

Mid-afternoon he saw Natalie enter the empty kitchen. He grabbed his empty mug and sauntered in behind.

"Hi, Mark!" Natalie said. She was wearing a striking burgundy dress that clung to her breasts and accentuated her narrow waist and curving hips.

"Hi. Err, Natalie, are you free tomorrow night? Do you want to go for a drink maybe? But it doesn't matter if you can't; I know it's probably too short notice."

I listened to Natalie weighing up her options. She was supposed to go clubbing with her friend Zoë and a bunch of other girls but...

"That's all right; I can make it. My friend bailed out on me, so I'm free," she lied. She'd have to call Zoë and let her know something else had come up, but it wasn't like Zoë didn't have other friends to be with.

I'd really hoped Natalie would have had a bit more

integrity but no such luck.

"Oh great!" replied Mark, as mini fireworks exploded in the pit of his stomach. "I can pick you up if you give me your address?"

"Sure. It's 3 Sheringham Court, just off Manning Road. Down the park end."

"I know Manning Road. Okay, see you around eight thirty?" He would have preferred to go out earlier but remembered, in the days before children, early wasn't cool.

"Yeah, that's fine. Thanks!" she replied, whilst thinking: *Blimey, that's early! Less time for getting ready and pre-drinks then.*

Natalie took her lunch out of the fridge, bending over provocatively to display a very enticing derrière, hoping Mark would be looking.

He was. He made himself another coffee, trying to keep his crotch out of view. *Oh hell, what am I doing?* he asked himself.

Exactly what I was asking him too.

***

On Saturday morning, Sasha went to the supermarket. As soon as she'd walked out the front door, Mark picked up his phone.

"Hi, Phil! Are you still alright to cover for me? Can I say I'm going for a drink with you tonight, please?"

"Mark, you dirty wanker! I knew you had it in you." Phil laughed loudly. "Course I can. Just don't do anything I wouldn't."

"Well, that's not difficult, is it?"

"Nah, mate! Have a good one and tell me about it later."

"Sure thing." There was no way in hell he'd ever tell Phil about it. "Thanks, mate. See ya."

I wanted so much to prevent Mark's evening from going ahead. With the greatest of willpower, I held back, keeping an image of the repulsive rule book in front of me. As you know, I'd been struggling with the "do not get emotionally attached" rule for some time now. An impassive observer, I was not, but I couldn't afford to meddle with Mark's actions, could I? I really needed to pass my Level III Guidance, and I'd be seriously risking it if I did anything now. In human form, I'd be slapping duct tape across my mouth right now and locking myself in a wardrobe so I couldn't do anything I'd later regret.

***

Later, the family went for a walk and play-about in the park. It was a pleasant afternoon but Sasha and Mark barely spoke to each other.

Sasha was still disgruntled with Mark's pathetic standard of job sharing and she worried whether he would have an affair. She didn't know whether to be relieved or anxious she could no longer "see" what he was thinking but she watched out for any telltale signs. He hadn't changed any habits or stayed late at work and he'd obviously been with Phil rather than a girl when he went out a few weeks ago because Phil came back to the house with him. She was expecting more of the same this evening.

Mark, meanwhile, was completely wrapped up in possible scenarios with Natalie. He knew how foolish and risky this was but his dick was doing the thinking and he was past caring. He'd given up trying to entice Sasha into making love as he was fed up with her moods and excuses.

What am I expected to do? he asked himself, trying to justify his actions.

For starters, sort things out with your wife, I was saying to his deaf ears.

***

The evening came round inevitably and I was still behaving myself, with a heavy heart (metaphorically speaking, of course). I'd made the rule book my screen saver on my tablet, and I clutched it tight as I watched and listened to all parties.

Mark realised he'd better not make any more effort for going out than he would if he were going down the pub with Phil – which meant pretty much do nothing at all.

He helped put the children to bed, then sat down to watch telly whilst Sasha was washing up in the kitchen. He wished he'd suggested seven thirty or eight rather than eight thirty.

"Why don't you go out now?" called Sasha irritably from the kitchen. Since you can't be bothered to give me a hand with the chores, she wanted to add.

"Phil decided to make it later," he replied. "He wants to try a new pub in town."

Sasha was in such a mood she didn't question why Phil

would choose to go out later, missing precious drinking time. Most unlike Phil.

Mark was still considering where he would actually take Natalie. He wasn't stupid enough to go to a pub Sasha was familiar with but he didn't know where else to choose. Maybe they could try Newport Pagnell or Bletchley. No, Pottersbury was more out of the way, so it would be a safer option. There was a choice of two pubs there if he remembered rightly.

Around eight fifteen, Mark said goodbye to Sasha. Chores completed, she was reading an article about a woman who'd had a baby without knowing she was pregnant. She barely glanced up as she mumbled, "Bye."

Mark sat in the car, having a moment of doubt. *What if this is the start of an affair? How can it possibly end well? Natalie could be a bunny-boiler. What if she tells Sasha and she kicks me out? Oh, fuck! Maybe I shouldn't go.*

He was ready to walk back in the house and say Phil had called off, but he had to adjust his boxers that were digging into his crotch first. As he rummaged around his tackle, straightening the cloth out, his dick reminded him of what he hoped to gain.

How about I talk straight to Natalie first? I can work out whether she'd say anything to Sasha. Tell her I can't risk not seeing the children. Lots of people have affairs for years and are never found out. Anyway, I don't want an affair. If I just have sex once, that would be enough.

***

Natalie's house was easy to find and he pulled up outside. He didn't want to knock at the door and have to make embarrassing small talk with a parent, so he stayed in the car, hoping she would come out to him.

She was in her bedroom keeping an eye out the window. After a respectable minute or two, she was out the front door and sauntering over to his car in skinny jeans and a cropped top, revealing a tanned stomach with a crystal belly ring glinting in the evening sunlight.

Mark didn't notice she'd put an attractive wave into her hair or she'd clearly made a lot of effort with her make-up; his eyes were trapped by the belly ring.

Natalie slid into the passenger seat and reached over to give him a kiss on the cheek, making his tummy do a triple flip.

"Hiya! Where are we off to, then?" she asked.

"Thought we could go to The Plume of Feathers in Pottersbury if that's okay with you?"

"Sure. I haven't been there for years but I'm not fussy. As long as it's got a bar and somewhere to sit, that's fine by me!"

"I think I can manage that," said Mark as they set off down the road. He was trying hard not to let his mind start questioning things again and concentrated on whatever Natalie chattered about.

And yes, I was responsible for his moments of doubt. It was all I dared do to intervene.

They reached the pub and walked in. Mark had hoped to start the evening off with a game or two of pool, but as it was later than he usually went out, the pool tables were all in use. Instead, they ignored the stares of the locals and managed to find a small table in the corner with a couple of stools free. He didn't notice it was next to the gents but Natalie wasn't one to complain.

Mark kept trying to find a way of moving the conversation round to what he wanted to discuss but it wasn't easy. It seemed Natalie could talk about favourite movies and music forever. He went off to get another round of drinks, vodka and Coke for her, just a Coke for him this time; he'd already had a pint. When he came back, he just went for it.

"Natalie, you know I'm married with children."

"Sure, I know," Natalie replied, crossing one leg over the other.

"Well, she can't know about us. Is that okay with you?"

"Yeah, why should I tell her? You don't need to worry; I'm not the bunny-boiler sort."

Well, that's one problem ticked off, thought Mark. "No, I never thought you were," he said out loud. *Liar,* he said to himself. "I just wanted to make sure whatever happens between us is kept just to ourselves. I couldn't bear to lose my children."

"Don't worry. Anyway, what are you talking about? Nothing's happened, has it?" Natalie said provocatively, holding his gaze and putting her hand on his left thigh, sliding it up a tantalising tiny bit towards his crotch.

Oh, Sweet Jesus! thought Mark as his dick sprung to attention. *I hope she'll be okay with the car.*

At 10.30pm, he asked her if she'd like to go for a

drive down some country lanes. *Was that too subtle?* he wondered.

"Where there might be a secluded lay-by, perhaps?"

Nope, not too subtle, he thought, a grin spreading across his face. "If it's your lucky night." He instantly cringed. *Why, oh why, did I say that?*

"Oh, yeah? We'll have to see whose lucky night it actually is then, won't we."

They went to the loo – not the same one, of course – and walked out to the car. Mark didn't really have a clue where to drive, but Natalie directed him out down one lane after another to a suitable lay-by.

"You know the best spots then?" he said as he slowed the car to a halt and switched it off, not sure he was particularly keen on her experience, though he couldn't deny he was grateful.

"Well, when you're seventeen and have nowhere to go, you soon find out. It's a long time ago but I haven't forgotten. Good thing, eh?"

"Certainly is," said Mark, wiping sweat from his brow. "Certainly is."

He released the lever on the side of his seat to lower the back, then leant over Natalie, gently resting his chest over hers, as he found the lever on her seat and lowered hers as well. He put his arm between her legs, stroking them briefly before his hand found the lever to slide the seat backwards.

Not that Mark could tell, but I could see his manoeuvring had set Natalie's senses alight. She hadn't had sex in months.

They began kissing and fondling each other. Mark was able to start fulfilling his fantasy, kissing Natalie's velvety-soft neck and working his way down to her cleavage. She had her hands up his T-shirt, stroking his back and chest, and scraping her nails just hard enough to provoke a skin-tingling reaction.

I'd now forgotten about staying in a wardrobe. I'd chucked the tablet inside instead. I zapped Mark a mental safety net: a vision of his wife laughing and playing with his young family. It was a flawless image of what he stood to lose if he continued down this adulterous path. In that fraction of time, he wondered why he was recklessly risking it all and whether one night of passion was really worth a lifetime of regret.

Just as Mark wavered, Natalie pulled him closer to her, moaning erotically in his ear. Natalie's breath sent a shockwave of nerve-jangling sensations right down Mark's spine. My image of his precious family evaporated like a morning mist. He wasn't even aware he'd made a choice as he groaned out loud. Mark was past the point of no return.

Sweet Dreams

I whizzed back to Sasha.

Bored, tired and fed up, an early night was beckoning. All the psychic and healing things were great but when they weren't happening and the children were in bed, she was left with a gaping hole where a loving partnership should be fulfilling her.

This isn't how I thought my marriage would be, she thought gloomily to herself as she got into bed. She kept turning from one side to the other, trying to switch off her brain and fall asleep.

I had one final opportunity and it had my training tablet hammering against the inside of the wardrobe door in protest. For a split second, I contemplated what had happened to Oswald when I'd intervened but it wasn't the same. No one would be murdered by this plan. I zapped Sasha straight into a very deep and lucid dream.

In her dream, she was in the middle of a dense, dark forest wearing only a nightshirt. Her feet were bare, so twigs and pine needles were painful beneath her feet as she tried to escape the foreboding interior. A frosty breeze taunted her as she stumbled nervously onwards, shivering and wishing she were fully dressed. The darkness was menacing; she imagined some savage beast might burst out of the bushes at any moment with vicious claws to rip her flesh apart. She tried to run, pumping her arms but her legs were refusing to move. She could no longer make out the trees around her.

"I can't see – I need light! Somebody help me!" she screamed into the void.

"Make it yourself," I said in a deep, booming and hopefully mysterious voice. Of course, she didn't know it was me orchestrating this dream. I cast a metaphysical ring round Sasha in her bed and a similar one round Mark's car, linking them together.

"Is that possible? Can I really make light myself?" she cried.

She poured all her energy into the space in front of her. And slowly but surely, something was happening. A narrow thread of lustrous silver, a mere promise of greater brightness, was flowing from her eyes. Sasha concentrated harder and harder.

I can do this. I can fix this, she told herself.

The thread became a cold, white band, glowing with steely purpose. Sasha forgot about running and put all her efforts into manifesting a magnificent light. The band expanded into an arc of luminescence, becoming a vast cone of the brightest, most awesome light from the narrow origins of her pupils to a broad beam of powerful brilliance, transforming the whole forest in front of her into a safe haven.

Creatures tiptoed into the lit open space before her. Instead of scary beasts, a benign family of bears padded towards her. A doe and her fawn delicately stepped forth, squirrels and badgers, hares and rabbits, all coming her way. They were exuding the exquisite love she recognised from her NDE, and Sasha's fear was replaced by wonder. The light was now all-encompassing and Sasha sank down onto velvety-soft grass to welcome the beautiful animals into her outstretched arms. She was overcome with relief and affection, stroking the animals and enjoying their nuzzling.

Before long, Sasha slipped seamlessly into a dreamless state of recuperation.

Thank goodness, I thought with relief, rather exhausted from the effort involved in producing Sasha's vision. Now for the second stage.

***

Back at the lay-by, the windows had become as steamy as the occupants. Mark had managed to undo Natalie's jeans and grapple them down over her hips before exploring her nether regions. Natalie's own fingers fumbled at Mark's waistband and he sucked in his stomach to help her unbutton his jeans and pull down the zip. As she slipped her delicate hands inside his boxers and sought his erection, he started sliding himself over her when, out of the darkness, a blaze of light pierced through the car windscreen. A tinny little tractor with incongruously impressive spotlights was trundling towards them.

What the hell? thought Mark as the tractor continued into the lay-by, facing his car head-on and lighting them up like a search beam homed in on its quarry.

Mark sprung off Natalie, much as if he'd just discovered she'd sprouted a penis. He fell back into his driver's seat, stuffing his rapidly deflating dick inside his boxers and yanking up his jeans. Breathing heavily, he raked his right hand through his hair and squinted blankly through the window as he tried to gather his thoughts. He couldn't see anything until the tractor driver switched off their lights and then he was just aware of the thrum of blood pounding in his ears. He adjusted his seat back into its driving position.

"I'm really sorry, Natalie," he said, his previous passion now replaced by raw remorse. "We should never have started this."

Natalie straightened her clothing quickly and sorted out her car seat. She didn't have as much to lose as Mark by being caught *in flagrante*, but she was a bit pissed off with the interruption. Mark was a more considerate lover than she had dared to hope for and she had been aroused.

"Well, it's up to you, I guess. No harm done." She was trying her best to sound nonchalant.

"No, no harm done," Mark repeated pathetically. "Now how the hell do we get out of here?"

Natalie laughed in spite of the situation and gave Mark directions as he started driving to get them back onto the main road. When they finally stopped outside Natalie's house, she leant over and gave him what she hoped was a lingering seductive kiss on the lips. It had as much effect as a warty toad might.

"You know where I am if you want to try again."

She stepped out of the car, swaying her hips sexily as she strolled up to her front door. Mark didn't look up once as he made the quickest three-point-turn ever and accelerated away.

His brain was playing a continuous loop of the moments leading up to the tractor's arrival, followed by the bright lights and his hasty retreat.

"Fuck, fuck, fuck!" he kept shouting as he impotently tried to break the visions.

He got home around 11.30pm, which was still a plausible time if he'd been out with Phil. Relieved, he slipped into the house and tiptoed to the cloakroom. After having a pee, he splashed soap and water over his face. In the bedroom, Sasha appeared to be breathing deeply. Mark inched into bed beside her and prayed for the oblivion of sleep.

Job done, I dared to believe. Even spirit guides can be naïve sometimes.

***

The first image in Sasha's mind when she woke the next morning was the blissful second stage of her dream. It was still so clear and unusual she had to talk about it.

"I had a really weird dream last night," she said as they were eating breakfast. She described the fear, followed by the light creation and interaction with the animals. "It was like a transformation from evil to good," she said, smiling at the memory and crossing her hands around her arms, giving herself a hug.

"That's nice," said Mark. Though seriously creepy that her dream matches the tractor spotlight changing things for me. Coincidence or what? He pulled his dressing gown tightly around himself.

I preened with smug satisfaction.

"How was your evening, by the way?" Sasha asked.

"Yeah, fine. Nothing special," said Liar-Liar-Pants-on-Fire.

Sasha felt a stab of mistrust strike her chest, causing a sharp intake of breath, but Noah ran up to her, wanting her to fix a rubber tyre back onto the wheel of a toy car. As Sasha concentrated on the task in hand, the warning was lost.

**

Sasha's mum and dad had invited them all over for Sunday lunch. Pauline was still under par but insisted she just wanted to try to act like normal.

"It's like you felt after your accident, love," she told Sasha.

"Yeah, I get that but don't overdo things. You're still in the middle of treatment. Can I give you another healing session, since I'm here, please?"

"I don't see why not. How about you men go and get the washing up out of the way whilst Sasha and I have some me-time."

Sasha loved the way her mother could get her dad and Mark to do jobs around the house without sounding bossy. If only she could do the same.

They made sure the children were occupied, then went up to the bedroom to escape any interruptions. Pauline lay down on her bed and closed her eyes while Sasha repeated the healing routine. She felt more and more confident each time she performed it and was certain the sensation in her hands was down to actual healing.

"Do you think this might be helping, Mum?" Sasha asked.

"I think so, love. You've all noticed that I'm more myself after these sessions and it makes me feel, I don't know, a bit lighter." Pauline made little speech marks in the air with her fingers when she said the word "myself". "And I'll just be glad when everything's back to normal."

"I'm sure you will. And that's what I'm trying to do with the healing, Mum – to clear you of cancer completely so it doesn't come back ever. Let's just keep on doing it, eh?"

"That's fine by me. It feels rather indulgent, like going to the spa or having a massage and it doesn't cost me a thing."

"Trust you to think of that," said Sasha, pleased her mum had enough energy to be jokey.

Organising Humans

There was one week before the Dennings would be going on holiday so Sasha wrote a plan of everything she needed to do and started making piles of holiday clothes. As the weather had returned to the unpredictable British summer climate, she needed to pack for hot or cool and dry or wet days, plus towels and swimwear. She mustn't forget the beach games and Mark's favourite snorkel, which he always insisted on even though he probably wouldn't use it. They would need entertainment for the children for when they were in the apartment and all the baby bits and pieces for Violet.

I just hope we can fit everything in, Sasha fretted.

I knew she'd manage just fine, so I set my next plan in motion. Of course I should have waited for Sasha to ask for help but that was looking as likely as Mark offering to do more housework. When Sasha and the children were sitting down eating lunch, I prompted Rosie.

"Mummy," she said, "can we play Left-Right?"

"Please," said Sasha automatically.

"Please, please, please," said Rosie.

"Oh, I suppose so. But not for too long," Sasha replied, sighing. She'd really need to focus now.

I did like it when a plan fitted together. I might not be good at following rules but I seemed to be a natural at organising humans.

Once in the car, Rosie and Noah called out left or right when they approached junctions.

I let the children lead to start with and noticed they were heading into Newport Pagnell.

As they stopped at traffic lights, Sasha's attention was drawn to a man crossing the road in front of them. He had a wiry figure and his head was bent down, like he had a lot on his mind. Suddenly he turned, frowning straight at Sasha as he passed in front of her car. She broke eye contact, shuddering with revulsion. Had he deliberately glared at her? He gave off such an evil aura. But why would he? She didn't know the man.

I did though. Part of me was chuffed at how Sasha accurately picked up Clive's character (showing she hadn't lost all her awareness yet) but the other part was far from happy. This encounter, however insignificant, wouldn't have been a coincidence but I didn't know why it happened or who had engineered it.

Sasha continued on – with a little assistance from moi – and she was soon travelling into the countryside. On their left, she could see a large care home set back from the road. It was a sprawling, imposing two-storey building with a landscaped garden and a driveway leading into a good-sized gravel car park. A large sign dangling from a post stated "Country Life Care Home".

"Leff!" shouted Noah, so Sasha turned down the drive. She pulled into a parking space with the intention of turning around and leaving straight away.

It feels like I should be here. Why? she wondered.

I sent her what you'd consider to be a lightbulb moment.

Oh no, Rebecca probably works here. Well, I'm not doing it. I can't. Sasha pushed the gearstick into reverse.

I wasn't giving up that easily. I tuned her into her NDE.

Young Sasha was in the playground at school and saw a sturdily build girl called Rebecca knock Carina to the ground. Carina got up and ran straight to the adult on duty, telling her what Rebecca had done. Sasha went over to offer her support.

"Liar," cried Rebecca, as Carina was saying Rebecca had been mean to her when the opposite was the truth.

Sasha placed her arm around her sister's shoulders and declared, "No, she's the big fat liar. She should pick on someone her own size, if she can find anyone that big."

Rebecca turned away and the supervisor left for the next issue. Normal playground activities resumed; incident dismissed.

Spirit Sasha zoomed in on the embarrassment and anguish Rebecca struggled with internally. It wasn't the first time she had been called fat and it wouldn't be the last: crisps, biscuits, cake and chocolate were Rebecca's go-to in a mean world. Her weight continued to rise in spite of (or because of) children's taunts and judgemental adults who tutted sanctimoniously amongst themselves.

Observer Sasha whizzed through the thread of Rebecca's progress.

At university, Rebecca was told by a very drunk girl in the ladies' toilets she could lose weight easily if she stuck her fingers down her throat after every meal to make herself throw up. Rebecca tried it the next day; it wasn't so difficult and suddenly she had the answer to her prayers for losing weight. The answer became a compulsion and the pounds started to fall away. She even lost her appetite for the first time ever, as the sour paste of food coming back up was far less appealing than the sensations of it going down.

Rebecca's health deteriorated. Her throat was always sore, her teeth weakened and she caught numerous coughs and colds. Life hadn't improved and her weight fluctuated like the weather. Rebecca scraped a third in her media studies degree in the end and didn't know what to do with her life. She returned to her childhood home where she had very little interest in anything other than watching telly. A family friend helped her get a job at a local care home where she stayed because it was convenient, even though it only paid the minimum wage. Some of the residents even seemed to like her.

Sasha came out of the flashback wracked with guilt but still reluctant.

I presented the idea of her pretending her dad had dementia and she was scouting for places for him to stay.

I suppose it would get it over and done with and at least it's the last mission, she thought. *And then I can forget about it once and for all.*

Sasha got the children out of the car and strapped sleepy Violet into the pushchair. It didn't occur to her to wonder why her children always seemed to be on their best behaviour when she was trying out something new lately.

Of course I was being instrumental, though I hope Hebron didn't hear me admitting that.

"Okay, my darlings," Sasha primed Noah and Rosie, "we're going to have a look at this place to see if we like it in case Grandad and Nanna want to move here one day. Please try to keep quiet and save any questions until after we get back out again. You can tell me what you liked about it after we get back in the car. Is that okay?"

They nodded, not really understanding but willingly being swept along by their mother's enthusiasm.

Sasha walked them inside. There was a reception desk ahead of her, to the left of which were a couple of closed white doors. To the right, Sasha could see through a short corridor and open double doors into a large communal room with plenty of high-backed chairs that were mostly occupied by elderly residents. She could hear a television blaring further down the room and a member of staff was helping a resident drink through a straw.

Sasha straightened her back and walked up to the reception desk with what she hoped was just enough swagger to look like someone who was used to getting results. Not that that sort of person would probably have three children in tow. She almost wavered but she couldn't walk back out now; that would be even more embarrassing.

A plump lady in her late forties or fifties was sat behind

the desk. She was wearing a name badge with 'Geraldine' printed clearly on it.

Geraldine looked up at Sasha over the rim of her designer-style glasses. "May I help you?" she asked.

"I do hope so," said Sasha, forcing her voice a little louder. "My father has dementia and will need to move to a nursing home in the not-too-distant future. I wondered if I might have a look at your facilities, please."

"Have you made an appointment?" asked Geraldine laconically, even though she knew full well there was nothing booked in.

I got Sasha to think of films where the lead actress successfully bluffed and flattered their way through tricky situations.

"I hadn't actually short-listed this place, as it happens, but I was driving along and spotted your sign, so it was a spur-of-the-moment job. Of course, I could just stick to my original choices and forget about yours, if it's a problem, but I did quite like the look of this place. It seems very well managed. I'd be extremely grateful if you could squeeze me in now, please."

She put on her best attempt at a professional smile whilst hoping there were no visible traces of baby-related splatters on her clothes.

"Mummy…" started Noah.

"Not now, sweetheart," Sasha whispered, starting to blush. With her post-flash-back psychic boost, she knew her son was about to ask, "Who's the fat lady?"

"Here, Noah – you can hold my keys if you're really good and quiet!"

"Hmmm. May I just take a few details, please? Your name, address and contact number."

"Sasha Denning. 34 Donnington Close, Milton Keynes. 07633 739249."

Geraldine filled in the empty August 20th segment of the diary, followed by "speculative viewing". She then stood up, her hips and knees having stiffened from being in one position for too long, and walked awkwardly to a door behind the counter, where she called into the void.

"Rebecca, would you come and show Mrs Denning and her children round, please? She's considering Country Life for her father."

As Sasha stood waiting, I took a moment to reflect on how far she'd come because this was such a transformation. Before the accident, she would never have entered a strange place without an invitation. And she'd certainly never have put on a façade of a confident businesswoman to get what she wanted. I really needed to stop being aware of the things she wasn't doing and concentrate on the positives.

The Rebecca-person ambled through the far doorway. She had a conservative, unassertive look and wore the light blue uniform house-coat Sasha had already noticed the other members of staff wearing. It was rather tight on her out-of-condition body, as if it had shrunk in the wash, or she had put on weight since being provided with the item.

Sasha smiled warmly as she introduced herself. "Hi, I'm Sasha."

The colour in Rebecca's cheeks drained away. When

she was approaching the reception desk, she'd thought this woman might have looked the tiniest bit familiar. However, when she heard the name "Sasha", she thought of the nasty girl in primary school who had a sister with some equally uncommon name. It would be just her luck for this woman to be the same one.

Rebecca led Sasha and the children into the day-care room and reeled off facts about the staffing, the range of care that was provided and the number of residents. She then showed them a recently vacated bedroom and explained about the relevant facilities available.

Best not tell them the resident popped his clogs yesterday morning, thought Rebecca. *Might not give the best impression.*

I could see she was sorely tempted to, though.

Not that it would have mattered; Sasha was picturing a prone elderly gentleman in the bed, his spirit wafting up and away. Her right hand wanted to make the sign of the cross in front of her, which made her think he'd been Catholic.

They moved to the kitchens, then to a large dining room and a further lounge. Sasha asked whether Rebecca could show them the gardens too. It was here she finally felt she could talk, out of earshot of staff and guests.

"Rebecca, I've got a big confession to make to you," she said.

"What do you mean?" Rebecca took a step back.

"You probably don't remember me from primary school but you were in my sister's class. Well, I had a near-death experience in June where I saw lots of things that happened in my past. I saw the time at school, when I was spiteful about you to my sister. I had no idea at the time what I said could have a lasting negative effect on you and I'm really sorry."

Rebecca didn't know how to deal with this. She wanted to tell Sasha to fuck off and mind her own business but she also had to fight tears of self-pity. "Yeah, well, there's nothing you can do about it," she said.

"I know," said Sasha, though she really hoped this wasn't the case. Mr Taylor had also been antagonistic but things hadn't worked out so badly with him. "I was wondering if maybe you'd like to meet up for lunch on a day off? I bet we've got more in common than just the grotty primary school. I'll probably have the kids with me, but they're pretty good if I have some things for them to play with. It could make a change from the usual routine for both of us; what do you reckon?"

"My day off is Thursday," Rebecca blurted out before thinking, *what the… where did that come from? Why the hell would I want to socialise with her?*

"Okay! I can do Thursday." And Sasha's thoughts were: *Why didn't I suggest after the holiday? I'll really have to get organised now.*

Ooh, I'd forgotten what fun it could be to manipulate conversations. I also put a massive effort into softening Rebecca's opinion of Sasha. For her to start liking someone she'd always resented? Really not easy.

Rebecca asked, "Do you know The Bell Inn in Pagnell? It has a children's play area and they do good pub grub. We could meet there, if you like." *OMG, I'm still doing this! What's wrong with me?*

Sasha was tempted to tell Rebecca it was fine by her if she changed her mind but was astute enough to keep things from getting any weirder.

"Yes, that would be perfect. Are you okay with 12 o'clock or is that a bit early?"

"No, that's fine. We can beat the lunchtime rush."

I had to get Rebecca to embrace the idea. If I didn't, I knew she wouldn't turn up on the day. I made her reason that she could do with a new friend and Sasha seemed to have a kind aura about her, no longer anything like when she was younger. Everyone could change; she herself felt kinder than she had when she was younger.

Surprising herself, Rebecca decided she could probably trust Sasha. At the same time, she couldn't help thinking she was having the most peculiar day.

They walked back into the reception area and Sasha thanked Rebecca for showing her around. To Geraldine, she said, "I'm impressed by what I've seen and especially by your lovely staff. We will hold out for as long as we can before moving Dad to a care home but I am certainly going to make Country Life my number one choice now. Thank you so much."

When she got to the car and had the children all strapped in, she slumped back in her driver's seat and closed her eyes for a moment. That had been something, hadn't it? How on earth had she pulled it off? And how good had the children been? She set off for a playground on the way home to reward them and celebrate ticking off the last mission.

Sasha's cheerfulness usually rubbed off on me but

not so much this time. I'd been acting rashly rather a lot lately, so I was constantly expecting Headmaster Hebron to come tell me off, but I was still waiting. It would have been easier if he'd just get on with it.

What Do I Mean?

On Thursday, Sasha headed to The Bell Inn. She'd been there once or twice before and was familiar with the layout. There was a separate entrance on the east side of the building for the children's play area.

She arrived just after midday and took the children straight in. She couldn't see Rebecca but she found an empty table with four chairs near to the little gate that led into the play area and parked Violet alongside one of the chairs. She let Rosie and Noah go play after telling them to stay close to where she was. There was a ball pool enclosure and a double-level padded structure with steps, slides and soft obstacles to run around. This was the toddler version and it was small enough that Sasha could see into all parts of it from her seated vantage point. In front of the climbing area was further space for toy vehicles to be driven along a colourful road mat. While Noah and Rosie raced around, Sasha spooned dollops of food into her youngest's eager mouth. All being well, Violet would be overcome with fatigue after her meal and fall asleep in the pushchair for a while.

By quarter past twelve, Sasha had looked at her watch a dozen times. Had Rebecca changed her mind about meeting up? Sasha's tummy was starting to grumble and she wanted to order food and a drink but thought it would be impolite to do so before Rebecca got there. Conversely, she was aware that she hadn't bought anything yet but now she had to finish feeding Violet. Sasha looked at her watch once again and huffed. She got out a ripe banana, peeled it and broke it into a few pieces in a plastic bowl. Using the back of a child's fork, she roughly mashed it up and started feeding it to Violet. Nowadays, she'd normally let Violet have a try at feeding herself, but this usually ended up with her wearing as much food as she ate. Not ideal in public.

I'm sure she's not coming, thought Sasha. *She's probably gone back to thinking what a horrible cow I am. I'll just have to get our lunch when Violet's done.*

At half past twelve, Sasha picked up her purse and called Noah and Rosie over so they could order lunch. While they were in the queue to be served, Rebecca burst in and rushed over.

"I'm really sorry I'm late," she exclaimed. "I'd promised to take my mum to her doctor's appointment at eleven and there'd been some emergency or something at the surgery meaning she had to wait over an hour. I got here as quick as I could."

"Don't worry," replied Sasha. "I did wonder if you'd changed your mind, but I'm glad you didn't. Good timing for ordering lunch too."

Whilst keeping a close eye on Violet in her pushchair, they made their selections and sat back down at the table.

"So how are things?" asked Sasha. "Do you enjoy your job?"

"It's all right, you know. And a lot of the residents are lovely; they appreciate having someone being kind to them."

"I didn't get the impression Geraldine was very nice," said Sasha.

"Oh, she's okay. As long as you let her know she's the boss, she's really a pussycat."

"That's good then. Look, I've got to explain a bit more to you as I only mentioned the smallest part of my near-death experience previously. If you don't want me to carry on at any point, because I know this is quite sensitive, please just tell me to stop."

"Sure," replied Rebecca, staring at her knees, waiting for the let-down. It always happened.

"When I said I'd no idea how much my cutting remark and other people's comments had hurt you, that was the case when I was alive, I mean, before the accident. However, my life review went into so much detail, not just from my own point of view. You know, it doesn't make sense how I could have seen so much, which would have taken so long in normal time, yet I came back to my body in what was probably only minutes after the accident happened. Oh, you know what, I'm sure I was shown how it was possible and how everything worked when I was over there but I can't remember it now."

Rebecca wasn't finding it easy to follow Sasha's train of thought but at least she'd moved off talking about her. Not for long enough, though.

"Sorry – I got sidetracked," Sasha continued. "It showed me lots of images of your life too, from that time in school when I called you 'fat' – and I'm not surprised you got upset because you weren't that big, not that that was relevant – it was really horrible of me. I saw how you'd comfort eat biscuits and junk food and then your weight did increase. I also saw you at university being told how to make yourself throw up, which led you into bulimia and health issues. You didn't have anyone around you to remind you of all your good qualities and you sank into a pit of self-loathing and loneliness. I felt so sad because I could see you are a genuinely caring, giving person. Life could have been so much better if only you'd been given the praise and encouragement you deserved when you were little."

"Yeah, then maybe I could've stayed little," said Rebecca, trying to cover her deep discomfort at Sasha's words. It wasn't easy to hear her life being dissected, even if good things were being said for once. It was all she could do to hold back the ever-ready tears.

Sasha laughed along gently with Rebecca's joke. "I was also given the impression you will be a lot happier if you start doing something you're interested in, just for your enjoyment, not for anyone else." *I don't know where that just came from but it sounds good,* she thought.

"What do you mean?"

What do I mean? Sasha mentally asked, hoping for a swift answer.

I was tempted to say, "Do I have to tell you everything?" but that would have been unfair. I fed her the right words.

"Well, is there anything you'd like to take up as a hobby, say, going to evening classes? The council usually puts on lots of courses. Actually, I've just remembered…"

Sasha paused as she followed my direction to rummage through the changing bag. She found the now-somewhat-crumpled leaflets from the library.

"Look, here are a couple of courses I spotted among the brochures in the library. Do you like art or pottery?" Sasha smoothed the paper out with her fingers.

"Well, I wouldn't mind. I'm not very good at painting but I quite fancy pottery. I don't suppose you'd go along with me, would you?"

"Gosh, I hadn't really thought. My life revolves around the children at the moment. But maybe I could; I'll have to ask Mark. I was planning to start going to healing every week – I'll have to tell you about that too – so he might not be so keen on me going out twice a week without him. But I guess this wouldn't be for so long. How many weeks is the course?"

Rebecca scanned the details. "It's for six weeks, on a Tuesday from 6.30pm to 8.30pm."

"Well, I'll try then. Would you go anyway?"

"I dunno…"

Sasha didn't need my help to sense that Rebecca was highly unlikely to go on her own.

"Okay, do you want to swap phone numbers, then I can let you know? And it would be good to meet up for lunch again if you want to."

Rebecca was a little overwhelmed but she couldn't help feeling Sasha was genuine. To have someone interested enough to ask her for her number and want to do things with her was the lift that she needed. At this rate, Sasha might even be forgiven.

"Yeah, that'd be good. You can tell me more about the rest of the near-death experience if you want to; it sounds really interesting."

"I'd love to. I never know whether people are going to think I'm a dodgy nutcase when I start to tell them and I'm still trying to get my head around it all."

They finished their lunches, chatting more generally, and then arranged to meet a few weeks later, with Sasha promising to let Rebecca know about the pottery class.

Sasha thought she had finished her mission at last, but I knew that wasn't the end of it. Why wasn't she asking me for help yet? I knew most humans go through life unconscious of their spirit guides but she'd met me face-to-face for goodness' sake. It had been laid on a plate for her. I now doubted she'd ever ask for assistance from anybody – human or spirit. The mission hadn't helped and I was beginning to doubt Hebron's wisdom. Was there anything else that could be done?

All Set?

The next day, Sasha took the children shopping in the morning and packed the suitcases in the afternoon.

Kevin and Pauline had agreed when Sasha and Mark first got Georgie they'd look after him whenever needed. Georgie was now used to being taken round to their house when Sasha and Mark went on holiday and, thankfully, Pauline didn't think it would be a problem to have the cat with them under her present circumstances. In fact, she suspected it would be quite therapeutic to have him curling up on her lap. So Sasha packed a box with cat food, bowls and the litter and tray.

After lunch, she pushed a reluctant Georgie into his travel box that she strapped into the car between Rosie and Noah. He meowed all the way, which they found hilarious; Sasha rather less so.

On arrival, Georgie was released from his cage. He sniffed around cautiously, found his basket which Pauline always put out for him in a corner of the lounge, then turned his back on it and stepped upstairs.

A few days earlier, Pauline had got so fed up with her hair dropping out she'd asked Kevin to shave her head. He'd initially protested but eventually Pauline wore him down and, as gently as possible, he complied. Although she had to get used to her shocking new reflection in the mirror, Pauline was relieved to sort it out. She had a variety of scarves she'd bought over the years and had ordered a wig too.

When Sasha saw her mum wearing a pink scarf with a pattern of yellow and orange flowers on it, she was careful to react positively.

"I like the scarf, Mum. It's lovely and cheerful."

"Oh good, darling. You know, it feels much better to have got rid of my remaining straggles of hair at last. And I don't have to worry about clogging up the plug hole when I shower anymore."

With the train track out and Kevin voicing Sir Topham Hatt, the children were soon giggling in delight. Pauline and Sasha took this as their cue to follow Georgie upstairs for one last healing session before the holiday.

***

"Are you all set for Butlins, then?" Pauline asked Sasha when she sat up after the healing.

"Pretty much. And the weather should be all right most days from what I've seen of the forecast, so I'm sure we'll be fine."

"Is everything okay with you and Mark?"

This took Sasha by surprise. She didn't confide in her

mother about her personal life, unless it related to one of the children, and it wasn't like her mum to spring this on her.

"Err, yes; why do you ask?"

"Well, you just seemed a bit distant with each other when you came over on Sunday. Not like normal."

"Was that me or him that didn't seem normal?"

"Well, Mark was very quiet and pensive and you weren't your usual self either. I wondered whether you'd had a row."

"No, we hadn't; we just haven't been very close lately. Don't worry, Mum – I'm sure it's just normal married life."

Sasha wasn't at all confident inside but she wasn't about to give her mother anything else to worry about.

"Well, I hope so, love. If you've got any problems, you need to talk to each other. You can't expect everything to keep being wonderful without putting in some effort. The only reason your father and I are still together after all these years is because we've talked through our disagreements, even when it's been tough. And you and Mark are so well-suited to each other, you don't want to start drifting apart. Anyway, enough of the lecture – I'm sure you'll work it out."

Pauline stood up and walked downstairs, making it easy to put an end to the conversation. She didn't want to butt in, yet she was becoming increasingly worried about them.

Sasha followed her mum, aware of the agitated beating of her heart.

Tainted Love

When Sasha and Mark prepared for holidays in previous years, the excitement and anticipation was palpable. This year, rather less so.

Saturday morning, with the car packed to bursting point, they all piled in and set off for Butlins. The children were excited because everyone kept telling them what fun they would have. The parents, however, weren't actually as excited as they made out although Sasha was looking forward to fewer chores. She'd have been a lot happier if they'd been going full-board but she'd conceded that self-catering was more practical for feeding Violet.

Sasha's mind was occupied with wondering how she and Mark would get on for a whole week together, twenty-four-seven. He'd been particularly grouchy over the last week, snapping at her or the children for the slightest of things and she was finding it nigh on impossible not to snap back.

Mark was thinking about the holiday as he drove along: We'd normally have sex on holiday but Sasha's turned colder than the North Sea. And the kids are going to be hard work now Violet doesn't stop moving around. I've definitely got to get the snip. Not that there's any danger of getting Sasha pregnant at the moment.

He was still suffering from guilt and pent-up frustration. He kept replaying the events of the last Saturday night over and over in his head, especially the lovemaking fiasco in the car. He would slap himself on the forehead when he was alone. His feelings for Natalie had turned one-eighty: lust to disgust. At work, he tried to avoid her. And he now scoured the job vacancies. There was no way he was planning to discuss things with anybody. He could imagine Phil's reaction to the tractor; he'd piss himself laughing.

Mark turned on the radio to put a stop to his dismal thoughts. They had around two and a half hours' travelling time, not including comfort stops.

"Tainted Love" by Soft Cell was playing.

Oh, bloody brilliant, he thought crossly.

Mark was about to change the radio station but Sasha was the entertainment master and she put a CD in the player.

"The Wheels on the Bus" began, and Sasha encouraged the children and Mark to sing along with her. Even "Tainted Love" would have been better. At least Sasha passed round snacks at regular intervals; he couldn't complain about her planning skills, that was for sure.

When they were driving round Peterborough, Sasha happened to glance outside as they were passing some billboards. One advertising Bernard Matthews' turkeys caught her attention.

Oh no, she thought. *Bernard! I'd said I'd speak to Mark about the bakery accounts on holiday. I wonder how easy that will be…*

Two emergency toilet stops, a lunch break and almost four hours later, they arrived at the holiday resort. Mark stopped the car near the reception area to get the keys and directions to their apartment. The children were bouncing in their car seats by the time he returned and drove them up to their allotted dropping-off space.

I wish I had half their energy, he thought glumly.

The apartment consisted of two bedrooms and an open-plan kitchen/dining/living area. A cot had been added to the twin room so the children could all be in one room. There was the kitchenette to the left, a table with four chairs and the high chair they'd requested in the centre of the room and a couple of small sofas and a television by the window at the other end.

Sasha got some toys out for the children to play with while Mark brought everything up to the apartment and drove the car off to the parking area. She unpacked and then they sat down with coffees, a resort map and information sheets to make a rough plan for the week. Daily entertainment was available to take the children to, plus the swimming pool complex and a fairground area.

Once Mark and Sasha had sketched out their plan, they all went to the swimming pool, where they had a lovely time splashing about in the shallow end. Tensions eased and they looked like the quintessential happy family. When their fingers and toes started imitating prunes, they showered and changed before taking a wander around the complex to find out where everything was.

They found the main Skyline Pavilion area which, from my vantage point, was a huge white tent with various peaks at odd angles – I hadn't seen anything like it – and spotted lots of things to do and places to eat. It was the first time I'd really looked at a holiday village and I was surprised by its size. There were multitudes of buildings, a fairground, go-kart track, a fascinating giant tap that looked like it was hanging in midair and more. The tubes coming out of the swimming pool building were like big bright worms entering and exiting a metal box.

The resort seemed vast, from a child's little legs' point of view, so they didn't try to explore it all that afternoon and wandered back to their accommodation.

While Mark kept the children occupied, Sasha made up dinner with pasta, a big jar of bolognese sauce and a bowl of salad on the side. She cut Violet's portion up and put her in the high chair.

Mark brought Rosie and Noah to the table and they all sat down to eat. Being together made a welcome change to their usual routine. They chatted about what fun they'd had and told the children about the different things they could look forward to. Rosie couldn't wait for the arts and crafts; Noah got excited about the puppet show.

After dinner, Sasha cleared the table and washed up while Mark played with the kids and put the television on. Sasha read them a story and put them to bed; Mark opened a bottle of beer each and sat down on the sofa in front of the telly. The rest of the evening passed in virtual silence and when it came time for bed, Sasha deliberately took so long with her ablutions Mark had fallen asleep before she slipped into bed.

Thank goodness for that, thought Sasha, who was definitely not in the mood. *He could have washed up at least or even changed Violet's nappy. The man does nothing!*

I'm not sure I'd ever seen Sasha feeling as fed up as this, and I really, really wanted to persuade her to talk things over with Mark, but I held myself in check. It happened occasionally.

Fair Play

Over the next few days, Mark and Sasha explored the resort, taking the children to many of the options for the under-fives as well as the swimming pool and the kiddies' fairground. At least the children were having a bright and sunny time but thunderclouds were looming over their parents.

I watched the storm finally erupt the third evening when they were in bed.

Mark moved closer to Sasha and put an arm around her, daring to hope for a positive response. But Sasha removed his arm and got up, declaring her need to go to the loo.

"Are we ever going to make love again, Sasha?" Mark demanded grumpily.

"You tell me, Mark!" she spat back.

He wasn't expecting that. "What do you mean, 'you tell me'? You're the one who decides whether it happens, not me."

"You don't get it, Mark, do you?"

"Get what exactly?"

"Why I don't want to sleep with you."

"Well, I'm not psychic, am I?"

"No, and it's probably a good thing I'm not any more either."

"What's that supposed to mean? I've got no idea what's going on in your head!"

"No, and that's the problem! You never notice how pissed off I am that you do nothing around the house. Even here, would it hurt to share the chores? Wash up? Change a nappy? Make up a bottle of milk, perhaps? Help get things ready to go out each day? You can't use the excuse that you've been working all day here. It's one big holiday for you but I'm still working my arse off, as usual. It's not exactly fair, is it?"

"How am I supposed to know if you don't ask? You never said!"

"I don't ask for help. I shouldn't have to. Besides, you can see just as well as me what needs doing, if you bothered to look. You even said, after I'd come out of hospital, you couldn't believe how hard it was to look after the children and the house, and I stupidly thought things would get better. But no. You let my parents do most of it. You've got it easy, going off to work in an office for the day and expecting everything else to be done for you. You're not the only one working, you know. I'd rather be sitting at a desk all day than everything else I do. And then you expect me to be happy to have sex at the end of it all. You really think I'll be in the mood when you're sitting on the sofa and I'm still washing up? And I'm too knackered from doing everything anyway."

Sasha was as shocked as Mark at her outburst; it was so uncharacteristic of her. She heaved a massive sigh and thought miserably, *I should have handled that better; I've never had a go at him like that before. At least I've finally told him what's wrong, but what's the point? He's never going to change.*

I wanted to say, "Don't be so sure", because Mark's brain was chugging away, but I kept schtum.

Mark walked out of the bedroom to get a glass of water. He was still aggravated at the situation, but his anger was ebbing. He wanted to feel justified, but there wasn't much he could say in his defence.

"Well, maybe I will start doing more then," he said gruffly as he walked back, "but only if you tell me what you want me to do though."

Sasha couldn't resist a little smile. "I'll try," she said in a softer tone. "You can start with washing up if I'm doing the dinner. Or you could even make dinner yourself sometime. And getting in a take-away doesn't count."

Her skin started to prickle, and she felt hot all over – wasn't that her asking for help? She really shouldn't have said anything.

Mark was oblivious. "Fair play. Do I have to get the Hoover out too?" he said, putting on a humorous whiny voice this time.

Sasha stared at him.

I stared at Sasha.

"You bet you do! And the duster is in the cupboard under the stairs."

Thank goodness!

"Not the duster; please, not the duster!" Mark flailed his arms in front of his face like he was fighting off a duster attack.

Sasha laughed, in spite of her misgivings. This was a reminder of happier days before the burdens of everyday strife had become so heavy.

"Anyway, let's get some sleep now." She leant over and gave Mark a quick kiss before settling down to get to sleep. He wasn't getting laid that easily, and besides, she needed to analyse what she'd just said.

Mark closed his eyes and months' worth of tension dissolved from his face. At least he finally knew why Sasha had been so cold towards him and he could work on that. It was a fair cop; the imbalance seemed blindingly obvious now. He wasn't particularly looking forward to doing the work but he knew it was only right. However, it didn't resolve the corrosive feelings that were still eating away at his guilty conscience.

If we'd sorted this out a while back, I'd never have looked twice at Natalie, he thought. *Just forget about it, mate. You can't say anything to Sasha.*

***

The next morning, Mark helped prepare breakfast and clear up afterwards. He even offered to change Violet's nappy, which he soon regretted. Next time, he was going to try out his snorkel for protection from the disgusting pong.

I noticed Sasha smiling more and even laughing with

Mark. It was such a relief to watch the family as they genuinely enjoyed a day full of activities and then treated themselves to dinner at one of the fast-food restaurants. This was followed by a visit to a child-friendly bar afterwards for an hour or so, where Sasha enjoyed a gin and tonic whilst Mark had a pint of beer. Even the children were feeling the benefit of their dad stepping up to the plate, with both parents being more relaxed and attentive. Maybe they'd managed to solve the chore-sharing issue but she'd still had a problem asking for help. Hebron had made it clear to me that Sasha did need to overcome the help-hurdle.

Mark was sensible enough not to expect an immediate change of heart when it came to horizontal affairs. Sasha was relieved he didn't try it on that night, as she wouldn't have been impressed; so far, he'd just made one small step in the right direction – not a giant leap for mankind.

They had a second day of shared responsibilities and happier hearts. Mark helped in one way or another with all their meals, plus he tried using the snorkel for the next stinky nappy and was delighted with his own ingenuity. He washed up the dishes after their chicken curry, helped put the children to bed and settled down to another evening of telly and beers with Sasha.

Well, that wasn't so bad after all, he thought. *Piece of cake!*

Sasha was so happy with the way things were turning out. If only I could have said something ages ago, things would never have got so bad, she thought. This is what it should be like, after all.

Not just said something, but asked, I wanted to remind her. Still, baby steps...

Sasha took a big, satisfied swig of her beer and looked at Mark with the first stirrings of desire she'd felt for a long time. She shimmied over and cuddled up next to him on the sofa.

"We could have an early night, if you like," she said, looking up at him through her eyelashes.

"Oh, but I really wanted to watch the end of this," replied Mark, trying hard to keep a straight face.

"Liar!" she exclaimed as she pretended to smack his cheek.

Mark caught her hand and pulled her onto him, wrapping his arms around Sasha and kissing her deeply. Without letting go, he stood up and carried her to the bedroom. They undressed hastily and dived under the covers, revelling in the first moments of affection they'd shared for a very long time. It was like being reunited after years apart and their capacity to satisfy each other was still present.

Afterwards, Mark lay next to Sasha, speculating how close he'd got to messing his life up. Even though the night with Natalie in the car had been exciting, erotic even, he would have been such a fool to have traded it for the passion and security he shared with his wonderful wife. He shuddered involuntarily at the thought of how close he'd got to having sex with Natalie.

Sasha's satisfied, almost trancelike state was on the frequency at which she read minds and Mark's little shudder catapulted her into his mind. And there was that woman from the office except now she was topless and Mark was think-saying "Natalie – ughh". Although it was perfectly clear that Mark's tone wasn't expressing desire or love, all Sasha could focus on was the image of the semi-naked woman. Jesus Christ, that woman had disgustingly perfect breasts. So why was Mark thinking about her right now, in the afterglow of lovemaking? Oh God, had he slept with the bitch?

"Who... the hell... is Natalie?" she said in an unnaturally low and deliberate voice, staring straight ahead.

Mark froze, the blood draining from his dumbstruck face.

How the fuck was this possible?

He stared at Sasha, his eyes as big as a bush baby's.

"Natalie?" he asked weakly. A tiny part of him wanted to confess everything and the rest of him was screaming: *Don't say a word! It will ruin everything!*

"Yes, *Natalie!*" Sasha hissed at Mark. "You were thinking of someone called Natalie just then, and that's not the first time. When you first came to see me in hospital, all you could think about was this stupid big-boobed girl at work. I presume that's Natalie?"

"How on earth? Are you psychic or something?"

"Yes – no – well, kind of. For fuck's sake, I'll tell you about that another time. *Natalie!* Are you having an affair? Do you love her?"

Mark groaned. He wanted to deny Natalie even existed but somehow Sasha seemed to know about her. Lying would only make things worse, he was sure. He was going to have to admit what had happened and just hope Sasha's reaction wouldn't be too extreme.

"No, I'm not having an affair – it didn't go anywhere near that far. And, no, I definitely don't love her. The thought of her makes me feel sick. I haven't told you yet but I'm looking for a new job just to get away from her. She flirted with me, and I ignored her at first, but…" Mark hung his head. "…I guess I got attracted to her after a while. I'm sorry."

"You disgust me!" Sasha raised her knees up to her chin and wrapped her arms around her legs.

"I'm sorry! I wanted you but you wouldn't let us make love. I was frustrated and she kept coming on to me. I held off for so long…"

Oh, what a hero! thought Sasha viciously.

"…then the last time I went out to the pub, it was with her. We started snogging on the way home but nothing happened."

"Really? Why ever not?" The sarcasm flowed from Sasha's mouth like molten lava.

Mark winced. "If you want to know, a tractor suddenly appeared in front of the car and lit us up like a Christmas tree. Even more, actually; it was like a spotlight on us and it brought me to my senses. I stopped – we hadn't actually had sex – and I took Natalie home. I've barely spoken to her since, and thank God I don't have to work directly with her. I've felt so damn guilty it got that close. I know I'm an idiot – I've been kicking myself ever since – and I honestly don't want anything more to do with her."

Yes, you are a big fucking idiot, said Sasha silently.

It struck Sasha it was probably no coincidence Mark was interrupted by a bright light as she recalled her vivid dream that night. It was an interesting thought but there were more pressing matters.

"So, if you really don't want anything more to do with her, why the hell were you thinking about her just now?"

"I was thinking how lucky it was that nothing had happened with her, that I hadn't spoilt our marriage by sleeping with her. If you felt me shudder, that's because I was revolted by the thought of her," Mark said with conviction.

Sasha had been watching his body language intently. There were no tells to suggest he was lying. But the actual truth was that he very nearly had committed adultery. Just because he'd got stopped by the tractor or whatever didn't suddenly make it all okay.

I've had it with him; he's just ruined our marriage, Sasha thought rashly. *How can I ever trust him again?*

She went to the bathroom and sat on the edge of the bath as she tried to plan what to do next.

Mark was trying to stay awake, nervously wondering what Sasha was thinking, and he opened his heavy eyelids when she returned to the bed. Sasha glared at him and settled on the furthest edge of the bed, facing away from him.

Mark sighed heavily. It was clear Sasha wasn't going to say anything further. He fell asleep almost straight away which infuriated Sasha even more as she lay wide awake, consumed with self-pity and rage.

You Are Joking Aren't You?

I could sympathise with Sasha's reaction. At the heart of the issue of Mark being unfaithful, he should have made it clear to Natalie he wasn't interested and he should have found a way to discuss his marital problems with Sasha. He had let her down badly.

Sasha wasn't at fault for Mark's weakness but she'd had the power to prevent it happening. If she'd asked Mark to help more around the house, I was sure he'd have done so and their lives would have been much more fulfilling. Her biggest weakness was clinging to her vow regarding asking for anything for herself. Martyrs were overrated in my opinion. Good communication seemed to be one of the biggest hurdles for humans in general, let alone Mark and Sasha. If Sasha hadn't tuned into Mark at that inopportune moment, everything would have been on an upward trajectory; they'd resolved their issues and Mark was never going to make the same mistake again (although he'd still have his guilt to bear). Instead, she was consumed with him being unfaithful and her views on infidelity were inflexible, so I was in a sombre mood as she awoke the next morning.

Sasha opened her eyes and looked around; for a moment, she wasn't sure where she was. Then the horror of last night flooded back into her consciousness and her stomach clenched.

Oh God!

She looked over at her husband, who was lying on his back, his eyes shut and his mouth ajar. She grimaced, remembering how humiliated she'd felt when she'd found out that her ex, Liam, had been cheating on her. How could it be happening again?

She tried to deal with the children as if it were just another lovely day but she only spoke to Mark when necessary and with a frosty edge to her voice. She packed the bags, separating Mark's belongings into one suitcase and squashing everything else in other cases and bags.

In the car, Sasha kept the children entertained and Mark kept quiet. He could hardly expect them to discuss the issue in front of the children and it was clear that general chit-chat was off the agenda.

When they arrived home and the children were out of earshot, Sasha thrust Mark's suitcase at him and told him to gather whatever else he needed so that he could leave.

"You are joking, aren't you, Sasha? Can't we talk this over, please?"

"There's nothing to talk about. You clearly wanted to fuck Natalie, so now you can go and do it. I don't know how we'll manage, but we'll have to find a way. You can have the children every other weekend."

"I don't want Natalie. I only want to be with you. I love you, Sasha. This is a bit of an over-reaction, isn't it? I never had sex with Natalie."

"Only because some stupid tractor stopped you."

"I was glad it did – honestly. I knew I'd made a mistake, but thank God the tractor came when it did." Mark could hear how pathetic this sounded, even though it was true.

"Yeah, the tractor came instead of you."

Mark could feel the venom in Sasha's words and he stopped arguing. Maybe when he wasn't there, she might just miss him and realise she'd made a mistake, then they could talk again. At least it was a glimmer of hope. He called Phil and arranged to stay there for a short while, then packed his work clothes and other essentials into another suitcase.

Mark hugged the children and fought back tears – how he would miss them. Then he turned to Sasha. "You said you were psychic," he spat at her. "Well, you're not very good if you don't know how much I love you." He slammed the door as he left.

Sasha burst into tears and slid down the wall in the hollow hallway. This wasn't what she wanted but she didn't know how to make it better. Letting Mark come back just wasn't an option, however much her heart told her otherwise.

I so wanted to encourage the heart side but the rulebook was back in charge.

Sasha texted Michelle to ask her to come over but she wasn't available before next weekend. Sasha thought about Meena and other friends but didn't feel up to explaining everything to anyone else at the moment. She'd just have to get by on her own.

She called her parents and asked if she could pick up Georgie the next day. The plan had been that she'd have picked him up soon after they got home but Sasha didn't want to go round with her face swollen by tears and she certainly didn't want to discuss the issue with her parents. She told her mum Mark wouldn't be with them, just before saying goodbye.

At least she had the children for company and she hugged them tightly and played with them in between dealing with the unpacking, washing and sorting out dinner. Loneliness and heartache took turns at stabbing her in the gut.

***

In the morning, Sasha told Rosie and Noah that Daddy had gone away for a while.

"Is he on holiday again?" asked Rosie.

"No, sweetheart."

"Will he be back for dinner?" asked Noah.

"No, Noah. He won't be back for dinner. But you will see him soon. I'm just not sure when at the moment. Let's get ready to go round to Nanna and Grandad's. Are you excited to see Georgie again?"

Sasha watched the children pick what they wanted to take with them. She was dreading the moment she would have to explain things to her mum and dad. When Liam had left her, the shame of not being as good as the new woman had been overwhelming. What would they say about her actual husband lusting after someone else? Maybe they would think it was all her fault, that she wasn't a good enough wife.

Round at their grandparents' house, Rosie and Noah raced off to find Georgie. Sasha was momentarily distracted from her predicament by her mother's appearance. Pauline was wearing a flattering wig and you'd hardly have noticed anything wrong if you didn't know.

"You're looking good, Mum," Sasha said as they hugged.

"Thank you, darling," Pauline said. "I think the wig's better than my own hair." At her first opportunity to catch Sasha alone, she asked, "So why isn't Mark here?"

"We've split up, Mum, but I don't want to talk about it."

"Oh, I'm so sorry, love. You know I was worried for you before you went away. Are you sure you don't want to talk about it? Talking can really help."

"No thanks. I don't see anything helping. Let's go do the healing, okay?"

Pauline rolled her lips tight together and they trudged upstairs in silence.

***

The weight of responsibility pressed down on Sasha as she waded through all the domestic chores alone. It became clear that Mark had helped more than she'd credited him for – sure it wasn't enough but it was much better than nothing. And she was lonely once the children were in bed; she missed having him in the house. She recalled how they'd chat and laugh together before things turned sour, and tears slid down her cheeks until her skin burnt.

The future was a constant concern. She considered selling the house and moving into a smaller place, where the children would have to share bedrooms, the kitchen would be tiny and there would only be one toilet in the house. More than likely, it would be terraced with noisy, irritating neighbours. Sasha also felt guilty for a moment because Mark had already got his own three-bedroom house before he met her, then she reminded herself she wouldn't have made him move out if he'd kept his dick to himself. It was his fault, not hers.

She knew she ought to go back to work, but she would have to find a job that would fit in with school hours and holidays, which was very unlikely unless she got a teaching assistant job. That wasn't likely with her lack of experience and the number of other parents and young adults all applying for the limited posts. In any case, it paid a pittance. If she went back to her admin work, which wasn't a high-earner either, she'd be working for almost nothing once childcare costs were deducted. It could have been okay if her parents were able to help with the childcare but she couldn't ask her mum under current circumstances. Nothing seemed possible.

At the beginning of the week, Sasha prepared for Rosie and Noah returning to school for the new academic year. Normally she would look forward to the first day of term, comparing notes with her friends at the school gates, but not this time. She didn't want to tell anybody about becoming a single mother. And what was worse was that Rosie was now in Reception Class, so Sasha would have to take both her and Noah in the morning, collect Noah at lunchtime and go back after three o'clock to get Rosie.

On Wednesday, Sasha almost asked her dad to do the school run so she could avoid everybody. But the desire to give the children words of encouragement and hugs goodbye as she left them in their new classrooms won over. On the outside, Sasha was upbeat as she walked them to school with Violet in the pushchair but inside, she was numb.

She chatted to Meena briefly and waved at other mums from a polite distance before making a quick getaway. Avoiding personal conversation each day was tiring and by Friday afternoon, she was so relieved she wouldn't have to do it again until Monday. Sooner or later, though, she'd have to confess.

The stress of putting on a normal cheerful façade in front of the children and everyone else was taking its toll. She lost her appetite and withdrew further and further into herself. Everything was so very hopeless and she had to buy extra boxes of tissues to mop up all the tears.

Raiding the [Memory] Bank

I was pretty miserable with the whole situation too. I didn't suffer fools lightly but Sasha was one fool I made exceptions for. No doubt too many exceptions. If she could put her pride aside, she'd soon see what a mistake she'd made. And of course if she'd asked me for help, it could all be sorted. Same old story.

Day after grindingly slow day, I sat back and watched her struggle on her own. I also watched a miserable and grumpy Mark round at Phil's and at work. Phil was on the verge of telling Mark he'd outstayed his welcome.

I had to keep reminding myself about the rules because what I was considering this time would be just as bad as the dream sequence. I'd worked out a way to make Sasha ask Mark back. This was a no-no. No. No. No. It crossed my mind that Hebron would be fully aware of my dilemma should he choose to be. Oh, I did hope he was fully occupied with some other trainees on the other side of the planet.

It took me another week in your timescale before I

caved in. The more I thought about it, the more convinced I was I'd already blown my graduation chances. If Sasha was going to be the last human I got to work with, I had to do my very best for her. From my point of view, that meant getting her and Mark reconciled. I had such a good plan I even convinced myself it would be for the best and Hebron might just see the sense in it.

As soon as Sasha was in bed that evening, I sent her straight to sleep. I was quite the expert at this now. Then I entered Sasha's memory banks in the same way you might visit the reference section of a library. There were heaps of tedious memories to wade through but I persisted; I knew just what I was looking for. I also delved into Mark's memories as he lay in his bed at Phil's to pull out the pertinent pieces.

I saved all the memories on my tablet (yes, of course it's far more advanced than your technology – the outside of them is pretty much all they have in common) and lined them up before rousing Sasha back to consciousness and placing a few images into her mind. There were several of her getting annoyed at Mark for letting her do all the work at home, where she wanted to say something to him about it but wouldn't let herself. To go with this, I showed her Mark telling Phil about trying to help with the ironing and how he didn't dare do it again. Then I showed her a couple of images where Mark tried to initiate sex and she turned him away. This was followed by a snippet of Mark's conversation with Phil in the pub, when Mark was saying, "I wouldn't look twice at Natalie if Sasha and I had a sex-life but Sasha won't come near me anymore. At least Natalie seems to want me." Finally, I made her revisit the post-coital scene on holiday where Mark was musing over how much of a fool he would have been to risk losing Sasha. This time she saw the whole of his thoughts and emotions, with his revulsion towards Natalie.

It actually seemed to be working. Sasha was still indignant and humiliated Mark got close to being unfaithful but clearly he'd only looked Natalie's way when he'd felt abandoned by Sasha.

I continued with the memory presentation by casting a vision of Mark changing Violet's nappy on holiday with the aid of his snorkel. That successfully lightened the mood, making Sasha long for Mark's good sense of humour at the same time as reminding her he'd begun to do his share of the chores. I was on a roll now.

On then to Mark in the doorway, accusing her of not knowing he loved her. That made Sasha try to tune in to Mark there and then, to see whether indeed she did have any psychic abilities left. I felt like Maria in The Sound of Music, in the scene where she's putting on the Little Goatherd performance, twiddling all the puppets' strings.

In perfect synchronicity, I turned to Mark and threw him some images of their wedding day and the births of their children when Mark was overcome with love for his wonderful wife. It had the required effect of wrenching his heart and he started to cry. I couldn't have hoped for a better response. I managed to boost Sasha's psychic abilities so she could see for herself how much Mark loved her. And then I shut the image down pretty swiftly, just in case his resentment bubbled up, which might have put a dampener on things.

Oh God, thought Sasha. *What have I done? He really does love me, and I chucked him out – all because of my stupid pride. I'm such an idiot. But can I actually trust him again?*

"Yes," I said to her. "As long as you both keep communicating and you talk your problems out, he'll never look at another woman again."

"Ooh, is that Zinnia?"

Of course Sasha was on the psychic boost and heard me for once. I quickly reminded myself not to say anything that completely overstepped the mark, like actually spelling out that she needed to ask for help – just in case there was the slightest possibility of graduation.

"Yes, it is," I said to her. "Remember, I'm always here by your side, ready and willing."

That was very, very close, but not exactly saying, "Ask me for help".

"Thank you, Zinnia. Gosh, this is really strange. Well, everything has been really strange since the NDE. I can't believe I can hear you and talk to you. You're still there, are you?"

"Yes, I'm still here," I said, doing the equivalent of rolling one's eyes.

"Gosh, there's so much I should probably ask you about but my mind's gone blank. I don't know what to say."

"Think about what I said to you, Sasha."

"You said you're still here."

"No, before that." Boy, this girl could test my patience.

There was a long pause as Sasha tried to make something out of me saying I was always beside her, ready and willing. She really didn't get it.

"I said Mark will never want to have a relationship with another woman as long as you both keep communicating and you talk your problems out."

"Oh." Another long pause. "Are you sure, Zinnia?"

"Yes, I'm sure." I shouldn't have said that because nothing is fixed in stone, but honestly, I was getting to the stage of saying anything Sasha wanted to hear.

"I should tell Mark he can come back then, shouldn't I?"

"That certainly seems like a good idea to me." *Hallelujah!*

Sasha's smile was broader than the Amazonian River Basin. She must have heard my "hallelujah" as well. She grabbed her mobile and called Mark, rousing him from his slumber. Actually, I had to give him a poke so he didn't miss the call.

"Hi, Mark. How are you?"

"I've been better," he said blearily. "What's wrong?"

"Nothing exactly. I've been thinking and, well, maybe I over-reacted a bit. Do you want to come back to talk things over tomorrow?"

Mark would normally have said something witty like, "I'll just check my diary", but he wasn't stupid enough to do it now. Plus, he hadn't been in the mood for joking lately.

I hastily sent him another image of the two of them together when times were better. He reacted like Pavlov's dogs, salivating at the sound of a bell.

"Okay," he said. "What time?"

Sasha knew it would be difficult to talk in front of the children, so she reluctantly stopped herself from suggesting the morning.

"You could come round for dinner and spend some time with the children before they go to bed and then we can talk after saying goodnight to them."

"Fine by me. I'll see you then." It was going to be the longest Saturday morning and afternoon ever.

"Bye." Sasha had been about to add "love you" but clamped her mouth shut just in time.

Job done. I was quite worn out by all the interaction and glad to pull back now. I hated to think about what Hebron would have to say about this latest misconduct.

As Long As I've Got My Snorkel

Sasha had coffee ready when Mark dropped onto the sofa after saying goodnight to the children and handed him his favourite "I Love Daddy" mug. She sat down at the other end, bending her legs up on the seat and hugging her mug for comfort. She didn't know where to start and emotions were bouncing inside her body like a game of ping-pong.

"Have you missed us?" she asked.

"More than you could imagine," said Mark. "It's been really hard getting up every day pretending to be okay."

"Oh." Sasha's guts were really curdling with guilt and pride. She had to get to the point or risk throwing up. "Look, I know I probably should have let us talk it out at the time but you made me feel like I was no longer attractive enough to you and that really hurt."

"You'll always be more attractive to me than anyone else in the world, Sasha. You're beautiful! Even if you weren't, it's not only about looks. I love you for who you are: the best wife, the best mother and my soulmate. I don't want to find anyone else."

"Are you sure you wouldn't sleep with Natalie – or anybody else – if you had a chance to do so without getting caught?"

"No way. I'd honestly avoided Natalie at the start when she was flirting. I should've given her the cold shoulder but the longer it went on that you and I had no physical contact, the more I got frustrated. It got harder to resist – though I know I should have. It wasn't that I wanted to sleep with Natalie – I just needed sex and you kept turning me away. I should have talked to you about how I felt but I didn't know how. I've learnt the hard way, Sasha. I'll never be an idiot again. If we get any more problems, I'll try to talk to you before things get so bad. And I've applied to two different jobs. Got an interview next week."

"Well, that's good, I guess."

"You've got to talk to me too, Sasha. I can see I should have been doing more around the house now, but if only you'd mentioned it earlier. You're going to think this is really dumb, but housework just wasn't on my radar. I need to be house-trained, I guess."

"You're right. That is the dumbest thing. But I just can't ask for help."

"Maybe not the brightest thing either, if you don't mind me saying."

"It's okay." Sasha was aware she was keeping any negative emotions at bay for now, and it looked like Mark was doing the same. That was a good thing. "We could agree on certain jobs. It would be easier to start off that way." In her mind, this wasn't actually asking for help but it was close enough to make her grimace and almost change her mind.

"Start off? Are you saying I can come back?" Mark's eyes widened, and he reached out to touch Sasha's arm. The contact felt good to Sasha, and she steeled herself to continue.

"Yes, though I can't jump straight back into trusting you again. And I definitely won't be able to jump straight back into having sex either. Is that a problem?"

"Well, obviously I want us to get intimate again but I understand it will take a bit of time. Once you realise you can trust me, do you think you will?"

"I'll have to or it will all go pear-shaped again. It will definitely be better if you're doing much more at home. Like, maybe you could make dinner at the weekends as well as help with the housework. And take turns at the nappy changes when you're home."

"Okay, as long as I've got my snorkel."

"Yeah, I saw that. Does it actually help?"

"A little bit, but mainly it makes Violet giggle instead of wriggle which definitely is good."

"You know, we ought to be able to make it work, don't you think? But there is one other thing I've got to tell you about that I know you're not going to agree with. Please listen to me and try to be open-minded."

Oh, great – just when I thought it was going well, Mark was thinking and his mind raced over possibilities – would he have to sleep in a separate bedroom? Had Sasha joined that church and become a devout Christian?

"You told me you don't believe in near-death

experiences but I had one when I was in the accident."

Well, he hadn't anticipated that. Mark paused before carefully choosing his response.

"Okay, so tell me what happened then."

"Well, first of all, I was floating above the accident and I could take in everything that was happening below. I didn't even question how I was there – I was pleasantly detached. It was only when I panicked, because it hit me that I'd died and the kids were alone, that I was whisked up and away."

"Like in a tunnel, going towards a light?" Mark fought unsuccessfully to keep the sarcasm out of his voice.

"Yes, and stop being cynical."

"Sorry."

"You know, there's probably a reason everyone says it's like that. Like maybe that's actually the way it happens."

Or like you've got that idea already in your mind, so that's what you choose to believe. Out loud, Mark said, "Just carry on." He tried hard to keep his face neutral.

"Well, Gran was with me and we saw a number of spirits who spoke to us. One of them was my great-grandad Henry, who had children with him. Their parents were really struggling to cope with their deaths. It's a long story, but I was able to meet them after I came out of hospital and reassure them. It was really sad."

"You did? When was that?" Mark was more shocked and resentful that Sasha had done this on her own without telling him – she always told him everything, or so he thought.

"It was the day before Mum and I went to the spa. She drove me up to Salcey Park to meet with the children's parents and grandparents. The grandad, Arthur, is a cousin of Mum's she didn't know about because he'd been adopted."

There was too much information here that just didn't make sense and Mark couldn't imagine how Sasha could believe it all, let alone actually go meet these people.

"I also had a life review – do you know what I mean?"

"You're saying you saw some things that happened when you were younger?"

"Yes, and I saw part of your childhood. Your mum never made you do anything to help, did she?"

"No, you're right there. It was a cushy life, when I come to think about it." *And it isn't hard to predict either,* he thought.

"Anyway, I was told I had to help people when I came back, and I think I have. How much it's helped some of them, I don't know, but I have tried. And I've got one more person I need your help with."

"My help? What do you mean?" Mark asked, his eyebrows shooting upwards.

"It's a bit of a long story but it started with a spirit called Bernard Walker who has – had – a bakery in Newport Pagnell. His wife, Ursula, still runs it. Anyway, Bernard can see their office manager, Clive, is stealing money from the business. I had to go tell Ursula about it. Bernard said that looking at the bank statements for the last five years would show what Clive's up to. Ursula isn't confident with figures and I said maybe you could take a look at them since you'd know what to look for."

"Really? That's sixty months of transactions to scrutinise; do you even know what I'd be looking for?"

"Bernard said Clive had set up payments to go into his own accounts."

"Hmmm. It's a lot of work. We don't even know the people."

"Well, I sort of feel like I do now. I'll help if you tell me what to look for."

"And this is all based on what? You believing you can speak to dead people and you went to heaven and came back to tell the tale?"

"That's a bit rude, isn't it? There's a lot more to it than that. I could read people's minds when I first came back. I saw you thinking about Natalie when you were in hospital with me. I had been so pleased to see you and then there you were – thinking about some sexy chick with big boobs. And I saw you had taken her out to lunch and you only gave me flowers and suggested the spa weekend because you were feeling guilty. That's why I wasn't exactly feeling very loving, you know. Well, that and you never doing anything to help."

Mark's mouth dropped open. It didn't make sense that Sasha knew anything about Natalie but it still wasn't enough to convince him she had psychic abilities. There had to be a scientific explanation – there always was. Maybe his body language was just too easy to read. Or she'd spoken to someone at work who'd seen what was going on – although this was as unlikely as anything psychic. It did bring his guilty feelings back to the fore again, though.

"Well, if you get the paperwork, I'll have a look but I can't promise I'll find whatever's supposed to be dodgy.

If this bloke has been stealing money for some time, he certainly isn't making it obvious or the Walkers would have noticed it by now."

"Well, thank you for saying you'll help. Whatever you can do will be good enough, I'm sure. I'll let Ursula know. And do you want to move back tomorrow; it's a bit late tonight, isn't it?"

"Or we could leave it until next week… Only kidding – of course I do. I'll get everything together as soon as I've showered and had breakfast. Phil was kicking me out at the end of next week anyway; I'm sure he'll help me pack."

They both spontaneously moved towards each other and hugged tightly. When Mark got up to go, he gave Sasha a gentle, lingering kiss.

"I do love you, Mrs Denning."

"I love you too, Mr Denning. It'll be good to have you back."

It wasn't going to be easy to overcome the trust issue, but Sasha felt hopeful. There was no denying he'd acted like an idiot but she wasn't the smartest either.

The Call

The next morning, whilst Sasha was waiting for Mark to arrive, she made the call.

"Hi, Ursula, it's Sasha here. Sorry it's taken a bit longer than I'd meant but I've finally spoken to Mark and he's happy to take a look at your accounts, if you still want him to."

"Oh, that's lovely, Sasha. Very kind of him, and yes, please. I've made copies of the bank statements and I'm happy to drop them round. When would be best?"

"Well, we'll be out most of today, so how about tomorrow? You could come round after six, as Mark will be home by then and he can ask you anything he needs to know to get started."

"Okay, dear, that's lovely. Do you want to give me your address, please?"

Sasha gave her address and directions, saying goodbye just as Mark arrived with his belongings.

"You know the bank statements thing," she said to him. "I've just arranged for Ursula to bring the paperwork round tomorrow night. That's still okay with you, isn't it?"

"Yeah, of course," Mark lied. He couldn't believe he'd agreed to it, but he wasn't going to risk spoiling things by saying so.

Actions and Consequences

Part of being a spirit guide involved looking ahead to anticipate what was lined up for our charges. I'd been blocked before when I'd try to see what Bernard had to do with Sasha but this time I was taken straight to Clive.

He was hunched, headphones on, in a corner of his sitting room, facing the bugging equipment on a desk. August had been predictably dead but Clive's adrenaline was surging as soon as September came. He could feel his blood pressure rising each consecutive day as he checked Ursula's calls until the sixteenth of September.

"You fucking bitches," he said to the empty room.

Actions he could take and possible consequences if he didn't get his plans right whirred through his mind. He shut his eyes as ugly memories of his two years in Pentonville Prison resurfaced. Painful encounters, fighting, negotiating with the bigger bastards, seizing opportunities to establish himself in the hierarchy. A snarly smirk grew on his face. Those wankers underestimated him – at first. As if carrying an offensive weapon was the worst he could do – what a pathetic thing to convict him on. But that was all they had and, instead, poncy Jimmy Wallace was doing time for bumping off the snitch. As if he'd ever. Still, nice one, Jimmy. Nice one, you filth, for stitching him up. Clive's cackles bounced off the walls of the dingy room. There was no way he was letting this Mark geezer get hold of the accounts. And once he was out of the picture, Clive would keep watching Ursula in case she tried anything else. His plan was risky but his job was worth fighting for.

This was serious. How could my naïve, kind Sasha and her husband get mixed up with a low-life like Clive? Mark was a fool but he didn't deserve what Clive had in mind.

***

On Monday, Clive arrived at work with a spark plug spanner in his rucksack. He propped the internal office door open to see when the shop was busy enough with customers to keep Ursula and Felicity at the front. As soon as this happened, Clive closed the door quietly, put the premises CCTV cameras on pause and took Ursula's car key from the hook where she always kept it. He slipped silently out the back, lifted the bonnet of her car, pulled off the HT leads and disconnected three spark plugs. He eased the bonnet back into place and relocked the car. Returning inside, he put the key on its hook and sat back down at the desk, heart pounding, moisture prickling his forehead. He wiped the sweat away with the cuff of his sleeve. Part One was ticked off easy enough, not that he hadn't had excuses up his sleeve had he been caught in the act.

Part One down, Part Two to go, he said to himself, grinding his teeth together.

***

Ursula finished the pasty she was eating, sitting at her desk in the office. She looked out the window to check the cloud situation – it had been raining off and on all day and she didn't want to get caught in another downpour. Maybe it would be sensible to put her jacket on.

She took the bundle of paperwork out of her drawer and put it in a carrier bag. Gripping that in her left hand and picking up her handbag, she walked out the back door of the building, locked up and got in her car. On autopilot, she clicked her seat belt into place and started the engine – or, at least, tried to. The engine turned over but didn't ignite.

Damn, she thought. Why tonight of all nights?

Ursula kept turning the key until she heard chugging and then just a click each time. She gave up and rang Sasha. "I'm really sorry but my car won't start. Do you mind if I come later in the week? I don't fancy waiting for a mechanic now, I can just walk home and deal with it in the morning."

"Oh, what a shame," said Sasha. "but I'm sure Mark won't mind coming to you to pick the paperwork up. It doesn't take long to get there. Hang on just a minute."

She called out to Mark, "Ursula's car won't start. You don't mind popping over there to collect the paperwork, do you?"

"No," said Mark, with a shake of his head.

"Oh, that's really kind of you. Tell him to drive round the back," said Ursula. "He can park in Clive's space next to my blue Skoda and ring the bell by the back door. I'll be in the office there."

"Okay. He'll be along soon."

Mark faffed around for five minutes before he sighed and set off. At least he was familiar with Pagnell and could picture the side road to turn down behind the bakery. It wouldn't take too long.

***

Clive had been perched on the edge of his sofa, listening out for either of Ursula's phones.

Yes! He punched the air in triumph. There had always been the risk Ursula would have called out the AA there and then, which would have been a pain – though a backup plan was that he'd "happen" to be passing and would sort the car out for her before the AA got there – but he'd judged her character well enough. The weakest part of the plan was Mark offering to drive instead but it had worked. Maybe the gods were on Clive's side for once. He picked up his rucksack and a balaclava. He put on a navy baseball cap, sunglasses and a brown leather jacket (less conspicuous when cycling, he'd decided) and walked out the back door where his bicycle was propped up, ready to go. He'd already paced the route: four minutes to ride to the lane at the back of the bakery at a steady pace. He intended to keep calm and collected.

Clive cycled along until he reached the top end of the lane where there was an old bench on the verge. After he'd padlocked the bike to a lamp-post, he sat on the bench where he could keep an eye on any vehicles that entered the lane from the main road. That was the way Mark had to approach the back of the row of shops – unless he literally went round the houses and that was really not likely. And in which case, he'd drive past him anyway. Clive pulled out his mobile and pretended to be studying it.

It wasn't long before a car arrived and was indicating to turn into the access road behind the shops. A man was driving. Clive stood up, folded his jacket into the rucksack and sauntered down towards the shops. Keeping out of sight, he watched this man get out of his car, which was parked right where Ursula had directed, in Clive's space.

***

Mark walked up to the building and looked at the door closest to the blue Skoda. He checked the nameplate by the door. Reading "Bernard's Bakery", he pressed the bell and waited.

Ursula opened the door. "Hello, you must be Mark. I'm Ursula."

"Pleased to meet you." Mark proffered his hand.

"Oh, do come in. I'll just run you through the statements so that you can see what's what. Would you like a cup of tea, dear?"

"No thanks; I'm sure this won't take long," said Mark, hoping the intention was clear.

As Mark disappeared through the door, Clive quickened his pace and slipped into the access road. He contemplated swapping his baseball cap for the balaclava but it wasn't fully dark yet and he didn't want to arouse suspicion. Anyway, the CCTV would still be out of action. Clive reminded himself that he must intermittently disable the CCTV a few more random times. He'd worked out his plan several weeks previously and had already done it two or three times a week so it couldn't be connected to the time of the sabotage. Putting gloves on, he slinked up to the side of Mark's car, keeping out of view from the office window. Quickly, he bent down to the front wheels, one at a time, and located the brake pipes. He snipped clean through them with a pair of bolt-cutters, then used a small squirt gun to apply highly corrosive acid to the ends and haphazardly on the pipes. That should eat away at the metal and make it look like the pipes corroded away on their own accord. He splattered more acid along the undercarriage in a way that should make it look like the car had driven over something. In no time at all, he'd crawled away, wiped his tools clean and bagged everything up safely in the rucksack.

He was prepared for the next day, when Ursula would inevitably tell him about her car not working whilst complaining about having to walk from and to work; he'd offer to have a look at her car. He'd reconnect the spark plugs without her seeing (he could always send her in to get some kitchen towel if she tried to hang around) and go back to his house to get a set of jump leads to start her flat battery, being the dedicated employee that he was. And he'd be ready with sincere condolences if she happened to hear about any unfortunate car accidents.

Walking nonchalantly away up the road, Clive retrieved his bicycle. Along his route home, a sauntering lad glanced up to see a grotesquely grinning cyclist approaching. He flinched as Clive glided past.

DON'T GET IN YOUR CAR

I'd taken the precaution of seeking out Bernard before the events unfolded. He had a vested interest and I thought it would do him good to have a companion next to him if he was watching Ursula in case things went as badly as I feared.

As we watched Clive sabotaging Mark's car, Bernard wailed, knowing he had precipitated Mark's situation. He was determined to intervene, if he possibly could, which was fine by me.

Sasha was sitting on her sofa with a magazine on her lap. Bernard stood in front of her, shouting in her face and trying to shake her shoulders but he wasn't having the remotest effect. Sasha was engrossed in an article on a pop star's turbulent life.

It would have been hilarious to watch under different circumstances. Now it was excruciating. If only Sasha had made some effort to communicate with me when her energies were strong, she'd have been able to sense Bernard. With hindsight, I should have spoken directly with Sasha when we were introduced to each other in her near-death experience. That way, she might have remembered me better and been more inclined to call on me. But it had been such an unusual situation and my superiors just wanted to show Sasha I was there for her rather than delay her return with a cosy chat. Mistakes happen – even in heaven. And telling her a few days ago I was always by her side, ready and willing, was clearly too subtle. She certainly wasn't aware that now would be a very, very good time to put a plea my way. I made a mental note to ask for someone a bit more astute next time – as if I'd get a next time.

Bernard was still flouncing around impotently.

I'd already ignored Rules One, Two and Three with Sasha, so did it really matter if I meddled one more time? I wasn't going to get to graduation anyway, and more to the point, Mark was in mortal danger.

I increased Sasha's perception until she finally became aware of Bernard jumping up and down in front of her, his arms flapping like a young albatross testing its wings.

"Oh my God – you took me by surprise," she exclaimed out loud. "What are you doing here? In fact, what are you actually doing?"

Bernard stopped flapping. "At last! You've got to help your husband. Clive has sabotaged Mark's car – he'll have a serious accident unless you can warn him."

"Really? Are you sure?"

"Of course, I'm sure. Clive's got criminal history and he's a dangerous man. He's done this to stop Mark looking at the accounts. If Mark dies, it works perfectly for him."

"Dies?" cried Sasha. She grabbed her phone and texted Mark, her fingers flying over the letters.

DON'T GET IN YOUR CAR.

IT'S NOT SAFE. CALL ME X

***

Ursula was thumbing through the bank statements with Mark, explaining names and abbreviations so he would understand who and what the debits and credits related to. He heard his phone ping but there were rather a lot of different names and abbreviations to remember so he ignored it. When it pinged a second time within a minute, he turned his phone off and put it in his jacket pocket. He was determined to get home as quickly as possible and he would check his texts when he was in the car. Whatever it was could wait a few minutes.

Ursula handed him the paperwork and he was ready to leave but she kept on chatting about what a good employee Clive was and how she really hoped this would all come to nothing. Mark just wanted to get back to his comfy sofa and he inched towards the door.

***

With three texts and no responses, Sasha called Mark's phone, wondering why the hell she hadn't just called in the first place. But the call went straight to voice mail.

"Answer the phone, damn you," she cried. If spirits were telling her Mark was in trouble, it really must be serious. She grabbed a tissue as tears erupted.

***

Mark eventually managed to say to Ursula he'd be in touch and no, it was really no trouble at all. He jumped in his car, chucked the bank statements on the passenger seat and reversed out of the parking space. Forgetting all about his phone as he mused over the task ahead of him, he turned slowly onto the side road. There was no traffic at the next junction so he was able to pull straight out onto the main road. *At least I'll be home quickly,* he thought.

***

Sasha paced up and down in her sitting room. Bernard was no longer with her but the tension was ramping up around and within her.

What should I do? I can't drive up there leaving the children alone. It would take too long to get them awake and in the car. Why didn't I ask what was done to the car? Mark's probably already left by now. What can I do?

"Ask me for help," I refrained from saying. With good old hindsight, I really should have shouted it at her.

***

Mark slowed down a little at a mini roundabout though he didn't need to fully stop.

Strange, he thought. *The brakes feel spongy. That's a bit ironic if Ursula's and my car both play up today.*

He drove on towards the first main roundabout and indicated to turn left. He could see a lorry approaching from the opposite direction; it was closer and had right of way. Mark put his foot on the brake but the pedal was worse than before. He pressed down harder and the pedal hit the floor. *Fuck!* His car wasn't stopping.

There was now a car alongside his right and railings on his left. There was nowhere to go but forwards. He yanked the hand brake up but it had minimal effect. Mark blared his horn to warn the lorry driver he couldn't stop and the lorry driver slammed his foot on his brake. The sheer weight and momentum of the articulated vehicle nullified the effect of the last-minute braking and it ploughed right into the side of Mark's car.

Realisation hit me at the same time. It was no coincidence Mark was involved in a car accident just like Sasha's. Hers happened when she'd driven onto a roundabout; same for Mark. Sasha's car was T-boned by a larger vehicle; same for Mark. As I'd mentioned before, Sasha's and Mark's souls went way back, entwined eternally. It would have been synchronicity to sigh over if it weren't so darned serious.

***

Back at home, Sasha was frantic. "Oh God! Bernard, Gran, Zinnia even – please look after Mark. Don't let him die. Please make it all right."

Finally, Sasha had asked for help, though still not for herself. I threw Sasha an image of her parents driving over as I concentrated on putting forward a good case to the archangels.

As soon as Sasha pictured her parents, she grabbed the phone to ring them.

"Dad – can you come round immediately? I'm sure Mark's had an accident and I need to go out to find him. Please don't ask – just come over right now to be with the children."

Responding quickly was drilled into Kevin from his years of medical situations.

"On my way," he said before shouting, "Pauline – emergency at Sasha's – you coming?"

Pauline dropped her book and rushed to put her shoes on. The couple left as swiftly as firefighters on call.

Sasha was hovering at the front door and jumped into her car as soon as Kevin and Pauline arrived.

"I'll call you," she shouted back as she sped off.

She followed the route Mark would have taken and saw emergency vehicles on the roadside by a roundabout. Much as she desperately wanted to believe otherwise, there was no doubt in her mind this was what Bernard had warned her about. As she pulled up, her stomach was already roiling and her ears were buzzing. Then she recognised Mark's car entangled with a massive lorry and screamed, "No!" The flashing blue lights of a police car competed with those of an ambulance in front of her.

Sasha leapt out of her car. She pushed through the people at the side of the road, yelling, "That's my husband in there!"

A policeman stepped in front of Sasha and restrained her firmly.

"Stay back. You think your husband's in the car or lorry? You can give me his particulars."

"In the car. His name is Mark Denning. He lives at 34 Donnington Close, Milton Keynes. Oh God, this is really serious, isn't it?"

Her legs were turning wobbly as she stared into the wounded heap that had once been Mark's pride and joy. She could just make out a paramedic placing a brace around Mark's head and his face was being covered by an oxygen mask. She thanked God she could see the oxygen mask – at least that told her he was alive, didn't it? The side of the car was so dented in, Sasha thought he would need to be cut out of the wreckage. Now she had first-hand experience. Sure enough, a fire engine was blaring its way through the traffic.

Sasha slumped to the ground and put her head in her hands. She tried hard to focus through the dark mist which was impeding her sight. So many thoughts were flashing through her mind.

This looks as bad as my accident and I almost died. Well, I kind of did for a while. Please, please, please don't let Mark die – I know he's a pain in the butt but I couldn't face life without him. Just when we've sorted ourselves out. If only I hadn't said I'd help Bernard. I'm such an idiot.

The policeman looked down at Sasha and quietly stepped back to make some notes. Tears poured down her face as she texted her mum – she couldn't trust herself to call and speak coherently.

Mark's been in crash.
Waiting for him to be cut out of car.
If they let me, I'll go in ambulance with him.
Will text again.

Pauline responded by asking where the accident was and advising Sasha she and Kevin would come up to collect Sasha's car as soon as they'd got her neighbour to stay with the children.

Sasha watched the firefighters at work. It must have been like this for me. I barely remember the firemen. I wonder whether Mark is aware of them.

Some subtle change seemed to be happening in the scene though. She was only catching glimpses of Mark through the moving bodies and equipment, so she stood up for a better view. This was just in time to see a paramedic exchanging the oxygen mask for a different mouth covering. He was now lowering his head to Mark.

"No!" Sasha cried out as she watched in horror at the paramedic breathing into Mark's mouth.

The paramedic was pumping Mark's chest with frightening force as the other paramedic raced to the ambulance and rushed back with a defibrillator pack.

Sasha ran towards the scene. It felt like one of those slow-motion dreams – damn her leaden feet. The policeman materialised before her and she collided with his outstretched arms.

"You've got to keep back," Sasha distantly heard him say. She was fighting an increasingly dense fog in her head, intent on smothering her awareness.

"Mark needs me," she croaked, falling to her knees. The policeman's legs were callous steel bars in a prison cell window.

The atmosphere changed again. Now all sound ceased. The defibrillator was no longer in use. A barely noticeable luminescence softly spiralled up, away from Mark. The paramedics stood back as the firefighters severed the last of the deformed metal and pulled the car open. Sedately, Mark was placed onto a stretcher and a blanket rolled over his body. Sasha surrendered to the fog.

It could have been decades later as far as she was concerned but, in actual fact, minutes passed before Sasha came to, aware her parents' arms were now around her, and their tears melding with hers.

"He can't be gone," she whispered.

Suddenly, the desire to be next to Mark overwhelmed her. Shrugging off her parents, she jumped up and rushed to the ambulance where its doors were still open.

"Please let me sit in the ambulance with him," Sasha called in.

"It's really not a good idea, love."

Sasha recognised that firm but kind voice.

"Jackie, you rescued me at the end of June when I had a car crash with my children in the back. You know I'm not any trouble. I just need to be with my husband now, on his last journey. You've got to let me," she pleaded.

Jackie looked at Sasha. Ah, yes, she was the woman from the T-boned car with the three backseat kids.

"Josh, I'll ride in the back," she called to her partner as she indicated a seat Sasha could take, facing Mark's body.

"It's not often I see my patients again," she said as the ambulance moved sedately back to the hospital. "You had to be cut out of your car too. What are the chances?" She couldn't help saying to herself, *I can think of better family traditions.*

"Yeah. So can I," agreed Sasha.

It was clear the boost I'd given Sasha in order to see Bernard hadn't worn off. This was a blessing – momentarily distracting her.

She was receiving a vision of Jackie with a new girlfriend, looking blissfully happy.

Whilst Jackie was wondering with horror whether she'd actually joked about family traditions out loud, Sasha blurted out, "I take it you're not with Zara anymore."

"Shit – did I tell you about Zara? No, we broke up a month ago."

Jackie never spoke about her relationships to strangers, and not to all that many acquaintances either. How did this woman know about Zara?

"Oh, well, I'm glad you've moved on – she wasn't right for you, was she?" Sasha knew it was too much but she couldn't stop jabbering away to suppress the horror. "And I can see you're really happy with someone new."

"Well, thanks for the vote of confidence – I think," said Jackie, squirming. Some people were just plain weird.

Maybe she'd stop letting them ride in the ambulance with a patient, deceased or alive. Could a call-out get any weirder?

"Honestly, I'm not just saying it to be kind." Sasha was still going on. "I had a near-death experience when I had my accident; that's when I saw how things were between you and Zara. You had your doubts, and rightly so, it seemed to me. Now I just got an image of you with someone else and you look so happy together. I hope it works out better for you."

"Yeah, me too," said Jackie, to humour the crazy lady.

All the while, I was in deep discussion with Hebron. I was pleading the case for Sasha and Mark to continue their current Earth-journey together, but Hebron seemed to think it was more important to dissect my transgressions. And this actual confrontation was just the icing on the cake as far as he was concerned.

Really? I thought. *Can't we just get on it?*

Conversation dried up. Sasha couldn't hold reality back any longer. Now outrage at the injustice of losing Mark was welling up inside her.

Damn Bernard! Damn the NDE! Everything was fine before then.

It had been far from fine, from where I was standing – oh, you know I don't mean physically standing – but Sasha was searching for a scapegoat.

If I'd never had my crash, there'd be no Bernard and we wouldn't have lost Mark. If Mum hadn't called me to get her, I never would've been on the road. Damn her and the stupid cancer!

Immediate guilt walloped her anger away.

How the hell could I think that? I'm sorry, Mum.

Self-pity consumed Sasha for a while before common sense seeped in.

I'm so stupid. As usual. This is actually Clive's fault. I'll have to tell the police but how the hell will they believe me?

She took a deep breath.

If I hadn't imposed my ban on asking for help, things wouldn't have gone bad with Mark. And I could have asked Zinnia for help ages ago. Then maybe…

Sasha berated herself a while longer, then started to question her vow. She revisited the scene in her life review where she reacted to her friend Kya's injuries and made her vow to never ask for help again.

My God, I actually thought I was to blame for what her mother did to her. That's like blaming my mum for Mark's accident. And I've kept that stupid vow all my life! How pathetic can you get?

Her thoughts segued towards the angel who'd been such a reassuring presence of unconditional love and support during the life review and she wrapped the sensation of comfort he'd given her round herself like a warm blanket. Suddenly she was struck with a lightbulb moment.

I've got to be kinder. Still to everyone else, of course, but also to me. I make mistakes, but honestly, I've got to stop punishing myself…

In her mind she shouted out a declaration: *I'm not really a bad person! And I'm going to start asking for help for anything from now on.*

She gave a little embarrassed chuckle at her internal dramatics, and Jackie's head jerked up in alarm.

Then Sasha opened her eyes and couldn't help focussing on the pale replica of her husband lying prone in front of her. Reality crushed her like she was an empty tin can.

Through a fresh wave of sobbing, Sasha whispered to me.

"Zinnia, I'm going to change. I can't cope without Mark; I need your help. Please do anything you can to help me get through this."

Hebron turned to me sharply with new instructions. So this was what he'd been waiting for. I thanked him with all my metaphorical heart before concentrating back on the scene in the ambulance. There was work to do.

A new urge filled Sasha's mind and forced her to reach out, through a fresh torrent of tears, towards Mark.

"It's really not a good idea…" Jackie's protest petered out as she examined Sasha's face. Behind the tears was rigid determination, dread and something else, almost other-worldly.

Sasha was thinking her unexpected urges usually produced positive results yet this was pointless. Nevertheless, her arm seemed to have a mind of its own. She instantly recoiled the moment she touched Mark's hand. It was cold and smooth and alien.

The urge (yes, of course I was controlling it) insisted she try again and she reluctantly wrapped her fingers around his as saline rivulets cascaded down her face.

Mark's hand was warming up.

It must be my heat getting absorbed into his skin, Sasha rationalised, squeezing his hand more firmly. *At least he feels normal now. It almost felt like he squeezed me back.*

And then there was a sound. Like an intake of breath. Sasha's and Jackie's heads swivelled to stare at each other for a moment, then Jackie jumped over to Mark and pulled the blanket off his face.

He blinked once in the light, letting out a low groan. Involuntary screams from both Jackie and Sasha shattered the air and startled the poor man; his eyes burst open.

Trying to bring her rapid breaths back to normal, Sasha focused on Mark's face. Their gaze locked together and a perceptive connection fizzled between them. Sasha's heart burst with jubilation.

"You'll never believe what's happened to me," whispered Mark hoarsely.

"Oh, yes, I will," Sasha replied radiantly. "Oh, yes, I will."

$\int \sigma...$

"So, Zinnia," Hebron said. "Sasha got there in the end."

"And not a moment too soon," I replied. Things would have been unbearable if she hadn't had her lightbulb moment in the ambulance.

"She's been thoroughly tested and her strength of character finally came to the fore."

"I was doubting whether she'd ever get there; she wasn't the most confident of characters." Where was our conversation leading? I was waiting for Hebron to berate me for all the rules I'd flouted.

"Not at first, but her confidence grew substantially, as I'm sure you were aware."

"Yes, I was," I said.

"Sasha wasn't the only one lacking confidence, was she?"

Uh-oh – here goes.

"You've been oscillating between self-doubt and throwing yourself into fixing Sasha's problems, Zinnia,"

Hebron said. "You had the book of rules for guidance but there were times you blatantly ignored it."

"I'm sorry," I said, turning away. It would clearly be a waste of time trying to justify the decisions I'd made.

"But you'll be surprised to hear I actually commend your choices."

What? Did I hear him correctly?

"You consistently showed a clear understanding of potential consequences, weighed up your options and made the right choices at the right times. Sasha and Mark's outcome could not have succeeded without your interjections."

Well, you could have knocked me down with a feather. Wow!

Hebron was smiling broadly now at my reaction – and use of an idiom. "And I am pleased to say you have passed Level III. You are a capable young spirit guide."

"Hallelujah!" I cried, pulsating with delight.

"You'll continue to be Sasha's guide until the end of her human life and I suspect it will be a very rewarding partnership. I'm sure she'll make more use of you now."

I wrapped Hebron in the biggest hug ever, even though he was more of a hearty handshake kind of soul.

After being stuck in the doldrums of Sasha's life before the accident, this stage had been like sailing in a tiny dinghy on a wild sea; I was so relieved we'd reached tropical waters together.

Hebron reminded me that even tropical waters had their stormy moments but the glimpse of the future he projected looked pretty good to me.

About the author

Jay Jacobs, a writer and mother of two, was inspired to write after her sister shared the account of a little boy's near-death experience. Exploring a wealth of similar stories, uncovering a fascinating and life-affirming perspective, this journey ignited her creativity, resulting in an uplifting novel intended to inspire and resonate with readers seeking hope and transformation.

Acknowledgements

My thanks go to my first reader, Clare Lloyd. She was far too polite to tell me how basic (aka rubbish) my first draft was but has always had my back.

I joined a Curtis Brown Creative Edit & Pitch course in the Autumn of 2019, thinking my book was good to go (it really wasn't), where one fellow student suggested I add some dimension to the plot – thank you so much! Thanks especially to Kathy Baird for beta reading and to Deborah Price, Emma Steele, Paul Davidson, Ronan Rooney, Benje Williams, Rob Ward, Denise Spencer, Felicity Cowie and all the others.

Thank you Rachel Brimble, a lovely author who gave me my first professional editorial feedback.

I took a selective CBC course in September 2022 for a different novel but when a group of us kept in touch, it was *Back For Good* that I concentrated on. Fellow alumni Caroline McCarthy, Cathy Bridge, Emily Scott, Emma Robertson, Melissa McCarthy, Skye Stranger and Susan Swabey – thank you for being wonderful beta readers, cheerleaders and genuinely wonderful people. I wouldn't be writing this if it weren't for you!

I joined Susan at the *I Am Writing Festival* in Bristol, May 2023, where I met more lovely writers and gained further insight into the industry. Big, big thanks to the organisers, Sarah Snook and Elane Retford of iaminprint. co.uk, who've gone above and beyond with their support; I cannot recommend them highly enough. Sarah, I'm sure your feedback was instrumental to my success. Thank you Alice May, D.A. Connors, Hazel Meredith-Lloyd, Kristienne Brandreth, Lucy Andrew, Richard Clarke, and Shaney Lloyd: my Writing Sphere compadres – we're all there for each other and I'm lucky to have you in my writing life.

To Scott Pack, author, editor, publisher, question-setter and no-nonsense guru of all things writerly has also helped me along the way, with great tutorials and individual feedback. Also, Kate Wells who shared her writing journey, encouraged me when I was wondering whether I'd ever break through and answered my concerns.

Then I met Anna Lucia and Rosie Radcliffe when approaching the publishing stage, who've generously shared their experience (being a bit ahead of me in the process). We share a beautiful bond of mutual support. Thank you Book Sisters!

My gratitude goes to The Book Guild who were just what I was looking for in terms of publishing.

Finally, to my eagle-eyed sisters and my friends who've always been there for me and, of course, my amazing children. It's been a long road but for once I was never tempted to give up. Here's to happy endings!

Note from the Author

All medical information in this novel has been researched but not verified so it may vary from current practises or what you might expect. The breast cancer procedures are based on what appeared to be standard in 2018.

The information about spirit guides and other dimensions is my own interpretation and may differ to others' beliefs. I have built up my ideas – which no doubt will continue to develop – based on reading hundreds of near-death and out-of-body accounts and other sources. There has been some slight adaptation for the novel based on readers' expectations.

Almost all the accounts state that the next dimension is one of unconditional love. The most common purpose for us choosing to be humans (yes, it does appear to be a choice) is to love and be kind, closely followed by learning from experiences. I hope this book helps to gently encourage us to be compassionate to all others (not just human beings) – and ourselves.

I thank my spirit guides (and other souls) and ask for support on a regular basis. I believe they help me through my hard times and share my happy moments; in fact, I think they're helping me to be happier than I've ever been before. Wishing you all the best with yours!